I0762161

House of Snakes

Jennifer L. Kelly

This is a work of fiction. All of the characters, organizations, and events portrayed in this novel are either products of the author's imagination or are used fictitiously.

Library of Congress Control Number: 2018908631

BOXERBULL BOOKS

Cleveland, Ohio

ISBN: 0-9992017-2-7

ISBN-13: 978-0-9992017-2-5

Dedication

To Kari—Thanks for being my friend, reader, cheerleader, confidante, fellow Whovian, yoga buddy, candle shop rep and just all around awesome person.

Prologue

It was the part she both loved and hated. The adrenaline and anticipation would coalesce in her veins, flooding her body in a rush of nervous energy. She wiped the long black strands of hair that had become plastered to her forehead and cheeks.

It was hot. Why was it always so damn hot? The cold stone of the building pressed against her spine, providing relief through the thin t-shirt she wore. Of all the stupid towns. They had to pick this one. This podunk town in the middle of nowhere with its too nice people and their too sweet, small town accents.

She watched through the trees, hazel eyes turned toward the road. The sun was just beginning to dapple across the asphalt road. Her skin sizzled with the heat of not just the town, but the unused energy that was dousing her blood. A cool breeze tickled the back of her neck, causing the little hairs to stand on end.

She checked her watch with its worn brown leather bands, twisted and tied in an attempt at what they called *boho-chic.*

An attempt at normalcy.

A car engine rumbled down the road. She closed her eyes. Sweat slowly dripped down her spine. Normal was one thing she was not. One thing she could never be.

A second engine. This one belonging to a newer model car. Its garish yellow paint job came into view as it roared down the road coming from the west. She knew without looking that the license plate read SGR-HNY and there was something lacey and feathery hanging from the rearview mirror.

The other engine—deep like a growl—coming in the opposite direction, from the east. An old sedan missing a hubcap and with a radio that would cut out without fail at the best part of any song, until its driver gave the dashboard a solid *thwack* with his fist. Then the station would abruptly change.

This was it. Her heart pounded in her chest, blood rushing to her head, senses coming alive with the hunt. Even though the cars were about a mile away from each other, she could hear the thud of the fist on the dashboard, the tinkling laugh of SGR-HNY and the too-loud, obnoxious pop music that emanated from the speakers.

Yes, she thought. *This is just right.*

No, she argued. *This is so wrong.*

She clenched and unclenched her sweaty fists, fingernails leaving half-moon indentations on her palms. The breeze picked up whipping her ponytail against her sweaty cheeks.

The music grew louder. SGR-HNY accelerated up the road toward the high school. The old sedan groaned down the road toward the high school. This was the part she loved. The anticipation.

SGR-HNY's shiny yellow paint job roared closer, preparing to make a left turn into the high school's driveway which was slowly filling with cars. Just as the sedan came into view, preparing to make a right turn into the same driveway. They were too far away. Their owners worlds apart, but their cars seconds away. It was all she needed.

The pop music caught on the wind and she could see SGR-HNY laugh at something the passenger had said, turning her head ever so slightly, rising sun reflecting in her too large, bug-eyed sunglasses.

Drenched in sweat, she flicked her wrist.

SGR-HNY turned too late, her face frozen in surprise as she careened into the old sedan.

Brakes screeched. Metal crunched. Piercing the stillness of the early morning air.

And still she watched, fascinated, as the yellow SUV plowed into the sedan, taking the turn too fast and braking too late. SGR-HNY lost control and the SUV caught the gravel driveway before rolling over into the ditch. Wheels up, still spinning.

She kissed the worn, silver charm around her neck. Time seemed to slow around her. People were running in slow motion toward the collision. The sedan still spinning before it came to a stop like a child's toy.

She ran, long legs pumping, sweat dripping down her spine. She only had minutes before the time enchantment would wear off and normal time would resume. But she was good at what she did. So the girl wasn't worried.

Leaping across the grass and sliding into the ditch, hazel eyes darted over the occupants of the SUV. SGR-HNY had blood across her forehead and smeared down her cheek. She must have hit her head on the windshield, which was a web of cracks. Her sunglasses were gone and her blue eyes were vacant and unfocused. The other passenger—a boy with shaggy blonde hair—a surfer type in a land-locked town—groaned beside her, fumbling with his seat belt before he yelped in pain. Most likely something was broken.

She was running out of time. This would have to do. If he saw anything, it would be dismissed as delirium from the pain of the broken bones or the trauma of the accident. With a deep breath, she reached through the broken jaws of the driver side window, oblivious to the jagged glass scraping her arm. But no blood was drawn.

This was the part she hated.

Biting her lip, she carefully placed her fingers into the girl's chest, feeling for the broken breast bone. SGR-HNY gasped and when she did, the girl plunged her fingers into her chest. Past her blue and silver cheerleading uniform with its silver Spartan warrior embroidered onto the front, past her pale skin and into her flesh. She closed her eyes, feeling around inside the cavity until she found what she was looking for. It was warm to the touch and when she coaxed it, it came willingly.

Sliding her hand back out of SGR-HNY's chest, the warmth came with it and when her hand emerged victorious with its prize, the shimmery golden orb seemed to wink at her. Fumbling with her free hand, she opened the small leather satchel at her waist and slid the orb inside. It left a shimmering trail from her waist back to the girl's chest.

She chided it, pulling a small knife with a black blade and a worn bronzed handle from her waist, she sliced through the shimmery gold tendril, connecting the glowing orb to the girl.

When she did so the girl let out a sigh, and her breath became shallow. Almost non-existent. The once shimmery gold tendril quickly shriveled and turned black before disappearing into dust on the cool morning breeze.

Satisfied, she sheathed her knife. She heard a shout. The enchantment was wearing off. She took several steps back, disappearing into the dark shadows of the trees. Quickly pushing any loose strands of dark hair back into her ponytail and feeling the cool morning air sweep over her damp skin.

And just like that the enchantment ended.

Shouts broke out over the still morning air. Feet running. Tires squealing as cars came to a stop, their occupants leaping out.

For the second time, she kissed her charm necklace and, taking a deep breath, whipped out her cellphone and dialed 9-1-1.

"9-1-1 State your emergency."

Her voice came out unrecognizable. It was several octaves too high. Too much bubble, not enough mirth.

"There's been an accident in front of the high school." And before they could ask her any more questions she hung up.

Pocketing her phone she backed away into the cover of the woods. School started in thirty minutes and she still needed to change out of her sweat-drenched clothes. She always looked a wreck after a Taking. Maybe she could fake a doctor's note and get a couple of extra hours of sleep. She was exhausted having to get up before sunrise. Not to mention the surge of adrenaline and its aftermath were already taking its toll on her body.

Her stomach began to growl at her in protest. And she bid it to shut up. Because she was all too familiar with the twisting of her gut and the slight sense of nausea that accompanied it.

This too was the part she hated. Tamping down the shame as it tried to claw its way up her throat. Her eyes burned, but she shook her head. It was part of the deal. She'd done the best she could. She chose someone who deserved it, she told herself, ignoring the part of her that begged to differ that nobody quite deserved that. Besides, she had been gentle, and heck, she'd even called 9-1-1 afterward. Surely, that had to mean something in the cosmic karmic bank account.

Tucking the charm necklace beneath her t-shirt, she headed deeper into the woods, walking parallel between the road and the high school. Her boots made no sound on the grass and dirt path she walked. No one would notice her. No one ever did.

Except this time she was wrong.

Someone had noticed.

Before she'd run down to the scene of the crime, someone had been watching her.

Keeping to the shadows, he'd watched as the strange girl had flicked her wrist in the air as if pulling some imaginary strings, right before the two cars had collided. Right before he saw her slow down time all around her as she raced down the hill toward the overturned SUV. He'd followed her, keeping far enough away for her not to notice, too concerned with the job that she was doing. He'd watched as her sinewy muscles worked through the back of her sweat-dampened t-shirt, how her black hair clung to her neck and cheeks. She was the most fascinating of creatures.

Hidden behind a tree, he'd watched as she'd leaned over the twisted metal and through the broken glass of the driver side window, reaching inside before carefully—almost lovingly—pulling something small and glowing from inside the SUV. She'd gently placed the glowing thing into a small leather satchel attached to a belt at her waist. Then he'd watched as she'd taken a strange knife and severed the shimmery golden tendril before it dissolved on the wind. When she turned toward him, he'd fallen further back, into the cover of the school building's shadow.

The sun was just beginning to crest over the horizon, and the morning light dappled her cheeks and made her hazel eyes seem to be alit from within. Like fire. She had turned back toward the accident, flipping out her cellphone and he heard her voice—well, what he assumed was her voice—but it had a strange cadence to it, as she had called 9-1-1 and reported the accident.

And when she pocketed her phone and silently took off through the forest to who knows where, he had followed.

Chapter One

Vic was beautiful.

In a terrifying sort of way. She walked down the halls of Olympia High School with a sort of swagger and yet, in the blink of an eye, she could blend into the background, barely noticeable. It was an eerie ability. One that set the other students on edge.

They'd whisper about her, but she pretended she didn't mind. Her black hair? Totally a drugstore dye job. Her tawny skin, the color of coffee made with too much cream—obviously it came from a bottle. Those hazel eyes? The ones that turned colors depending on her mood (gray when she was angry, gold if delighted, and a pale shade of green rimmed in brown any other time) had to be contacts. Because no normal person had eyes like that. And just who did she think she was anyways? Walking around with her ripped jeans, flannel tied around her waist, fitted t-shirt, and black Chucks.

To say in a town of *Leave It to Beaver* types that Victoriana Haden stood out was an understatement. But that afternoon, no one paid particular attention to Vic as she made her way to her locker, carefully pulling out books for fifth period English and sixth period Latin. She's always had a natural affinity for languages and typically enjoyed her afternoon classes, when she was more awake. Usually she spent the mornings dozing on and off through math classes and science labs until it was time for lunch.

Two willowy girls in blue and silver cheerleading uniforms—Spartan silhouette blazing across their chests—walked by, blonde heads pressed together like Siamese twins. Vic couldn't remember their names. Something like Terri and Sherri. Or maybe it was Carrie and Sherri. Their hushed voices drifted over to where Vic stood, looking busy as she shoved her backpack into her locker.

"Mariana totally texted me about it in third period," whispered Carrie. Or was it Sherri?

"I can't believe Lauren's in a coma! And tonight is the big game against the Cougars." Sherri's voice sounded disbelieving, as if anyone could have the audacity to enter into a coma on the same day as the big game.

Vic pushed a strand of black hair behind her ear. She didn't need to strain to hear as the two girls headed down the hallway. Much to her chagrin, Vic's hearing was beyond excellent.

"I heard Eric is super freaked out by it. He was there you know. When it happened. Somehow he only has a concussion and a few broken fingers," Carrie continued.

"A total miracle."

"Totally."

"It will be a miracle if we win tonight."

Carrie's high-pitched laughter floated back down the hall, as if they weren't just talking about their friend and fellow cheerleader. "Totally."

As the girls rounded the corner, Vic let out the breath she'd been holding. She closed her locker, and pressing her books against her chest made her way to Mrs. Williamson's fifth period English class. The late pass from the office was crumpled in her sweaty fist.

She climbed the steps at the end of the hall catching bits of conversations. The words *coma* and *accident* jumping out at her like a jab to the gut each time.

That morning when she'd left the scene of the crime, she'd headed home. If you could call a huge house with one occupant a home. It was set back from the main road by a winding gravel driveway. The house was really old, but well-maintained. A groundskeeper came regularly and attended to the property's vast gardens, as well as regularly fixed anything that was broken or leaking or simply no longer working. He was an older man who kept his head down and his mouth quiet. Her father had hired him. Richard was his name and over the months Vic had crossed paths with him, she'd decided he was kind, but that she couldn't waste too many brain cells on it because he could also be a spy for her father. It was a shame really, but the list of trustworthy people was relatively short.

Namely, herself.

Still, Richard was as close as she had to a family while living here.

To make the house seem cozier, Vic mainly kept to the downstairs. When the delivery truck arrived with the furniture she hadn't even picked out, they'd simply set the bed up in what would normally be the living room. She had a stiff couch with an ornate, onyx back, upholstered in silver along with a high-backed chair that looked more throne than everyday household item. Obviously, her father had made the arrangements. Other rooms in the house had old furniture from the turn of the century, hidden under protective covers and those without covers had several years' worth of dust.

Vic had carefully pulled out the small metal box she kept under her bed. To unsuspecting eyes it looked like it was just some sort of lock box for money or other valuables, but it was so much more than that. It was Vic's last hope.

The box didn't use a key or combination, instead, Vic took her onyx-bladed knife and carefully pricked her thumb. Once a tiny, ruby-colored droplet emerged from the wound, she pressed it against the bat emblem that acted as the box's latch. She pressed her bleeding thumb to the bat, its sharp ears digging into her flesh. Its crystal-set eyes seemed to glow white hot, and Vic pulled back as the bat's head hinged backward and the box's locking mechanism undid itself.

Inside the box was lined with soft, red velvet. Right now it was empty. Her last trip to her father's had been fairly recent. The accident this morning was the first opportunity she'd had for a Taking. Carefully undoing the buckle of the leather satchel attached to her belt, she gently reached in and coaxed out the shimmering golden orb that she'd taken from Lauren.

It had been an easy choice. The day Vic observed Lauren tripping a freshman girl on the stairs, one of many transgressions Vic had observed over the last few months, then pointing and laughing with the other cheerleaders was the day she'd unknowingly become a Mark. Vic didn't like to Take from just anyone. She was careful—if not meticulous—in who she chose. The soul itself was always pure, it's why they shimmered so beautifully. It was the shell—the human body and its ego—that was tainted. So it was easy to Mark someone like Lauren. Even if Vic generally hated the process. She let out a shiver as the golden orb slid through her fingers, curious and alive. It made her feel like a monster. Taking.

Sighing and with great tenderness, she placed Lauren's soul gently into the velvet-lined box. The box would not only keep it safe, but keep it alive and well before Vic could take it to her father. But bringing just one would not be acceptable, and she didn't need to feel the burn of her father's wrath. She'd have to find more before she could return, before he'd *allow* her to return.

Gently, she closed the box. The bat's head snapped back down and its glowing, crystal eyes turned dark and empty. Standing, she nudged the box with her foot, back under the bed, and went into the downstairs bathroom to find a Band-Aid for her thumb. She didn't really need it, but it somehow made her feel better. More normal. Then she used the landline—who had a landline these days?—to call the school. She placed the cool metal of the bat charm around her neck—a gift from her mother before they were forced to part—to her lips. Her voice came out soft and sweet sounding, gentle and motherly, as she explained to the office that her granddaughter Victoriana Haden had a dentist appointment that morning and would be into school after the lunch period. And yes, she'd be sure to bring in a note from the doctor. Very well, thank you.

Vic hung up and snapped her fingers at a pen and notepad lying by the phone. Immediately the pen started to write on the paper, creating a header for a made-up dentist and writing out her excuse for why she was coming into school late. Her notes were never looked into anyways. People just thought Vic was sick a lot. Or crazy with grief since her mom died and her father was a workaholic. Neither of which was far from the truth. The rumors simply perpetuated the story.

While the note finished writing itself, Vic hopped in the shower, turning the hot water on all the way to wash Lauren's blood from her skin and the cloyingly floral scent of her soul from her fingers. Each soul smelled different, usually pleasant—some smelled like flowers, others like fresh baked-bread. Once, she had collected one that smelled like chocolate. That was a personal favorite. Vic was always amazed at the variety of aromas and often wondered what it said about the person, from which she'd plucked the shimmering golden orb. The sticky sweetness of Lauren's soul gave Vic the impression that it was young. That would certainly make her father happy.

Before she could further ponder that morning's Taking, she'd turned off the shower, threw on her over-sized bathrobe and barely stumbled onto the bed before she fell into a fast, dreamless asleep.

–

Now, however, she couldn't help but ponder Lauren's Taking as she headed up the stairs toward English class. It was lucky that Lauren hadn't died. Taking was a tricky business. Too many deaths could arouse suspicion. Vic had let her anger make her a bit careless. It was easier—*better*—when she Took from someone who wouldn't be missed. In a small town that was no easy feat. And she had a feeling that's how her father had wanted it. He had wanted it to be difficult for Vic, but if there was one thing she'd gotten good at over the last seventeen years it was outwitting her father.

Vic slid into her usual seat in the backrow just as the bell rang to signal the start of fifth period. She automatically pulled out her notebook ready to begin the boring process of diagramming sentences. It was only once she'd pulled out her favorite purple gel-ink pen and looked to the front of the room that she noticed Mrs. Williamson was not alone.

Standing beside her was a sheepish looking boy. No, not a boy, Vic considered. But not yet a man, she also noted. He was an entire head taller than Mrs. Williamson who was relatively tall. He had an angular jaw and a full bottom lip that Vic felt her eyes unwittingly drawn to. The classroom windows were open to let in the breeze, but it did little to stifle the eighty degree temperatures in early October. His eyes were a warm, golden brown—almost amber in color—framed by long dark lashes. The breeze ruffed his too long, chocolate-colored hair that curled beneath his ears and stuck out from his forehead in a just-rolled-out-of-bed kind of way. He must not have realized how unseasonable the weather was in Olympia, because he had on a gray sweatshirt with navy sleeves which he'd pushed up to the elbows. His feet were clad in beat up Chucks and Vic felt the slightest smile cross her lips.

Until a ruby red leaf swirled into the classroom from the open window and made its way unnoticed across the room before landing directly on her desk, where it promptly curled charcoal black at the edges before completely disintegrating into a pile of dark ashes. Rolling her eyes at the reminder and gritting her teeth, she swooped the ashes off her desk and onto the floor. She didn't need the reminder. Gods, she couldn't even smile without receiving a reminder from her father—or her father's spies.

She looked up to the window and out at the looming, giant Oak tree, but didn't notice anything strange. Sometimes her father sent nymphs, if they owed him a favor. She stuck her tongue out at the window as she turned back around and felt a flush race up her neck and bloom across her cheeks as she turned her attention back to Mrs. Williamson.

"...from Pacifica, California...that's quite a long way! So let's all give Callum—"

The boy cut her off with a sheepish grin. "Actually, Mrs. Williamson, just Cal is fine."

Mrs. Williamson tittered at him. "Well, aren't you the one. Okay, Cal, you can take the open seat back there by Miss Haden."

She gestured toward the empty seat next to Vic and Vic automatically slouched down a little, scooting the ashes on the floor with her foot toward one of Mrs. Williamson's many bookcases.

"Now that the pleasantries are out of the way, I'd like you to begin diagramming the sentences that I've written on the board. You may work alone or with a partner, but know if there's off-topic kibitzing then you will most definitely be working alone." She glanced at the clock as Callum—Cal—made his way to the empty desk. "In fifteen minutes, we'll *rendez-vous*. I'll be around to answer any questions."

Vic began carefully writing out the first sentence in her notebook when a shadow crossed her page and she smelled Mrs. Williamson's distinct scent of coffee, chalk, and vintage perfume. Mrs. Williamson liked to say she was a writer, but teaching is what paid her bills. Vic glanced up into the plump, slightly wrinkled face of her teacher. Mrs. Williamson was the teacher she liked best. She was often to the point and had kind blue eyes, often bloodshot from late night writing sessions. Today her long blonde hair was in a loose braid over her shoulder.

"Vic, you wouldn't mind helping Cal get acclimated would you?" She absent-mindedly dusted chalk off her fingertips and onto her black slacks as she spoke. Vic liked that Mrs. Williamson trusted her. It was hard to trust people. Most of all yourself.

"Certainly, Mrs. W. It's no problem." Vic made a point to smile.

Sometimes she had to remind herself, as if she'd forgotten how to do it. How had it happened so fast? The Takings had changed her. But it had to be done. There was no other way, she reminded herself.

"Wonderful. You're such a dear. Vic here is a master of the craft, you're in good hands, Cal." And with a conspiratorial wink, Mrs. Williamson floated back up the aisle to go harass Nick and Justin who were making a raucous in the front row over the evening's upcoming football game. The seemingly never-ending heat made everyone restless, especially in the afternoon.

Cal pulled the empty desk over, angling it slightly so it faced Vic's own desk. Most people didn't talk to her. She was friendly—or tried to be—when they spoke to her, but for the most part she kept to herself and, besides when she first came to town at the end of her junior year and they asked her prying questions to assess where and how she'd fit in, they'd gradually lost interest. She'd somehow become the loner kid who lives in the fancy manor down the lane with its elaborate gardens and a father who didn't seem around much. The kid who seemed incredibly smart and artsy and would go to whichever liberal arts college her father could afford. Which as far as they knew was any and all of them. So, for the most part, Vic was not usually on their radar. And that's just the way she needed it to be. She couldn't afford to get close to any of the students here. Not if she was Taking. Getting to know them and having personalities to go with the faces—with the souls—would make it altogether too difficult. And she had a mission. She would not—could not—fail.

Cal cleared his throat and Vic looked down, realizing she'd pressed the pen too hard in one spot for too long and now had a huge purple dot-stain over her sentence. Sighing she ripped out the paper, crumpled it up and placed it on the corner of the desk.

"So…" Cal tried as Vic meticulously rewrote the first sentence for a second time. "Vic's an interesting name. Is it short for something?"

She looked up. Cal had gotten out a composition notebook, all fresh white pages, and a black ink pen. He'd already copied the first sentence down and had it completely diagrammed out. For the second time Vic felt herself smile.

Cal grinned. His two front teeth were larger than the others. He was probably bucktoothed as a kid, before his face had grown around his mouth. "We already covered this at my old school."

"Victoriana," she replied to his initial question.

"That's an interesting name. Not Victoria?" He tapped the pen silently on his leg as if listening to an imaginary beat.

Vic shrugged. "My parents are kind of old-fashioned with a flair for the dramatic."

He stopped tapping and his eyes zeroed in on Vic's face. Like he was studying her. She hoped that she didn't have toothpaste on her chin. She'd slept all morning and then rushed out the door before she could sleep the whole day away.

"Yeah, I get that. Callum isn't exactly a common name around here."

"Or anywhere," Vic pointed out. Cal laughed and the sound came from deep in his throat. His right cheek dimpled when he smiled—not grinned—but full on smiled. Vic felt a tiny jolt in her chest. Somehow the air in the room suddenly felt stifling. "Mrs. Williamson? Would it be possible to open the windows a little bit more?"

Mrs. Williamson gestured at Nick to take care of it. As he got out of his seat, Vic noticed the silver numbers on his navy football uniform. For home games, the players wore their jerseys. 66. She blinked. And the numbers had rearranged themselves back to Nick's actual number: 56.

Hastily, Vic finished diagramming the sentences on her own as Cal looked over the schedule for his last three classes. When she was finished, he turned the print-out toward her so that she could see it. He didn't have sixth period Latin, but he did have seventh period History with Mr. Chauvice.

"Looks like we end the day together," Vic said in what she hoped was a friendly way. Gods, she was so out of practice talking with people—let alone talking with people of the opposite sex.

"Something to look forward to then," Cal said.

His eyes sparkled when he said it and Vic felt her cheeks flush again. This was not good. Not good at all. It had been a long time since Vic had allowed herself to make a friend. Besides Richard. Who wasn't really a friend, but her father's associate. And who was also seventy years old give or take a decade. Friends just complicated things. A lot.

"Yeah, Mr. Chauvice is really interesting. If you like a misconstrued version of history delivered in a raspy, monotone voice."

Cal laughed again and Vic felt herself instinctively leaning into it. As if on cue there was a commotion from the window as Elaine let out a yelp, barely scrambling out of the way as a rush of gold, orange, and crimson leaves came rushing through the open window that was just behind her desk.

The leaves poured in, as if someone had a giant vacuum cleaner on reverse and were pouring them into the room. They floated and swirled around the room, a crinkling cacophony.

"What in tarnation?" Mrs. Williamson asked, eyes wide in bewilderment.

Nick and Justin, and some of the other students, laughed, picking up piles of leaves and tossing them at each other. Elaine began to giggle, the leaves' unexpected appearance, suddenly reverting them all back to being kids again. Cal just stared bemusedly at the chaos around him as students laughed and threw leaves at one another while Mrs. Williamson used the paging system to call the office for a janitor.

Vic was the only one who didn't crack a smile. Couldn't crack a smile. It was another reminder. Wordlessly, she slipped her notebook back into a pile with her other things, carefully avoiding the black ash that still smudged the floor beneath her feet.

Chapter Two

She had tried to walk away after seventh period.

Really, she had. But she'd found that her legs would not obey what her head told them to do. When Cal called out her name, in his deep, friendly voice, she had willed her Chucks to continue on to her locker and ignore him.

Instead, she had found herself glancing over her shoulder, drawn to the magnetism of his voice. That was apparently the only encouragement he'd needed.

They'd sat on opposite sides of the room during History, and yet Vic kept feeling her eyes drawn to him. She'd caught him looking at her too. And to be honest, guys like Cal didn't look at girls like Vic in that way.

She blended in as best as she could. Didn't wear make-up. Didn't keep up with the latest fashions. She got good grades because it was what she expected of herself. Despite everything, once her mother was well again—once this was all over—and over for good—she wanted to go to college. Some days it felt like a pipe dream, but then other days…the days when she scored the highest in the school on the ACT or when she aced a particularly tough exam and Mrs. Williamson looked on her with such pride, that Vic thought maybe it wasn't such a crazy dream after all. But this. This was the craziest of craziest dreams. As evidenced by her father's none too subtle reminder during fifth period.

Cal fell into step with her down the hallway. Her locker wasn't far from Mr. Chauvice's room, so the walk was short. It was the end of the day, and as she opened her locker Cal leaned his shoulder casually against the locker to her left.

"So there's a football game tonight or something?" he asked, a lock of dark hair falling across his forehead.

Vic shrugged disinterestedly. Nick and several of his teammates walked by sporting their navy blue jerseys. Several of the cheerleaders towed behind, back to their chittering selves despite the events of the morning. To some extent, life went on. Vic wasn't sure if this fact made her feel relieved or sad.

She nodded in the direction of Nick's retreating form. "There's your answer to that. It's the homecoming football game."

For some reason this got a smile out of Cal. His cheek dimpled and Vic felt her eyes involuntarily drawn to his full bottom lip. She turned toward the interior of her locker and simultaneously shoved her books and folders inside while yanking out her backpack. None of the teachers had given homework because of the dance, but Vic intended to study for her Physics exam anyway and to work on an essay for Mrs. Williamson.

"Let me guess. Football games and school dances aren't

your thing?"

Vic flinched at being pegged so easily by a newcomer. She slammed her locker a little harder than she'd intended and began to walk away. But Cal was quickly two steps ahead of her. He began walking backwards in front of her down the hall and held up his hands in surrender.

"Hey now. I didn't mean any offense by it. You just seem kind of..."

She halted. Guarded. "Kind of what?"

The air was stifling as they made their way down the front steps of the school and onto the tree-lined walkway. All the trees were ablaze in shades of chartreuse, cinnamon, and gold. Vic paused, momentarily forgetting her agitation. Mesmerized by the beauty of it. She felt Cal pause beside her, his shoulder softly brushing against her own.

"Too cool," he said, but it came out almost like a sigh.

"Yeah, it is," Vic agreed, assuming he was referring to the breath taking beauty of the perpetual autumn that Olympia seemed to be locked in.

His laugh was low and warm, like drizzling maple syrup. "No, not that. I meant you."

She turned toward him. "Me? Cool? Sorry, new boy, but I think you have the wrong girl." With that she walked away heading toward the parking lot on the other side of the building, where her vintage mint green Ford F100 waited for her.

Cal's upbeat presence dissolved behind her and she shook her head in disbelief. This wasn't something she could let rattle her. Friends complicated things. Heck, people complicated things. She pulled her keys from the zipper compartment of her book bag, mindlessly stroking the smooth cylinder key chain that housed dried flowers—forever suspended in their perpetual stillness. It was another gift her mother had given her when she'd left home.

And despite the unnaturalness of the heat and the slowly unfolding autumn that Vic already knew would not be turning to winter, flowers and spring always made her think of her mother. A sharp pang unfolded from deep within her gut, surging like a serpent to wrap around her heart and squeeze. So much was at stake and she couldn't afford to mess this up.

Most of the parking lot was deserted, so her mint truck stood out against the barren, cracked asphalt. She came up short. There was someone leaning against the driver's side of her truck. Someone long and lean with muscles bulging out of a too-tight black t-shirt. Even from this distance she could see his arms were covered in full-sleeved tattoos. The breeze rustled his black hair which was usually swooped across his forehead in a too long style and kept short underneath. He had on dark denim jeans and black work boots.

Her heart quickened. But before she drew any closer, he pushed off the truck and winked at her. It was easy to imagine the meaning behind it, those green eyes she'd looked into too many times to count. Seemingly out of thin air, an all-black Harley-Davidson Sportster Iron 883 materialized. With a last meaningful look at her, he hopped on, opened the throttle and roared out of the parking lot.

Vic let out the breath she hadn't realized she'd been holding and finished walking across the parking lot. When she put the key into the door's lock, she realized she was shaking. Shoving her book bag across the smooth, white leather seat, she climbed in and slammed the door, pressing down the lock mechanism even though she knew locks wouldn't stop him.

Nothing could stop Asher.

When she was younger and more naïve, she thought she'd

been in love with Asher. But really one could never be in love with one of her father's associates, as he liked to call them. Or in Asher's case, more specifically, a hellhound. And that's what Asher was—had longed to be—and his wish had been fulfilled. After that, he'd dropped Vic like yesterday's news. It had broken her heart, conveniently so that when her father sent her to Olympia to help save her mother it had been easy to say yes. Maybe a little too easy.

She rested her forehead against the giant white steering wheel. But why was Asher here? What did he want? And then she thought of the leaves in English class. That wasn't one of her father's wood nymphs. That was Asher. Asher was giving her a warning. But was it actually from her father? Her stomach felt unsettled. She probably should have eaten something, but the Takings always made her feel a little too ill to eat. The last thing she'd had was the previous night's peanut butter and jelly sandwich. Cooking wasn't exactly her thing. And it seemed pointless for only one person.

Pushing thoughts of Asher aside and now preoccupied with the idea of filling her very empty belly, Vic turned the engine of the old truck over. The truck may have been more than sixty years old, but its engine was replaced with something top notch and more efficient. Still, Vic loved its slow, easy pace. It was a stark contrast to her life, and something she longed for. *Just get through now,* she reminded herself.

She pulled out of the school parking lot right where the accident had happened only hours ago. Everything had already been cleaned up, as if nothing had even happened. She turned left onto the main road and shook her head. Humans were truly curious creatures. Vic turned on the radio, searching through the stations until she found one with country music she liked. The goal of finding something to eat, pushed thoughts of Cal and Asher out of her mind—at least for now.

About a half mile from the winding drive of the manor, was a small, mom-and-pop general store with made-to-order sub sandwiches. Vic pulled up into one of the vacant spots out front and was just stepping onto the covered, wooden porch when she heard what sounded like someone panting behind her. Concerned, she turned, and to her surprise, found Cal, with a hand pressed to her truck and the other on his knee as he was doubled over trying to catch his breath. A red bicycle was laid in the dirt beside the truck, the front wheel still spinning.

"You. Sure. Don't. Make. It. Easy. For. A. Guy." Cal panted between breaths, sweat dampened the front of his gray sweatshirt and his dark hair was wind whipped, cheeks flushed pink.

Vic bit her lip, suppressing a smile. If he was going to go to this much trouble to talk to her...She nodded toward the store's entrance.

"Come on inside. I'll buy you a sandwich. They're the best in town."

Cal straightened up grinning. "Really?"

This time Vic smiled. "Really. And if you're extra nice, I'll even give you a ride home."

–

Cal was from California. Vic had never been, but from the sounds of it, it sounded like beaches, sunshine, and the sea. As he talked about his old school—cliques, classes, and California life—she wondered what it would be like to feel the ocean breeze in her hair and taste the salt of the sea on her lips. It had to be so much more refreshing than the stifling air of

Olympia. Vic often felt like she was suffocating, the air like grains of sand slowly filling her lungs. She'd talked little of herself, both happy and relieved to let Cal rattle on so.

Afterward, they stepped into the early evening air, which was still stifling. The sun wouldn't be setting for another couple of hours. Cal hefted his bike into the mint truck's bed, careful not to make any scratches—even though it was far from shiny and had a few dings and dents—Vic felt it gave it character. He climbed in beside her and shook his head in disbelief, that same lock of dark hair falling across his forehead, refusing to stay put.

"I can't believe this is yours," he exclaimed, gesturing to the white dashboard where Vic had attached a little vase with some wildflowers from the manor garden inside it. "I mean, it's great!" he awkwardly amended.

Vic shrugged as she angled the truck onto the main road. She didn't need directions. She'd already learned the small town like the lines of her hand, and when Cal told her he lived on Magnolia Lane, she knew it was only a few streets over from the manor.

"I like old things. Nostalgia. Sometimes I feel like it reminds me of simpler times." That was a loaded statement if she'd ever said one, but Cal had only looked over at her with his dimpled smile.

A comfortable silence stretched out between them. Vic wasn't one to share much. She wasn't used to having a friend, and basically sucked at small talk. Part of her felt as though she should ask him more questions, but she worried if she asked too many questions, he'd begin to ask the same of her. She was a horrible liar—one of her fatal flaws her father liked to say, not that she was going to be dying anytime soon. The daughter of two immortals, she wasn't exactly easy to kill. But she had become quite adept at omission.

When she pulled into the driveway of the white colonial house with its idyllic front porch, she felt a familiar pang in her chest. There were lights on inside, giving off a warm glow against the shade of the Sycamore tree in the front yard. The windows of the truck were down—no air conditioning—and she could hear the cadence of voices rising and falling from the open windows of the house.

Cal gave her a sheepish grin, misinterpreting the expression on her face as one of annoyance instead of longing. "I have five brothers and sisters," he explained. One of six. Vic felt a shiver run down her spine.

"I'm an only child," Vic replied, her voice soft as she tore her eyes away to focus on Cal. She heard a dog barking somewhere in the stillness of the in-between time. No longer afternoon, but not quite evening. Cal hopped out of the truck and withdrew his bike from the bed, laying it gently in the grass to the side of the driveway, before meandering back over to the driver's side window.

He put a hand on the window frame. The breeze rustled his hair and it carried the scent of him into the cab of the truck, something sweet and spicy like honey and cinnamon. It made her a little bit dizzy. Suddenly, she felt incredibly shy. And incredibly stupid, she chastised.

"Thanks for the ride," he paused, glanced at the house, then back at her, the light of the house reflecting in his deep amber eyes. This was the closest she'd been to him all day and it unnerved her. "I'd like to pay you back. For the food…and for the ride."

Vic felt her heart sink slightly. She waved a hand as if to say no big deal, but Cal continued.

"By taking you to the football game tonight. I get that

you're probably not a formal dance kind of girl. But I think it could be fun." She cringed, but he leaned in closer, his cheeks still wind-whipped from his manic bicycle ride to catch up with her after school. "At the very least you can tell me the ins and outs of Olympia High. Who to avoid…and who to get to know." His voice was low now and hitched on the last word.

Before she could stop herself, the words were already off her lips. "Okay. But only because you owe me. Then we'll call it even. Deal?"

The look on Cal's face was priceless. You'd have thought she'd just told him he'd won the lottery and a puppy and a new car and an all-exclusive vacation to go skiing in the Alps.

"Deal."

–

For the second time that day, Vic banged her head against the steering wheel as she sat in the old barn behind the manor. At one point, it had been horse stalls and someone had converted it into a garage. It was much too big for just the truck, but Vic found she liked to come out here and read in the lofts, which still smelled like hay and horse, but mixed with varnish.

What was she thinking? Going out with Cal. Was it a date? She dismissed the thought as she dragged her book bag off the seat and headed toward the house. You couldn't go on a date with someone you only just met. They were friends. No, not even that. She was showing the new kid the Olympia way. She imagined the principal, Mr. Beckerman with his balding, shiny head and three piece suit—complete with a chained pocket watch—saying the same thing. Mr. Beckerman reminded Vic of the human version of the White Rabbit in *Alice in Wonderland*, he was always frazzled with his glasses sliding down his nose. But he was kind, and that was always a win in Vic's book.

She let herself meander through the gardens. Inhaling the scents of hyacinth, lavender, and patchouli. She paused by the little fountain. A very forgiving sculpture of Poseidon. Truth be told he didn't have the six pack anymore with which he was often depicted. Naturally, he was still handsome, but in a much more wild way than the sculpture let on. He was on a chariot being pulled by seahorses. Water trickled from their mouths and was recycled back through the fountain. To her left was a small bench made of stones in case anyone wanted to sit and admire the fountain or listen to its soft, tinkling music. The gardens always helped to clear her head.

She pulled out her house key. Richard would already be gone. The little light beside the door was on, in case she returned home late. Richard often arrived early and left early. If she'd been home, he'd have made sure all her needs were attended to for the evening, before heading home to be with his wife. Richard was a good man. Much too good to be working for her father.

But that was the thing. You never knew what kind of deals, agreements, or pacts people would make with her father. Desperate enough people would bargain away their very souls if it was to cure a child or save a loved one. Or even pay off a simple debt. And her father would always come to collect, sure as the sun rises in the east.

When she let herself in, she found there was a plate of freshly-baked peanut butter-chocolate chip cookies on the counter top in the kitchen by the back door. Beside it was a yellow sticky note saying that Richard's wife, Anastasia, had made them just for her—and with extra peanut butter. Vic's favorite.

She tossed her book bag onto the small wooden table to

the left of the door, helped herself to two cookies and exited the kitchen into the front of the house. The large trees in the front of the house caused the living room to be cast in shadows, despite the remaining daylight left. If she was going to this football game with Cal, she'd need to pick him up in a couple of hours.

The living room housed her bed and the sofa, as well as a large screened TV that she never turned on, except to watch movies on particularly bad nights when she couldn't fall asleep after a Taking. A wardrobe was pushed against one wall, clothes spilling out of it. Shoes were in a pile on the floor. Mainly Chucks, a pair of boots, and a lone pair of black stilettos that Vic was pretty sure had a layer of dust on them to match the rest of the house.

She moved to turn the lamp on—in the corner by the TV— and that's when she felt it. All the air was sucked from her lungs as she felt the temperature shift in the room around her. There was movement behind her and suddenly she was very aware that she was not alone in the house. Someone was inside and—dammit—she hadn't even noticed! Getting caught up in Cal had made her careless. She had no weapon. Her dagger was in the box because she couldn't very well take weapons to school. Especially in this day and age. The half-eaten cookies grew soft in her sweaty palms.

Cursing silently, she turned the light on, secretly hoping that the light would push out the darkness. Like little kids who were afraid of the Boogeyman (who was very real and not very pleasant by the way, but essentially misunderstood) believed sleeping with the light on would keep the darkness at bay. The presence behind her didn't move, but she couldn't hear it anyway over the sound of her blood rushing in her ears.

Holding her breath she turned to face whatever was

waiting for her in the room.

Asher was strewn across her bed, tattooed arms behind his head, boots still on and his black hair mussed as if he'd just woken from a nap. His green eyes took her in—like they always did—as if she were a treat to be savored. If Asher walked the halls of Olympia High, girls would probably throw themselves at him. Literally. It irritated Vic that she had fell for it too. Asher was a user and by any means necessary. His eyes caught the crumbling cookies in her hand.

He grinned.

"I hope you were planning to share."

Chapter Three

"Why are you here?" Vic asked through clenched teeth.

She didn't move, as if her feet were glued to the old wooden floor. How dare he come to her home—to her bed no less—and ruin the safe cocoon she'd tried to build for herself. Away from him. And away from her father.

Away from who she was.

Away from who she is.

Who she is afraid of becoming.

Asher ignored the question. Vic could feel her heart pounding against her ribcage like a caged bird. She hated that Asher could have this effect on her. He'd made it clear before she left, that she had meant nothing to him. And she'd accepted that. Or at least she had tried.

"Who's the guy?" Asher asked, still reclined on the bed with his tattooed hands cradling his head. He appeared to be studying the intricacies of the ceiling.

This time it was Vic's turn to ignore the question. She took a deep breath and stepped forward, tossing the handful of cookies onto Asher's flat stomach. Gods, he was so attractive it made her hate him all the more for it. Although, the fact that he was a total ass kind of helped to balance it out. Not wanting to be near him, she sat on the throne-like chair that was caddy-corner from the bed and crossed her arms. Whatever it was he wanted, she didn't intend to make it easy for him.

Above the bed's headboard was a painting she had done—back when she had time—back before the missions—of a woodland scene with deer, squirrels, rabbits and birds cavorting. It was mostly dark, painted with deep earth tones, except for one ray of golden sunlight that cut through the canopy and illuminated the green space of animals. The sunlight reminded her of her mother.

Asher picked up a half of peanut butter cookie and took a bite. He rolled his eyes in mock pleasure and Vic felt her guts twist. The way he acted, you'd think his father was Apollo. Instead, he had been born from the River Styx. He had no lineage, except the river itself. Vic supposed you could say the keeper of the river, also named River Styx, could be his mother. But Vic doubted River would appreciate that much.

As Asher languidly ate the rest of the crumbled cookies, apparently not minding at all that moments before they'd been in her sweaty palms, Vic studied his tattooed arms, careful to look around disinterestedly lest he noticed. And gods, if he noticed, she knew he would not let it go. It appeared he'd added some more work to the skeletons in the desert scene. Some desert foliage of some kind, onto his left bicep. But Vic's favorite was the tattoo on his back—which she couldn't see right now and had no intention of ever seeing again—that was a beautiful raven-haired girl with crow's wings hatching from an egg. She'd always found it a peculiar choice, but Asher wasn't one for conversation so she'd never really asked what it meant. If anything at all.

Finally after he was done, he turned his gaze toward her. He looked her up and down and she felt goosebumps burst out on her arms. She felt self-conscious. Again, she was reminded of why she should have taken precautions. At the very least, she should have bound the house. She made a mental note of it, but there wasn't much that could keep Asher away. Especially if he had a message from her father.

He licked his lips. "I don't bite you know."

Vic recoiled. "Funny. I distinctly remember the opposite."

Asher laughed, a cool sanguine sound. "You used to like me."

"Key phrase in that sentence: used to."

Looking away, she rubbed her hand over the plush, velvety softness of the chair's upholstery. "What do you want, Asher? My life doesn't revolve around you, you know. You can't just show up at my house unannounced. We aren't...friends anymore."

The word felt strange in her mouth. Friends were not someone who set you on edge. Who made you feel afraid, but for a long time that's all Vic knew. That was her world. But this afternoon, she felt like she'd experienced something different. And she was both terrified and amazed by it.

"Oh, how you wound me so." Asher put a hand to his heart. But it was just playacting. Vic knew he didn't have a heart. Quite literally. The river ran through his veins and was tied into her father's power. It's what kept him alive. And tethered. He could never stay in the mortal world for too long.

He was propped up on one elbow now and leveled his green eyes at her, which sparked with curiosity and some other emotion that Vic couldn't identify. It wouldn't come to her until much later that it was envy. "Your father wanted me to check on your progress, that's all."

Vic scoffed. "And he chose to send you? He could have sent any of the hellhounds. Jacob, Chase, Brim…" Her voice trailed off as a realization dawned on her. Maybe, Asher had volunteered. She knew Asher had two sides to him, she was often trying to forget one and remember the other.

"Don't sound so surprised, Tor." She cringed at the use of the nickname he'd given her several years ago. He bit his lip. "Vic. Your mother…is not doing well. Your father is feeling desperate. It's been over two months since your last visit."

"School just got back in session. I had to find my bearings. You know as well as I do that if I Take too many, it could arouse suspicion."

"How many have you Taken?" He raised a dark eyebrow.

Vic tensed at the implication. "One since school's been back in session." It wasn't enough. She needed more. "But tonight, I'm going to the football game. Maybe…maybe I'll be able to get another. Two should be enough to tide her over for another few weeks."

Asher cast his eyes downward. "She's not doing well, Tor. I-I'm not sure it will be enough."

There was genuine remorse in his voice.

Vic felt nauseous. How could that be? Her mother had seemed on the upswing the last time she'd been home. Was Asher trying to play her? But the weather. The heat had stayed, the seasons unchanging. Until her mother was well, Olympia would be stuck in this strange summer-like autumn. It was beautiful, but it wasn't the natural way of things. There was an order for a reason. Vic liked order. No, Asher wouldn't lie to her about her mother. He loved Persephone as if she were his own mother.

"I'll get one more and then I'll come home. I-I need to see her anyways. We have a fall break coming up next weekend. No one will notice if I'm gone for a few days."

Her mind drifted to her mother. Persephone was a queen in every way. Blonde curly hair that tumbled to her waist, a raven-feathered crown and piercing blue eyes. She was the summer to her father's winter. How she was taken ill is incomprehensible. Immortals didn't get sick. They didn't die. And yet somehow, Persephone was dying. The souls were keeping the illness at bay, but they were only a temporary solution, as told to her by the Oracle of Delphi, who conveniently read tarot out of a head shop on West 5th. The souls kept the fever away and the hallucinations, but not the black, syrupy appearance that ran through her mother's veins and marred her papery, ivory skin.

Vic fingered the bat charm against her neck. It was one of her mother's many symbols and was a gift on Vic's sixteenth birthday. For comparison, her father had given her the onyx blade. Both were her most prized possessions, possibly for the same reasons.

Persephone.

After a long silence, both lost in their own thoughts, Asher cleared his throat. "I guess I should be going." There was an actual hint of sadness there beneath the casual bravado, whether for her mother or for her, Vic couldn't be sure.

He gracefully got up from the bed and Vic automatically stood, mirroring him. That was the type of presence Asher inadvertently commanded. He was both beautiful and frightening. It was an unnerving combination.

To get to the front door, he had to walk past where she stood. As he did, he paused. He was standing very close, Vic's nose inches from his chest. She was fairly tall at 5'7" but Asher was built like a brick wall. She could smell the distinct, familiar scent of him: leather and incense, with a hint of musk. It was a stark contrast to Cal's warm, fresh-baked, sweet smell, but she found herself leaning into the familiarity of it. Asher smelled like home. And despite all her gripes about it, Vic knew to a certain extent that it was where she belonged. The only place she could ever truly fit in. And more importantly, be herself.

Nervously, she peered up through her lashes at Asher. Once again, bolted to the floor when she should practically be shoving him out of the door. She'd been so mad at his audacity to come into her home, but now she found part of her not wanting him to leave. Maybe Asher wasn't the only one with two sides to him.

Very slowly, as if she were a skittish animal, he raised a tattooed hand and gently tucked a lock of hair behind her ear, the one lined from lobe all the way up the helix with piercings. His fingers were warm against her skin and she felt a hot tingle all the way down her spine.

"Be careful," was all he said and before she could even inhale the scent of him again, he was gone. Hellhounds moved eerily fast, and Asher was no exception. She heard the roar of the Harley as he started it and leaned her forehead against the closed front door. He'd even managed to somehow lock it behind him.

What did it all mean? Asher couldn't...he couldn't actually *miss* her. Besides, *he* had ditched *her*. But watching someone die can change people. She would know. She'd watched it more times than she'd care to admit. And she was no longer the same person that she once was. Each Taking changed her, took something of hers along with it.

As the Harley faded down the winding drive, Vic shoved herself away from the door and headed over to her wardrobe, purposefully ignoring the rumpled bedspread where Asher had been only moments before. She had a football game to get ready for.

Chapter Four

Vic had seriously considered taking her satchel and onyx dagger along to the football game, but she thought that if Cal caught sight of it that it may be slightly off-putting. She had the sneaking suspicion not many girls carried blades around Olympia. Interestingly, she had no idea why. Drunk guys and victory parties seemed the perfect excuse to Vic.

Not that she thought she'd need it with Cal. She drove along the winding road back toward his house. It was dusk now and the sky was cast in shades of indigo and midnight blue. It was also Vic's favorite time of day. The moment between waking and sleeping, dreams and nightmares.

Energy hummed through her body, one of the few fortunate side effects of being around Asher, of being near someone linked to her home. Taking extra precaution, she'd sprinkled some black salt around the perimeter of the house and along the window edges on the upstairs floor, even though she hadn't even been to that floor in ages. Something like height or windows wouldn't stop Asher from entering if he wanted to enter. She actually wasn't sure if the salt would either, but it was known for its binding and protection capabilities. Peace of mind had to account for something.

She drove with the windows down, the night air just as stifling as the daytime. The breeze blew her freshly washed hair back into her face, dousing her nose with a floral concoction from the general store shampoo. Truth be told, she wasn't sure how the evening was going to play out. She *needed* to find another soul tonight, but she was also a firm believer in where there was a will there was a way.

Asher's visit had set her on edge. The way he had acted so concerned not just for her mother, but for her. It was so un-Asher-like that Vic wondered if he was trying to manipulate her for one reason or another. Asher's motives were never clear cut as evidenced from his past behaviors. But, then again, she hadn't been home in several months. Maybe Persephone was no longer in homeostasis, but somehow worsening.

Vic shuddered at the thought as she pulled her truck back into Cal's driveway. She let the truck idle, unsure of whether or not she should go up to the door and knock. Or she could just text Cal and let him know she was here, except she hadn't asked for his phone number. She supposed she looked presentable enough. Her hair was washed and tumbled past her shoulders in slightly frizzy black waves. She'd put on a plum-colored V-neck shirt that contrasted nicely with her hazel eyes and tied a heathered-gray zipper hoodie around her waist under the presumption that it could get chilly, but she knew that it wouldn't. Until Persephone was better, she knew for a fact the weather wasn't going to change. The only problem was, no one else knew that.

Before she could decide what to do, Cal burst from the front door of the white colonial, golden light spilling across the porch and walkway. She could imagine his five brothers and sisters laughing together around the dinner table, maybe poking fun at him for doing something so cliché on a Friday night.

He was nothing but a silhouette against the doorway for a moment before he pulled the door shut behind him. Trotting down the driveway he called something over his shoulder, but Vic couldn't hear because the direction of the wind took it back through the house's open window.

He pulled open the passenger side door and climbed onto the white leather seat. Vic felt her pulse quicken, forgetting for a second where she was. His warm smell enveloped the cab of the truck and she wondered if it was some sort of cologne, or maybe his mother was a witch and baked him into her pies for him to be reborn from them each day. It sounded like one of the fairy tales her mother used to tell her at bedtime when she was a kid. She shook her head.

"Hey." It sounded more confident than she felt.

"Hey back," grinned Cal. As she backed out of the driveway she noticed he was more appropriately dressed than during the school day. He was still wearing the same Chucks, but instead of the heavy sweatshirt, he was wearing a navy, ringer style t-shirt with the outline of a silver Spartan silhouetted across the front. There was a silver watch on his wrist with a dark mother-of-pearl face that glowed in the fading light. It seemed slightly out of place with his casual attire.

He caught her glance and moved his wrist back and forth.

"A gift from my father on my eighteenth birthday. A reminder to not be late."

Vic turned onto the road, heading back toward the school and the football stadium. "A bad habit of yours?"

He grinned. "I'm working on it."

"Aren't we all?" Vic mumbled.

"Your hair looks nice," Cal said. She looked at him sidelong, then turned her eyes back onto the road. She did not want the soul she was Taking tonight to be his, especially as a result of her careless driving.

Cal misinterpreted her body language. "I mean, not that it didn't look nice before…"

Vic caught a red light and smiled. "Thanks."

His shoulders visibly relaxed. After the light turned green and the shadow of the school came into view and the lights from the football stadium, Cal admitted, "That's always happening to me. I always think I'm saying one thing, but it seems to come out all wrong."

She pulled into the parking lot that joined the school and stadium. It was already full and the game still didn't start for a half hour. Friday night in a small town was a football night. She knew that even if she wasn't usually a part of it.

"Maybe it's not so much that it comes out wrong, as it isn't interpreted the way in which you think it should be." She finally found a spot relatively far from the stadium entrance. "I hope you don't mind a bit of a walk."

Cal was already climbing out of the truck. "Nope not at all. Has anyone ever told you that you're kind of strange?"

Vic shoved her keys into her jeans pocket and made her way to the front of the truck where she fell in step beside him, their shadows elongated on the asphalt and the tall lamps casting their faces in sickly yellow shadow. Not like the warm amber light from inside Cal's house.

"Did that come out wrong?" Vic asked, glad that he couldn't see the quirk of her smile in the darkness.

"Maybe you *interpreted* it wrong."

"I don't think so. I took it to mean that you find me wildly magnificent," she teased.

He grinned. "That's exactly what I meant."

They reached the ticket gate and to her surprise Cal paid for her ticket. It wasn't much—the game was only one dollar for students—but it was the gesture that she appreciated. Did it mean this was a date? Before her mind could wonder further, Cal turned to her.

"I owe you for showing me Sal's. That sandwich was probably the best I've ever had in my whole life. But don't tell my mom I said that," he chuckled.

"My lips are sealed."

They made their way through the sea of navy and silver, stopping at the concession stand to pick up some gummi bears for her and popcorn for him, then continued to the bleachers. The home side of the field was covered in silver, white and navy t-shirts, some parents near the front row held signs with their child's name and jersey number.

Cal chose a seat off to one side, slightly away from other people. Which was okay with Vic. She wasn't a huge fan of crowds. And all this enthusiasm could be a little overwhelming. People were on their feet cheering and the game hadn't even started yet.

There were some kids from their History class in front of them and some faces Vic recognized from around school, but with which she had no names to attach. Several people were waving little felt pennants and one guy even had a navy and silver knit beanie on, even though he was shirtless and sporting the Y of Olympia in blue paint across his torso.

They stood, Vic chewing on gummi bears and Cal popping popcorn as they watched the homecoming court be announced and step out onto the football field. The court's queen was a nice, quiet girl from Vic's Latin class who also somehow happened to be a cheerleader. She was so quiet, Vic wondered how she even made the squad. Maybe she had an alter ego, like Wonder Woman. The king was some guy that Vic knew played on the basketball team, she whispered as much to Cal, her breath warm against his ear. There was Elaine from their English class and Nick, along with two other people in different years, that Vic didn't really know all that well.

After the student MC in the broadcasting booth gave the rundown of the court, Mr. Beckerman stepped forward on the field with a microphone. He wasn't wearing his usual suit with its waistcoat, but gray slacks and a navy polo shirt with a silver Spartan embroidered near the heart. First, he thanked the homecoming court for their school spirit and said that the student body had chosen wisely—even though for the most part it was simply a popularity contest, Vic supposed in a small town everyone was popular to some degree or another.

Then the crowd grew silent, the jittering and movement stopped. Mr. Beckerman cleared his throat, and it was as if everyone sensed what was coming before it dawned on Vic.

"I'd like to take a moment of silence for Lauren and Eric before the beginning of tonight's game. As you all know, Lauren is a well-liked student and fellow cheerleader who would have been at tonight's game if not for the unfortunate circumstances of this morning. Eric also sustained injuries, but not life threatening ones. At this moment, Lauren remains in critical care and in a comatose state. Our Spartans will play in their honor tonight and we hope, as we bow our heads, that God will hear our prayers."

Vic wasn't sure she believed in a singular god, it was kind of difficult with the upbringing she had and given who her parents were, but she bowed her head anyway. Her guts were twisted with shame as a heavy silence fell over the people of the stadium. She stole a glance across the field and even the emerald and gold colors of the night's opposing team had their heads bowed. She wondered if the pounding of her heart could be heard in the thickness of the quiet. Someone sniffled a few rows ahead of her, followed by someone else to the right.

Cal had his head bowed and his lips moved in what Vic assumed was silent prayer. The shame she felt was laced with guilt because these people prayed to a God she was pretty sure didn't exist—at least not in the sense that they believed in it. The person they prayed to could not help them, could not save Lauren any more than the Earth could stop spinning. Sure there were gods, but they were many and not one. For her this was a fact. And she knew the palpable silence that grieved around her would only grow worse with the more souls she was forced to Take from this small town. Because she could not—*would not*—stop Taking until Persephone was well again.

–

The game was exhilarating, much to Vic's surprise. There was something contagious about the cheering and the competitive spirit that before the end of the third quarter, she'd found herself sucked in. Even letting a girl in front of them paint blue and gray streaks across either of her cheeks, the girl's fingers dripping with the cool thickness of the paint. Cal had taken an S on either side.

Vic found herself laughing and screaming out the Spartan's fight song alongside her classmates: "Spartan Warriors, descended from the sky, Spartan Warriors fight and die!" Really, it was rather morbid if one stopped to think about it, but in the spirit of the moment it seemed harmless enough.

The cheerleading squad front-flipped, back-flipped, and threw each other somersaulting in the air, as if they could reach the stars. The marching band dipped and jived, and the fans in the stands stomped their feet in the bleachers. Popcorn and cotton candy wafted on the breeze, wrapping their scent in the strands of her hair. Her hands were red from clapping so hard. They had creamed the other team 36-7. And Vic knew that the win had been hard-earned. She also knew that there were celebratory parties tonight, perhaps laced with just a hint of sadness that their classmates were unable to take part.

After the game, the crowd spilled onto the field and the football players dumped a bucket of ice water over the head of Mr. Beckerman who howled good-naturedly. Vic and Cal hung back near the goal post and watched as their classmates hugged, cheered, and generally jumped on one another. One guy in their Physics class was sitting on the horizontal bar of the goal post with a cowboy hat and the letter A painted on his torso in navy blue.

Cal caught Vic's eye and smiled. Suddenly, she wondered if this was how it was for him too. A part and apart at the same time. Here, even at home, Vic always felt like an outsider looking in. Sure, she could fit in just fine, but she never quite felt like she belonged. Maybe that was something Cal had sensed about her, and why he'd reached out to her in the first place. Perhaps it was a divine accident that Mrs. Williamson had paired them together that day. Serendipity. A fortunate accident. Vic liked that word.

Cal nodded his head in the direction of the parking lot, not even attempting to be heard over the blasting music and raucous hollers of their classmates. Vic nodded and they walked away from the crowd, passing the school mascot, dressed in a loincloth and fake muscle costume as he danced and brandished his shield, play-fighting with some of the younger kids who'd attended the game. They were all laughing. Happy. It warmed Vic from the inside out. This feeling was something she'd have to tap into later in the wee hours of the night when it wasn't yet morning. Sometimes the good feelings made the bad things easier to do.

Her ears rang with the aftermath of the evening's sounds, dulling any current noise so that it sounded as if her ears were stuffed with cotton. They reached her truck, but as they'd approached she'd checked the shadows beneath it and then glanced inside the bed, to be sure Asher wasn't somehow lurking. A hellhound was one thing, a jealous hellhound was a whole other thing.

Once they climbed inside, Cal gestured to his ears. "I feel like I spent the evening at a rock concert and not a football game."

Vic gave him a confused look. "What?" He frowned and she smiled. "I'm kidding."

"I'm sorry, did you just say you were kidding? Or did you say you could go for some pudding?"

Vic turned the key in the ignition and the engine purred to life. "That was a horrible joke." She gave him a pointed look before glancing in the rear view mirror. For just an instant she though she saw a pair of green eyes peering back at her, but when she blinked they were gone. Possibly one of

Asher's stupid tricks. Or possibly a trick of her own mind.

Cal held up his hands in mock defense. He had somehow acquired a Spartans knit beanie during the course of the evening. "I know. I know. I apologize." He rolled down the passenger side window as Vic pulled out of the parking lot and back onto the winding road.

"I don't know about pudding, but I know where we could get some ice cream." She glanced at him as the street lights periodically illuminated his face in a wash of gold. Gold. Gray. Gold. Gray. He had a sprinkling of freckles across his nose, maybe a memento from his California days spent in the sun.

"Now ice cream is something I can definitely get behind. Way better than pudding. Plus, if your ice cream choices are as superb as your sub sandwich choices, then I definitely have something to look forward to." He smiled and glanced out the window at the passing scenery.

There wasn't much to Olympia. There were lots of trees and wooded areas, which were some of Vic's favorite places, but there was also pastures and fields of wildflowers. A single stream ran through the town—which had once had an oat mill when it was first founded. The mill now stood abandoned, but there was a push to renovate it and make it a historic landmark. Now, the town subsisted on tourism and numerous campgrounds.

Vic thought the town was beautiful, with its snow-capped purple mountains in the distance. Close enough to frame a picturesque view, but far enough away where people could get away for a weekend of skiing in the mountains. The town was ordinary, but to Vic it felt like magic. She wondered if Cal could sense it too, with his pensive expression—eyes alert, lips slightly parted as he stared at the moonlit view from the passenger side window.

The ice cream shop was about a ten minute ride from the school, just past the turn she'd have taken to go to Cal's house. It wasn't a super popular place, there was also a Dairy Queen in the opposite direction from the school which was both cheap and convenient. But this place had the best mint chocolate chip ice cream. Vic's favorite part was that it was made with crème de menthe so it was tinged a pretty green color, dotted with milk chocolate chips. Just thinking about it made her stomach lurch and she remembered with Asher's surprise visit, she hadn't eaten anything since the sandwich earlier, except a couple of cookies.

As Molly's Milk and Creamery came into view with its white and pink awning shining like a sweet-toothed beacon on the horizon, Cal suddenly turned to Vic.

"Admit it."

Vic pulled into the parking lot, passing the sign with the giant cow wearing a pink tutu. "Admit what?"

"You had a good time tonight." He grinned as she pulled into one of the parking spaces beneath the sign. The light from the sign caught those freckles again. Vic decided she really, really liked freckles.

She gave him a coy shrug. "The night's not over yet."

Chapter Five

Vic pulled into the driveway of the manor and into the old barn. She wouldn't be taking the truck tonight. It was almost midnight and the moon hung like a thumbnail in the sky. She paused at the back door, carefully inspecting the black salt which still formed a line across the threshold.

She highly doubted something as simple as salt would keep Asher away, but he made her brain feel all muddled and she needed to be clear headed about this. The lock tumbled and she let herself in, she'd left one of the kitchen lights on earlier so she wouldn't be returning to a dark house. The plate of peanut butter-chocolate chip cookies still sat on the counter, so she decided to help herself to a couple, despite having just ate her weight in mint chocolate chip ice cream. Her sweet tooth was something wicked, in that way she took after her father. It was one of the few things they had in common. Actually, Vic could only think of three things: sweets, Persephone, and a temper.

The Takings made her crave sweets even more, as if all the sugar-laden goodies could fill the hollow void that they left behind. She was beginning to feel like two different people. One being her father's daughter and her mother's savior. The person who let Asher unnerve her. Then there was the other Vic. The person who got good grades in her classes and went to high school football games. The type of person who noticed the freckles sprinkled across Callum Bishop's nose.

She cringed and pushed away from the counter. She wasn't sure she could ever be that person, but her heart felt the inklings of wanting to be and she wondered if it was enough.

–

The woods at night were filled with sounds. The howls of coyotes and the hoots of owls, the gentle flapping of wings. It was still warm out, and already Vic's t-shirt was clinging to her, damp with sweat. The long walk isn't what made her sweat, but the anticipation of what she was about to do. Sometimes it would even make her feel physically ill just thinking about it, so she avoided too much planning.

Her leather satchel was secured around her waist and the onyx dagger was sheathed at her thigh. If anyone saw her, she'd probably look like a crazed lunatic. Obviously, she would not be mistaken for a hunter at this hour. Besides, not many people hunted with daggers. At least not for animals.

Luckily, the enchanted necklace her mother gave her was quite useful. The bat was one of Persephone's many symbols. Essentially the charm bent to Vic's will, obeying her silent demands. Her mother thought the Upper World was dangerous and thus had given her the necklace as protection.

Vic almost never took it off.

She crept along the sloped edge of the forest, there was a

ridge to her left and on the other side nothing but a field of wildflowers. Keeping to the shadows of the forest, she searched for one of the housing developments on the opposite side of the road. This is where she would find her Mark.

The development came into view with its fancy sign and kitschy name. The housing development seemed carved out of the forest, the woods backing up to the back yards of the houses. This would make her job easier. She needed to be close, but not too close. Just enough to keep the Mark in her line of sight. And then of course to extract the soul, she had to get very close. But not initially.

Rock music drifted to her across the otherwise silent neighborhood. A car passed on the road, going much too fast for what Vic knew was a rather windy stretch. She could have used this to her advantage. Changed her mind. But she decided it would seem suspicious if there were two potentially fatal car accidents in the same number of days. What she was about to do could be explained away. At least that was her hope.

She loped across the street and to the west, sticking to the wooded back yards, following the sounds of the music. Laughter soon drifted across the night, and it didn't take her long to find its source. She had been right. There was a house full of Olympia High students celebrating the night's victory along with the homecoming weekend. A party.

Cal had asked her if she was sure she didn't want to go to the dance tomorrow—no, not tomorrow, it was after midnight and the dance was tonight—and she had smiled and thanked him, but told him that despite the football game being fun, a dance was a little too out of her comfort zone at this point. He genuinely didn't seem to mind. She'd also mentioned to him that she would be out of town over the weekend. That she had to go and visit her mother, but would be back on Monday. He'd given her that dimpled smile before climbing out of her truck. The moonlight casting his face in pale shadows, he'd turned back toward the rolled down window and leaned in casually. His grin turning shy when he told her that he looked forward to hearing all about it in English class on Monday. She'd watched as he had ambled down the long, shadowed driveway, stopping to wave one last time, before disappearing into the idyllic white colonial.

The thought of Cal even caring how her weekend went made her heart skip a beat. She brushed her sweaty hair out of her face. *Focus.* Standing behind a large Sycamore, Vic observed the scene. The house had a few lights on. A groan wafted down to her from one of the open windows and she couldn't help but roll her eyes. She was pretty sure whoever it was would regret it in the morning. Daylight made nighttime choices often seem worse.

There were a few students out in the backyard, collapsed in chairs around a bonfire. There was an open pack of jumbo marshmallows spilled onto the grass near someone's foot. Vic felt relief that she didn't recognize anyone. Knowing made Taking harder.

They were all more or less cast in shadow with the eerie glow of the fire jumping around and sometimes illuminating them in a brief amber glow. She counted two girls and three guys. One of the girls and one of the guys sat huddled together and Vic suspected they were kissing. Empty beer cans were crushed at their feet.

Meanwhile, the other girl and the other two guys sat holding cans and talking in low voices. At least fifteen discarded cans were littered around them. She hated to take advantage of their drunkenness, but then at the same time felt like it served them right for being so careless under the guise of being young and free.

Actions had consequences.

Of that Vic knew first hand. Just not all of her consequences had been dealt. But she knew that it wouldn't be long before they came, rearing their head in all their wicked glory.

She creeped closer, a low stone wall separated the woods from the actual back yard, but it would be easy to hop over when she needed to. Now, she would just have to wait until the right moment. As she watched through the shrubs and branches of the woods, she once again felt like she was on the outside looking in.

Was this what so-called normal teenagers did? If so, then Vic felt very un-normal. She also couldn't see Cal acting like this. Casually kissing a girl with a lukewarm beer in his fist. The thought made her stomach drop. Granted, she didn't know him very well. But this sort of thing seemed more Asher's speed than Cal's. She bit her lip, hoping her thinking of Asher wouldn't make him magically manifest.

It didn't.

The making out couple got up and wandered toward the house, cans crunching beneath their feet as they went. Vic was far enough away that the music drowned out whatever they were saying. She wasn't sure how much time had passed.

Fifteen minutes maybe?

Her t-shirt stuck to the small of her back. And the knees of her jeans were dirty from kneeling on the ground. She was positioned in such a way that she could leap up at any second. Behind her she heard what sounded like a twig snapping and whipped her head around, hand poised on her dagger.

But nothing appeared and she shook her head, chalking it up to an animal.

Takings always made her anxious.

Finally, she saw her opportunity. One of the guys was slouched in the chair, his arm hanging limp, knuckles grazing the grass. The remaining girl had gotten up and disappeared around the side of the house. Maybe she was leaving or maybe there were more people out front. It didn't matter much to Vic either way.

The guy that didn't appear asleep, sat with his head hung low, nursing his can of beer. Before he could disappear too, Vic wiggled her fingers in the air, as if reaching for something, feeling for the energetic strings of the guy's soul. A familiar, warm sensation waved out at her. She quickly kissed the bat charm for its efficiency as much as for its luck.

And so began the night's Taking.

Once she had a strong hold on his energetic strings, Vic flicked her wrist. The guy gave a low groan, dropping his can of beer before tumbling out of the camping chair. He hit the ground on his hands and knees. He began to wretch—a horrible sound that Vic wouldn't soon forget—as he threw up beer and whatever else he'd eaten that night. The guy asleep didn't stir. Vic flicked her wrist a second time, and this time the guy gasped, falling forward onto his stomach, over top of his own sick. She saw him convulse once and knew that this was her chance.

She easily leapt over the stone wall and ran on light feet toward the limp figure. His head was lolled to the side and his eyes were rolled back in his head. The fire cast his face in a demonic glow. It was fitting for the situation. Taking a deep breath, she didn't hesitate as she pushed her fingers through his back, past bones and muscle until she felt the ebbing warmth of his soul.

Her fingers wrapped around it and she pulled gently. It came easily as if it wanted her to Take it. She didn't even need to cut any lingering tendrils. It was quick and clean. This was her favorite kind of Taking.

She unlocked her satchel and slipped the living orb inside. Its human shell had gone very still. Sweat dripped into her eyes. The other guy slept on in drunken oblivion.

Vic quickly hopped the stone wall and landed back in the woods. She kissed her bat charm and in a deep, male voice called out over the music: "HEY! HEY, GUYS! I NEED HELP BACK HERE! COME QUICK!"

The music cut and there was the sound of running feet. A few figures appeared from the door leading into the house's garage. Vic's voice had startled awake the other guy.

"Oh, shit!" someone said.

"Quick, call 9-1-1!" said someone else.

Panic and chaos.

She hoped it was enough. That the guy—a kid, really—wouldn't end up dead, maybe comatose like Lauren. That meant there would at least still be hope. No matter how little.

Before she could dwell on it any further, she took one last glance at the backyard, then turned and ran all the way back to the manor, until her legs had gone numb and she could no longer catch her breath.

–

Vic's sleep had been restless. The low-light had been a nightmare where bodies with barely any breath were stacked in a pile, vacant eyes staring off into the distance. Pale arms and legs set out at odd angles until Vic realized that the bodies formed a throne of what she'd come to consider the living dead. The soul—chi, spirit, life-force, conscience, personality—

whatever you wanted to call it, it was what made a person who they were. It was what made the souls so valuable, not as payment, but as medicine.

In the dream ten foot tall fires blazed around the throne made of the living dead. Everything was a garish mix of obsidian and scarlet. Sitting on the seat of the throne was a crown of bones and an onyx scepter. Her father stood off to the side in one of his black tuxedos, shoes so shiny she could see the fire reflected in them, even from where she stood several feet away. His black hair was slicked back and he'd grown a poetic-looking goatee. Set on his head was a halo of black crow feathers, a circlet, probably hand-woven by his bride queen. Her father had always had a flare for the dramatic.

She could smell the lavender of the soaps Persephone often made, wafting off of his olive skin and mixing with the smell of ash and brimstone. If he'd turned, she would have seen the leathery black wings that protruded from his back, like a bat's. The symbol of her mother. Usually, ever the one for appearances, he kept them neatly folded in two parallel columns beneath shirts and jackets, so that if you didn't know you wouldn't notice. That is until you said something that sent him off into a rage. Then they'd open wide as if they could swallow you whole. They terrified Vic.

Come, her father had said, *and sit upon your throne, my daughter.*

Vic's throat had tightened in the dream as if an invisible hand was choking her. How could it be her throne? What princess was fit for a crown of bones? She shuddered and staggered back.

You are the princess of darkness.

His voice was barely a whisper, but she still heard it crystal clear over the roaring and crackling of the fire surrounding them. She turned, the fire now formed a ring around them. Normal fire wouldn't harm her much, but this—this fire was not normal if it was conjured by her father.

Vic shook her head in disagreement. She was not cut out to be a princess.

This may be what her father wanted, but it wasn't what *she* wanted. This was not a quiet life on a college campus somewhere in the Above World, doing normal, college-y things.

Her father shook his head with a slight frown.

But you are not normal. You are not destined for mediocracy. You are destined for greatness.

Vic knew that's what she should believe, but she just couldn't get her heart to wrap around the idea. She should want to fulfill the role she was destined to have. To be the Princess of the Under World. Maybe even with Asher by her side or in her service. Her skin grew clammy at the thought of living in darkness once she'd begun now to see the light. Persephone would understand. She may have chosen to stay in the Under World half the year, but she'd still made a choice.

All Vic wanted was the choice.

The fire began to swirl around her, drawing closer. Vic began to cough. It leapt from behind her father, who spread his black wings wide and levitated just high enough so that the flames licked the wingtips of his shoes. The flames were alive: hungry and deprived, cresting over the throne of bodies. Vic watched helplessly as the vacant eyes stared at her, unfeeling of any emotion. Blank. Empty. Her father's fire was powerful, it consumed the throne, crown and all in a matter of seconds. All that remained was a pile of ash with Vic standing beside it, still surrounded in a ring of fire that was intent on growing tighter and tighter around her.

Her father's deep laugh echoed off the walls of the cavernous space, a laugh that haunted nightmares all over the world. A laugh so terrifying it could make your blood run cold. As if it belonged to the Devil himself.

–

She'd woken up drenched in sweat, her breath coming in short pants as if she'd been running again. Her hair stuck to the back of her neck. On the pillow beside her was a single, satin black crow's feather. Like a calling card from home.

It was nice of Asher to give her a warning of his arrival this time.

Immediately, she went into the kitchen and scarfed down two peanut butter-chocolate chip cookies, the sugary sweetness somewhat ebbing her unease. She didn't realize how much she was dreading going back until that nightmare.

The roar of a motorcycle filled the kitchen, where Vic still leaned against the counter, her sleepshirt plastered to her still sweaty body. *Shit. Shitty Shit-Shit.* She ducked into the bathroom and grabbed her pink, fluffy robe—a gift from her Aunt Aphrodite.

The back lock tumbled of its own accord and the door swung open. Asher's tall, muscular form took up the entire doorway before he let himself inside. His boot kicked the salt that lined the threshold and a flicker of annoyance crossed his sharp features. Rolling his eyes, he stepped over the line and into the kitchen. His green eyes found her just as she tied the robe shut around herself. He lifted an eyebrow.

"I did send a message this time."

Vic swallowed the lump in her throat. "I know. Thank you."

She didn't know exactly what else to say because being mad at someone like Asher was so much easier than being kind.

"Um, I need to hop in the shower really fast, but, uh, help yourself to some more cookies." She gestured to the plate on the counter and before he could respond scurried into the bathroom and locked the door.

–

When she came out of the bathroom, wearing a pair of old jeans and a fitted black t-shirt, hair still damp and in tight ringlets against her head, Asher was lounging across the fancy onyx-backed settee. She was relieved he wasn't lounging across her bed again, but then she was also irritated that he looked so at ease no matter where he placed himself in her home.

Kneeling beside the bed, she pulled out the metal box and placed it onto the sleek black coffee table where Asher had crossed his booted feet. She knocked his feet off with a shove.

"At least take your boots off if you're going to do that. I know for a fact you weren't raised in a barn but in a very nice stone-walled palace."

He ignored her statement, but didn't put his feet back up on the table. Progress.

She went about gathering a pair of plum-colored Chucks, her onyx blade, and her necklace. Asher rose without asking, taking the necklace from her fingers, and moving aside her damp hair to clamp it against her neck. His fingers brushed her skin ever so slightly and caused heat to bloom like a flower down her spine.

"Thanks." She turned to face him.

"Ready?" He rocked back on his heels as if he had all the time in the world. It was very un-Asher-like.

"I think so."

He picked up the metal box and followed her back into the kitchen. She noticed that he'd left the last cookie for her.

She glanced at him then picked it up and made her way to the door. "Be sure to lock it behind you. For mortals, locks can actually prevent people from coming in."

He rolled his eyes, but plucked the key from beside the door and locked it behind him before relinquishing it to her with a slight bow.

She pocketed it and walked over to the Harley-Davidson Sportster Iron 883. She watched as Asher took some belt like straps and attached the metal box to the front of the bike, near the handlebars. Then he straddled the bike and kicked up the side stand.

The bike roared to life. He gave her a pointed look.

There was no more procrastinating, so she crossed the driveway and threw her left leg up and over so that she could still touch the ground with her tip toes. She knew Asher had pegs for the back passenger, so she kicked them down with her feet.

However, he still didn't move until she placed her arms around his solid waist, clasping her hands in front near his belly button. Heat radiated off him and she knew he could feel the pounding of her heart against his back.

She hoped he thought it was because it had been so long since she'd been on a motorcycle and not because of her close proximity to him. The earthy scent of incense clung to his clothes.

He sped down the winding driveway, and at the very end before they hit the street, he jerked up onto the rear tire, the front wheel high in the air, which forced Vic to tighten her grip lest she slide backward off the bike.

Vic scowled, sure that he'd done that on purpose.

Asher let out a delighted whoop as the front tire made contact with the pavement once more.

They tore down the road heading south, the delicate light of the morning following them as they went.

Chapter Six

Mystery hunters and fans of the occult would say the entrance to the Under World was at the bottom of a river.

Maybe one that claimed too many innocent lives. Or they would say that it was deep within an ancient cave where macabre rituals were performed to summon the living dead. Or maybe even just the dead-dead.

But it was really much simpler than that.

Asher had turned off the main road and onto a dirt path. Loose earth sprayed behind them as Vic clung to his solid form. The feel of him was all too familiar.

They entered a field with a giant, twisting tree with flame red foliage, and an odd blackish-brown bark. A tree that seemed much too old, much too gnarled, and much too large to actually be real. Because it wasn't actually real.

It was conjured.

Several trees like this existed around the world, and the one before them happened to be the closest to Olympia.

Now, despite what you may have heard to the contrary,

one cannot simply stumble upon the gates of Hell. You had to either be summoned or accompanied by a hellhound. Even Vic couldn't come and go as she pleased.

Several crows sat perched in the knobby branches of the tree. Sunlight glinting off their shining wings. As Asher twisted the throttle, to a bystander it would seem the sleek, black motorcycle was destined to crash into the massive trunk of the old tree. But just as the front tire was poised to smash into the trunk, crumpling them both, the tree seemed to swallow them up instead, enveloping them in darkness.

The darkness was only momentary before the ground beneath them turned from the familiar Above World sienna color to a deep, rich burgundy. Brimstone choked Vic's lungs. Overhead, the sky was a purplish black and a glowing white star hung brightly. They zoomed by twisted, blackened trees and burnt out shrubs. A river—the Styx—flowed alongside them to the left, as if guiding whoever entered the Under World.

In the distance to her right, Vic could see shadowy, hunched over figures picking enchanted berries from black bushes. The figures were chained together like an old-fashioned chain gang.

Vic knew that no matter how many bushels they created, as soon as their work seemed done and relief was near, more berries would instantly materialize. The berries were enough to satiate her father's sweet tooth, but it was a punishment for a soul's minor transgressions. The liars and the cheaters.

The Mendax.

They continued to follow the churning river—it ran black and ice cold. The air was hot and stifling, pressing down on Vic's shoulders. Absent-mindedly, she rested her cheek against Asher's back and watched as the metal forgers came into view.

Hephaestus may be their god and overseer, but the fires of the Under World are what fueled their work. But these metalworkers were not like the living artisans who Hephaestus minded, these were the thieves and the abusers. People who lived their lives always taking and never giving, no matter how much or little, and the ones who used their power to exert dominance over others.

Black cauldrons of lime green flame were spread throughout this section of the Under World and figures more dead than living tended to them. The fires must be kept continually burning because they fueled the fires of Hephaestus's best in the Above World. As above so below. It was back-breaking work, continually stoking the fires every day, all day without stopping. But Vic did not feel bad that people who mistreated others were faced with such a grim task. The Abutens suffered what they deserved.

They continued on, the green flames both mesmerizing and terrifying in their beauty. It was not long before they reached Vic's least favorite section of the Under World: The Interemptor. Her skin broke out in goose bumps as they neared.

Iron cages stacked on top of one another rose beside the road. They were small, maybe two feet by two feet, and black-ash, skeletal bodies rested inside them. More demon than human or anything once living. The cages formed a tower that seemed to have no top. Vic knew that each day The Interemptor had one task and one task only. They were released into the River Styx, where they would sink because of the weights of their crimes—the most atrocious crime against nature—they would then have to claw their way back up to the surface, trying to resist the weight of the invisible chains. Each day they would fail. Each day they would try again. Dying only to die again another day. This was the fate of murderers, killers, and assassins.

Vic turned, pressing her forehead in between Asher's shoulder blades. His body was solid, but relaxed. She didn't know how it didn't bother him. To see the things that existed outside the safety of the inner domain. She knew that in each of the domains—there were only three, Dante apparently liked to exaggerate—it wasn't actual people, simply a husk that contained a tarnished soul. That's why they were so eerie. Their soul was sent here to repent for their Above World transgressions. To cleanse itself back to a pure state. But it still put Vic on edge.

Asher stopped just before the bone bridge that ran over the River Styx, which now crossed in front of them. A woman with dark skin and full, cherry red lips sat on a large boulder beside the river, idly sweeping her bare foot back and forth in its cool blackness. The river was like ice—a stark contrast to the fires and suffocating air that permeated the Under World.

At the sound of Asher's motorcycle she looked up, brown eyes—almost black—wide.

"Is that? No. But is that Asher and her highness?"

She scrambled up, the hood of her long black cloak slipping off her raven-colored hair. The cloak had matching thigh high slits on either side and was tied at the waist with a sort of golden rope. She grabbed her staff made of the same bark as the tree in the Above World and bowed slightly.

"Your highness."

Vic smiled. She hated being called your highness about as much as she hated being called Tor.

"Come on now, River. You know that isn't necessary. I'm glad to see you're faring well."

River was the Guardian of the Styx, thus named River Styx

herself. She never aged and always looked beautiful and mysterious with the ease and grace of a dancer. She presided over the penitence of The Interemptor, but Vic was pretty sure she saw it as a limitation of her talents. When she was particularly bored, she was known to simply morph into the river itself and disappear beneath its surface.

However, if anyone inadvertently tried to wander across the bridge and into the inner sanctum without the accompaniment of a hellhound, they'd feel her cyclonic wrath. If they weren't already dead, they'd certainly be dead after an encounter with River. She took her responsibilities seriously.

Asher gave her a nod and she bowed again, before Asher guided the motorcycle across the bone bridge—aptly named for the skulls and bones that created it—some crimes even penitence could not purify—and that were enchanted together in a spanning arch. When they reached the other side, Vic let out a relieved breath.

Sweat clung to the small of her back, and plastered her now dry hair to the back of her neck and to her cheeks. Towering black trees with purple leaves bloomed with juicy, blood-red pomegranates. These were her mother's trees, and the orchard lined the road on both sides. There were no thieves or abusers or murderers in this domain. All that resided on the other side of the bridge. A side of the bridge, her current comings and goings from the Above World excluded, she'd only visited once as a small girl.

From a young age Vic had not understood just what her father did.

She did not understand why some people avoided him, feared him even.

The bridge had been her boundary. As a young child,

she'd played in the river and talked with River, but never was she to actually cross the river.

Then one day, she'd been particularly angry—a trait that she wasn't very proud of—and had thrown a temper-tantrum, kicking her father square in the shin in the process, little fists balled up. She couldn't have been more than seven or eight. She hadn't gotten her way: but *why* couldn't she go past the bone bridge. There was a whole world to see and why did he insist on confining her to such a small portion of it?

Her father had grabbed her by the wrist, half dragging her down the lane away from their home—the inner sanctum—and across the bone bridge. And that was the day that Vic understood.

Understood just who her father was and what it was that he did. That it wasn't so much a choice, as an assignment that one could never resign from. Seeing the other domains had frightened her. She'd had nightmares for weeks, and then on and off for years afterward.

The father she had loved so much—who'd given her virtually anything she'd wanted—was also a man who could make others cower in his wake. He was the Ruler of the Dead, the Harbinger of Balance, the King of the Under World. The power he had both intrigued and terrified her. The fact that it intrigued her frightened her even more.

Asher pulled into the rotunda where other motorcycles, identical to his own were lined up, waiting for a hellhound to beckon. The rotunda was lined with pomegranate trees and in its center was a gigantic, onyx fountain with the likeness of her father and her mother, black water flowing out of their outstretched hands.

Her legs buzzed from the long ride, and Asher gave her a gentlemanly hand off the back of the bike. As she unstrapped the box containing her Takings, Asher walked up to one of the pomegranate trees and plucked off a piece of the ruby red fruit. Immediately, a new pomegranate grew in its place.

She tucked the box under arm and caught the fruit as Asher tossed it to her with a smile. He hadn't said anything since they'd left the manor and only later would Vic realize the reason why. He'd been concerned for her—for what she was about to be asked to do.

But for right now, she gave him a grin, surprised at how easy it spread across her face. Worlds away, it was too easy to fall back into old habits.

He extended his arm like a courtier and Vic rolled her eyes, but slipped her arm through his anyways. The onyx castle shone above them like glass, twisted spires disappearing into indigo clouds, it spread out in a half circle as if it was hugging the rotunda. Asher led her up the steps and to the arched doorway, with its clear crystal, skull-shaped knockers. But Asher didn't need to knock, at the slightest press of his fingers, the door swung open.

Some people would call it Hell.

Vic called it home.

Chapter Seven

What Vic wanted to do was to run up the winding, onyx staircase to her right and go straight to her mother's rooms. She pictured herself throwing open the door and crawling into the bed beside her, resting her cheek against her still beating heart.

But Asher had other plans, leading her gently into the foyer with its majestic ceiling graced with a chandelier of bone and lime green flames. The sound of the piano drifted to them, and Asher led her down the main hallway.

The walls did not hold decorations, they simply flanked guests like glossy black mirrors. Periodically, there would be a sconce made of bone with a dancing orb of green flame, but otherwise the decor was sterile and cold. To an outsider anyways. Vic knew where to look to find the warmth.

The hallway opened onto a set of double doors that were ajar. This is where the piano music emanated. Asher nudged the door open a bit wider and they slipped inside, the metal box still tight under the crook of Vic's arm. The study was lovely. It was all mahogany woods and black, satin paisley wall paper. Three of the four walls were inlaid with shelves of books. Vic spent countless hours in here as a child.

Her father's back was toward them. He sat at a baby grand piano in a brilliant, cherry red. His spidery long fingers danced over the keys. After a couple of minutes Asher politely cleared his throat. His boss finished the song—a whimsical, sad song that Vic herself remembered learning how to play, but couldn't remember which long dead composer it was by.

After the final note of the music settled around them with a blanket of finality, he turned toward them. His dark brown—nearly black—eyes lit up when they landed on his daughter. Immediately, he stood. He towered over Asher and was a formidable man. As in her dream, his black hair was slicked back and he had grown a goatee while she was away, but it was flecked with silver. He was wearing a pin-striped suit in a deep shade of emerald. A crow feather circlet around his head.

He closed the space from the piano to the door in four strides and pulled Vic into a rough hug, pressing her against his chest. The scratchy starchiness of his tailored ivory shirt, brushed against her cheek. Her eye fell on the gold medallion of the bident that rested at the base of his collarbone.

He pushed her away at arms' length, giant hands resting on her shoulders. It was now that she noticed the wrinkles at the corners of his eyes, the worry lines forming between his brows. These were bad signs of Persephone's progress.

His lips formed a sort of grimace. "It's good to see you, my daughter. Your presence has been missed." At this his eyes briefly went to Asher, who stood sentry against some bookshelves housing anthologies of ancient poets. Her father was a bit of a snob when it came to the arts.

She smiled back. Despite all the trouble he caused her—

the leaves in English class, Asher's unexpected visits—she knew that it was only because he cared. Well, that he cared and that he was desperate for a way to save her mother.

"It's good to be home."

And she realized that she meant it. Here, in the Under World, she was a princess. She was not someone on the outside looking in. Much the other way around. She was on the inside looking out.

Her father gestured to the four, leather armchairs to the left of the piano. Vic had spent many hours reading in their chocolate-buttery softness.

Asher did not make a move to follow. His face was impassive. Vic sat facing him, the metal box in her lap, with the bat clasp facing her.

"Are you hungry? Are you well?" Suddenly, a creature about three feet tall with red skin and black eyes emerged with a crack as if out of thin air. He was wearing a black bow tie and bowed to her father. His long, spear-like tail, was draped over his arm.

"My Lord."

"A plate of our best for the return of my daughter, but not something that will spoil dinner. We will dine as a family tonight."

"Very good sir." The red demon-creature bowed, then dissolved into thin air. Nothing but a lingering shimmer giving any indication of his presence.

"I'm always hungry and I'm doing well," Vic finally replied in answer to his questions.

It was very much like her father to plow forward without getting a response. He liked to get things done, and done fast, much to his own detriment. Usually, others were left to clean up the messes of his hastiness.

Vic glanced at Asher. "I really like school."

The corner of his mouth twitched slightly, but otherwise he stood stock still, his colorful tattooed arms crossed at his chest.

"Ah, but of course you do. You've always been one to appreciate art and culture. You do take after your father in many ways, but naturally, you also have the best of your mother."

The servant-demon reappeared. He held a tray laden with meats, cheeses, and wine. Before Vic could decide what she wanted, the creature slowly turned to stone. This was one of the house's enchantments. The creature would remain stone, essentially a statue holding a tray, until his services were no longer needed. He would then resume his normal form and disappear until beckoned once more. She chose a piece of prosciutto and popped it into her mouth.

Her father plucked a glass of merlot from the tray. "What's your favorite class?"

"It's a tie between English and Latin."

"Very good." He took a long sip. "And Richard?"

"Excellent. And I'm sure he'd send his regards if I'd told him I was leaving." She glared across the room at Asher, who could have been a stone statue himself.

"Have you been tending to your responsibilities?"

Vic chewed on a particularly rich, creamy piece of brie. She knew this was her father's way of asking about the Takings. Her responsibilities included not drawing unwanted attention, collecting the souls, and keeping them safe until she could return home.

She delicately tapped the box with a finger. "I have two since the last time I was home." She paused, testing the waters. "I didn't realize I would be summoned again so soon."

"Yes, well." Her father shifted uncomfortably in his chair. He was the King of the Underworld, the God of Below, the Monarch of the Dead. And yet, the mere implication of what this meeting really meant, made him look like Nick after he got a detention from Mrs. Williamson for throwing wadded up paper balls into the trash can like it was a basketball hoop. He rubbed anxiously at his goatee. "Things have changed."

Vic felt a sharp twinge in her chest. She knew this was why Asher had come for her. That this was the reason she'd been summoned so soon, but to hear the words from her father himself made it into a reality she wasn't sure she was quite ready to deal with yet.

"How so? Is Maman…unwell? Is she worse?"

The box felt heavy in her lap, its corners digging into the meat of her thighs. It suddenly felt like a piece of brie was lodged in her throat. She reached for a glass of chardonnay and took a long, icy gulp.

Her father leaned forward, resting his elbows on his knees and pressed his fingers into a steeple. It was a move she knew well. It was one of his more diplomatic poses, typically used when sharing undesirable news.

"It would seem that the infection, or whatever it is that she has, is spreading."

"But-but is she well?" Vic pressed. Panic was rising in her chest, clutching at her heart.

It wasn't a simple question. Because if her father was paying attention—which to Vic's chagrin he most always was—what she was really asking was if her mother was dying. If she was running out of the time it took to save her. She knew the Oracle was never wrong, but futures were not set in stone. Even those of the gods and goddesses.

He bowed his head for a moment, then looked up at Vic

and she recoiled at the site of tears welling up in his eyes. It was the worst possible reaction. Worse than the rage that her father was known for. Some called him Devil or Demon. Those in her English class would recognize him as Hades.

To Asher he was Boss.

To Vic he was simply Dad.

He extended a hand toward her. It was the hand that had his onyx wedding band burned into the skin of his ring finger, a vow that could never be broken except by death. A death that up until now, was certainly impossible.

And yet, here they were. She took his hand, her small fingers disappearing in his grasp.

"Come with me. Let us visit your mother and you can see for yourself that for which words escape me."

For the first time since Persephone was taken ill, Vic realized that she was the rope in her father's turbulent depths of anguish. She was his lifeline. And somehow she had to save them both before they drowned in a sea of sorrow.

–

Her mother's wing was not like the rest of the castle. Whereas the rest of the home was all sleek black edges, her mother's wing had walls of textured stone the color of sand, deep mahogany rafters, and indigo-colored clematis wrapped around driftwood tables and wooden beams. Vases and wooden boxes, nailed together by Persephone's own hands, hung from the walls and were filled with yellow and white daffodils and jewel-blue crocus. It was like entering a different world, the transition abrupt, only indicated by a runner of woven beach grass along the floor.

This was Vic's other favorite part of the house and now she knew why. It reminded her of the Above World. Asher trailed behind them, but when her father knocked softly on

Persephone's bedroom door, he fell back and placed himself against the wall opposite the door to wait.

Hades pushed the door open carefully, as if he were afraid of startling his wife. The crisp scent of hyacinth made Vic hold back a sneeze. Hyacinth was the one flower that she found somewhat overwhelming. Once her father opened the door and Vic followed him, still clutching the cold, metal box under her arm, she saw why the hyacinth struck her so.

It was everywhere.

Little petaled flowers in every shade of peach, purple, yellow, blue, white, and pink that you could imagine grew from the floor, their sturdy green leaves pressed against one another like tiny soldiers. The hyacinth grew from the walls and breathed from the ceiling in an ocean of lavender and cerulean.

It was the most beautiful thing Vic had ever seen.

Draped across the bed in a simple, white cotton dress was her mother, a sea of hyacinth beneath her making her ivory skin stand out even more against its white, peach, and orange backdrop. As she walked, the hyacinth seemed to part around her feet in its own attempt to not be trampled. Persephone's blonde hair was in long, loose curls. Even from where she stood, Vic could see that her hair had become brittle like the straw used in the harvests that were completed in honor of Persephone and her own mother, Demeter.

Her pale blue eyes widened at the appearance of her daughter, and she held up an arm toward her. The black veins standing out against her pale skin like lightning across a midnight sky. Vic tried not to show the worry she felt and instead forced her lips into a smile.

"Maman," she practically choked the word out as she reached the bed.

"*Amica mea*," her mother whispered and the words sounded slightly gurgled, like they were buried in quicksand.

Vic grabbed her outstretched hand, Persephone's long fingers that had spent hours weaving flowered crowns for her all the way up until she'd left for the Above World, found hers. They were cold as ice, and her mother's grip was not as strong as it once was, but Vic gave in as Persephone pulled her into a hug.

The familiar smell of her mother enveloped her: the smell of roses and sunshine was so comforting that Vic had almost forgotten. How could she almost have forgotten? Tears stung at the corners of her eyes. She pressed her forehead into the crook of her mother's neck, ignoring the river of black pushing up from the top of her white dress, savoring the satin smoothness of her skin.

Persephone brushed the hair back from Vic's forehead and planted a kiss, where a tiny flower immediately bloomed against her skin. Vic brushed her fingertips against it and they came away with the soft white and blue-striped petals of a Puschkinia. A Russian Snowdrop.

It was worse than she thought.

Hades neared, placing a hand on Vic's shoulder. He looked out of place in the space, his pinstripe suit and sharp features, against the pale colors of the flowers. Persephone's pale hand snaked out and grasped his free hand.

Where he was all fire, she was all ice. Persephone's body no longer raged with fire and Vic feared that this meant her body was no longer fighting back. The black syrup of her veins was stark against her paper thin skin. She wasn't simply dying, she was withering away to nothing.

Chapter Eight

Hades paced the floor of his office, a room down the hall from the study. They were alone. The demon creature-servant was gone, as was Asher, but Vic could sense his presence right outside the door. She could always sense him. Like attracted like after all.

A large granite desk stood near the middle of the room on top of a black plush rug. Green flames roared in the fireplace. Her father had tossed his suit jacket onto the leather duvet, and now the sleeves of his cream button-down shirt were rolled up to the crook of his elbows. There were various decanters and papers littered across the desk.

Vic pulled her blade from its sheath, using its tip to prick her forefinger. A tiny crimson drop pushed its way to the surface. She carefully pressed her finger to the metal bat. Its crystal eyes glowed white hot and when Vic pulled away the bat's head hinged back and the box unlocked itself.

Laying across the soft red velvet were the two souls which she had Taken. They glowed brightly, shining a shimmery gold light across her face. Hades paused his pacing to look up, his daughter's face captured in an otherworldly, angelic glow.

If he'd had an actual beating heart, it would have stopped at the sight of her. How delicately she handled the golden orbs, as if they were precious objects. He watched as she slid the shimmery gold orbs into one of the large glass decanters, they slid against the glass like molten lava. One of the souls had tendrils that wrapped around her long fingers, and ever-so-gently, she coaxed it into the glass decanter.

A second decanter held a thick silver liquid, it was Hades own blood. The thin line along the inside of his forearm now wrapped in loose gauze, stained with silver-turned-black droplets. As if mesmerized, he watched as his daughter emptied the second decanter into the first. His blood moved languidly and his dark eyes were transfixed as it slipped into the first container.

When it hit the golden orbs there was a hiss, like a soft wail. Vic's face remained impassive, but he knew that this hurt her. That he was hurting his daughter in order to spare his wife. But what choice did he have? This would not be the last hurt he would ask of her.

Vic felt her father's gaze on her as she took a glass stirring stick and gently swirled his blood so that it mixed with the shimmering gold life-force. As above, so below. The concoction was what the Oracle of Delphi had told them to do. She knew Hades was desperate. It was rare that he ventured out of his domain and into the Above World of his brothers' domain. But Vic hadn't realized until now just how desperate he had become while she was away.

The liquid stayed separated into two colors, a sort of yin and yang. Vic pulled a glass tumbler from the whiskey shelf behind the desk, and carefully poured the liquid into the glass. She cracked a pomegranate, using her blade to scrape the fleshy fruit away from the rind. It dripped like blood over her fingers and ran in rivulets down her forearm. She squeezed the juice of the fruit into the glass, the sliver-gold liquid immediately absorbed it.

Soul of the living, blood of a lover, fruit of the dead.

Her father snapped his fingers and a creature appeared, slightly different this time than the previous, his skin onyx like the walls of the castle itself.

"Take this to Persephone. Do not spill a single drop."

The demon bowed, took the glass from Vic, and disappeared just like that. She imagined him appearing at the foot of Persephone's bed and nudging her awake. All of the creatures—demon or otherwise—in the Under World loved and cherished Persephone.

In her usual short stays—half of the year—she brought joy and flowers in her wake. A kind smile here, a pat on the shoulder there. But now she was too weak to leave, could no longer keep to the cycles of the Above World. Her power had nowhere to go, so it bloomed all around her and against everything she touched.

Vic began to wash her hands in the wet bar sink, watching the red water disappear down the drain. When she turned, the decanters were gone and her blade was once again shining clean. The metal box was closed as if it hadn't just housed the souls of the living—souls that Vic had Taken. Her gut twisted in conflict. *Sometimes you had to do bad things to protect the ones you love*, she reminded herself. But the words felt hollow inside her.

Hades had resumed his pacing.

"I'm very proud of you, Victoriana."

He was the only one besides her mother who called her by her full name. His voice sounded gruff and he absent-mindedly pushed a hand through his hair, mussing it up so that two locks framed his forehead like upside down devil horns.

Vic didn't know what to say, so she sheathed her blade. She wasn't very proud of herself. The Takings were physically exhausting—she slept for hours—sometimes half a day—afterward, and she hated that she was hurting people she cared about in her own secluded way.

"That's why I'm sorry that I'm going to have to ask this of you."

The words caught her off guard. Hades had paused his pacing and was looking at her. The expression on his face was so broken that a terrified chill started at the top of her spine and snaked along to its base, despite the warmth emanating from the enchanted fireplace.

Hades pushed on, not waiting for a response. "As you can see your mother is..." He still refused to say the word. *Dying.* "Unwell. And each day she is getting worse. The youth of the souls will tide her over a few days, a week at most. But the weaker she becomes the more she needs to consume."

Vic's mind drifted to the room overflowing with hyacinth. The Above World stuck in homeostasis. Anger flared like a flame in her gut. "Who would do this? Why is this even happening?"

Hades shrugged. "I've no more answers than when you left. It's not a surprise that I'm not well-liked. But your mother is adored both in the Above World and the Under World. Who would want to take her life–and the life of an immortal no less—has left me perplexed."

"It's not enough."

Vic meant her father's research. Whoever his informants were, it wasn't enough. She knew of the chains in the castle basement, the tables that could stretch a man until he snapped. The iron mask that could make a sane man lose his mind; the only way to remove it was by beheading. Her father could get answers. He was the Lord of the Under World. He was a god.

Hades, however, misinterpreted her statement. Vic now stood on the other side of the table, leaning against it and her father closed the distance between them and clasped her hands which were swallowed up inside his larger ones. Her tawny skin not quite a match to his olive coloring. His eyes were desperate, rimmed in grief.

"That is why I must ask you to perform a difficult task."

Vic's mind reeled. The syrupy black veins that ran beneath her mother's butterfly-winged skin. Her straw-like blonde hair, the way she coughed and it was thick with mucous. Her mother was a goddess. And somehow she was dying.

The people of Olympia didn't even know she existed. That she gave them the beautiful springs and too warm, humid summers, that Demeter's sorrow during the six months she spent with her husband, resulted in autumn and winter. The myths weren't myths. They were real and they didn't even know. Would never know Persephone's gentle touch or warm smile. Someone needed to pay. These thoughts clouded her head and are why she was not prepared for what her father said next.

"There's a powerful soul among you in Olympia. Much more powerful than the souls that your mother has been consuming. This soul…I think has the power to cure her."

Little yellow flames flicked in her father's pupils. Little flames that flared as the hope in his heart flared. Twin flames. He and Persephone. As above, so below.

Hades pressed on. "I only know this because of Asher. You

wouldn't have known. Known what signs to look for. But Asher is well-trained in the strength of souls. Can smell their purity. The aroma of their peace." He closed his eyes and later Vic would wonder if it was out of regret or for dramatic effect. "I wouldn't ask this of you—I know how few friends you have—but your mother, she needs you. You must Take the soul of your new friend. You must reap the soul of Callum Bishop."

–

Vic's world spun out of control at the mention of his name. How could her father have known? What could Asher possibly know that she didn't? Flashes of red blinded her, her anger consuming her worry like Cal's name was the accelerant to her already simmering conflict.

She wrenched out of Hades' grasp and pushed through the door to the study with a bang, out to where Asher stood leaning, one knee bent with his foot pressed against the wall and arms crossed, in the hallway.

This was not fair. Not fair at all.

Before he could even register her reaction, she was on him like a wildcat. Biting and clawing at him, her rage so palpable that if she didn't let it out, it would surely consume her from the inside out.

"You, bastard!" she growled, her bent fingers finding the smoothness of his cheek where it met the corner of his mouth. Blood trickled out of the corner of his mouth and down onto his chin.

She pummeled at his chest. She was an uncaged beast and the anger curled off her in scalding hot bursts of steam. Asher tried to cover his face to protect himself from the hotness of her, the rage that was leaking out all over. She was an uncontrollable burst dam of emotions.

"You. Sick. Jealous."

She accentuated each word with a punch to his chest. She was about to add another colorful expletive when she was pulled back by strong arms that braced across her chest and pinned her own arms to her sides. She kicked and flailed, howled in frustration.

"Victoriana." Hades' voice.

"You can't believe him, Dad! He's just jealous that I've moved on without him. Cal isn't anything…" She was going to say special, but the lie froze on her lips. "He's just a regular mortal guy!"

Asher slowly pushed himself to his feet, wiping an arm across his bloodied nose and mouth, leaving a smear of red across his cheek.

"Asher knows things. Victoriana, please."

The rage was beginning to subside. Color was leaching back into her world. The dark brown of Asher's hair and his piercing green eyes which did not regard her with contempt as she'd expected, but with…with pity. She swallowed the lump in her throat.

"Let's go for a walk," he said. He glanced over her shoulder at Hades and she felt her father's arms release her.

She didn't want to go on a walk with this liar, this traitor. He'd seen—who knows what all he'd seen—and he'd used it to hurt her. To get back at her for things she didn't even understand.

"Fine. Walk."

She gestured in the direction of the front door.

Asher headed down the curving staircase, halfway down he paused and peered over his shoulder at her. A challenge of sorts. Despite her mind telling her not to go, she found her feet moving anyways.

She followed him down the stairs. The adrenaline receding. Her fingers hurt from hitting him which was basically the equivalent of punching a stone wall.

She felt a little bit of regret for losing control. When she got angry, it was like a match being dropped into a bucket of gasoline. Long ago—when she was as young as three or four years old—Hades had taught her how to control the insatiable rage that could ignite in her. He never said it was bad, but he did say it was weak to let it take control of her. She wondered if this somehow meant that befriending Cal—maybe even *liking* Cal—had somehow made her weak.

Asher stopped when they reached the orchard of pomegranate trees. It was one of her favorite spots to think or read, her spine pressed against the familiar bark, the green triangular leaves tickling her forehead. If she hadn't been paying attention she'd have plowed right into him.

"I'm sorry."

Two simple words. They wouldn't be enough. They were never enough.

Sorry was very un-Asher-like. Vic turned away, inspecting the plump, red fruits, her fingers still stained with their juice. It was underneath her nails like she'd been playing in pools of violet-red blood.

"I wasn't there because of you. I wasn't following you. Your dad wanted me to look for a soul that was more pure. More light-filled. I didn't know…I didn't know it would be some guy you'd end up liking!"

She couldn't argue there. There was clearly something she liked about Cal. He was gentle and kind, a bit silly. With horrible jokes. She continued to inspect the fruit. He was, at the very least, her friend. Her first real friend in the months she'd spent in Olympia—perhaps her first real friend in her entire life. And she'd only known him barely a week. It still didn't make it fair.

"You're asking too much of me."

Asher's voice was soft. "I'm not the one doing the asking."

Vic felt her knees give way and she crumpled to the roots of the tree, Asher caught her in a half embrace. She felt the tears coming before she could stop them, so she pressed her face into his shoulder, near the tear she'd ripped in his collar only moments before. She cried silently, twisting her fingers into his t-shirt, and he let her, arms wrapped around her back, but at the same time barely touching her.

Finally, after several moments when she sniffled, Asher took it as a sign that he could say more. "It's for something good, Tor. You know that. I know you—Hades, myself, all of us—would do anything to save Persephone. If there's even a chance that Cal's soul is pure enough to save her, then we—you have to at least try."

The vacant stares of the Taken filled Vic's thoughts. She could not—would not—do that to Cal. But by saying that she was most certainly dooming her mother to a certain death.

"Why him?" her voice cracked. "I'm sure there's someone else just as...pure, as you say."

Asher twirled a lock of her hair between his fingers. "Perhaps. But I think there is something more to your new friend. Something he hasn't told you."

She pushed back, palms flush against his chest, to better see his face. He tilted his chin so he was staring down at her, so close they could kiss. Earthy incense enveloped her, overwhelming her thoughts. She blinked to clear away the physical attraction. Asher was the only person she could physically assault and then moments later be held by him. He understood her, even when she didn't understand herself.

And she often hated him for it.

His eyes were serious, not joking or ridiculing. He might know something that she didn't or he may just be expressing a thought, but he wasn't teasing or manipulating. It was difficult for two people so similar to one another to deceive the other.

"And you know what that something is?" her voice was soft, barely a whisper, the spoken air landing on his lips. His Adam's apple bobbed.

"I don't. But..." He licked his lips and then broke his gaze, staring at the gnarled trunk of the tree instead. "But if you want me to help you find out, then I will."

An alliance. She couldn't go against her father's word, but if Asher could somehow help her to find a loophole then maybe Cal could be spared. "When does he expect me to return?"

"In one week's time. Two at the most. I told him of your...attachment. I think he understands he is asking too much of you, but he's desperate. We all are."

Vic nodded at the truth of his words. Time was something the immortals always took for granted because they could never run out of it, but now someone was turning the tables. And that gave Vic an idea.

If she could find out who—or what—Cal was, whatever secret Asher claimed he may be keeping, then that would save his soul. But it still wouldn't save Persephone. She needed to find out who had attacked her mother and why. All these months she'd thought her father's way was the only solution, but now, thanks to Asher of all people, she realized that there was another way, and just maybe, if she could find out the truth, everyone could be saved. Including herself.

Chapter Nine

Monday came quicker than Vic would have liked. She couldn't shake the sight of Persephone's frail form from her mind.

Asher offered to drop her off at school, but Vic passed, telling him to drop her off at home so she could grab her school stuff. He looked a little put out, but did as she instructed.

She climbed off the back of the motorcycle and he handed her the metal box. He was wearing mirrored aviators so Vic couldn't see his eyes, but he clasped and unclasped his hands like he didn't know what to do with himself. Finally, he placed them on the grips and glanced at her. The rising sun glinted rose gold in the mirrored lenses. A shiver ran down her spine, but Vic couldn't decide if it was a good shiver or a bad one.

She'd been fairly successful at avoiding Asher the remainder of her stay in the Under World. He was, after all, in her father's service, not hers. It gave her the space to contemplate Asher's kindness. Something she wasn't really used to in the first place. Could it really be something as simple as he missed her? Or that he loved Persephone and wanted to help save her? Vic doubted it. Nothing about Asher was simple.

"I'll do what I can from below, but you know we're going to have to compare notes at some point."

She nodded. She knew. "Give me three days. Come by Wednesday. Meet me here after school and we can share what we've learned."

He gave a subtle nod of his chin and without another word, roared off down the driveway. Vic let out the breath she'd been holding and headed inside to get ready for the school day.

–

She parked her truck near the east entrance, arriving just before the final bell. Admittedly, on purpose. She needed time. The one thing she was constantly running out of. She was hoping to avoid Cal until the afternoon when they had English class together.

It was reasonable to assume that Cal had no idea that he was something special, different from anyone else. Asher had only said that his soul was pure. One reason could simply be that he had never reincarnated before and that his soul hadn't had a chance to be tarnished. He was a new soul, quite literally. But then there was the flip side that maybe Cal somehow knew, and the thought tugged at her gut. She chastised herself. *Not every guy is a deceptive prick. Not every guy is like Asher.*

Vic made her way to her locker, lost in thought. The halls were practically empty, but her homeroom was just across the hall. In one weekend, both her father and Asher had managed to turn her life upside down. Not that it was ever right-side up.

But up until this point, Vic had managed. She'd blended in more or less, even enjoying herself to one degree or another. Being in the Above World was like being set free, and she could better appreciate why her mother loved it so. Even if Hades and Demeter hadn't demanded that she split her time, Vic was pretty sure Persephone would have done so anyways.

She was even on the verge of making a friend—an actual friend, except now there was the little problem of Taking Cal's soul. Which would only become harder the more she got to know him. Because what she already knew, she'd found that she really liked.

His easy smile. The fact that his Chucks were as worn as her own. How he was quick with a corny joke and appreciative of small gestures. The sprinkle of freckles across his nose.

The windows in the hallway were open and some dried, red leaves scattered down the hallway. But they didn't seem like a reminder from her father. Just some leaves. She had two weeks. It *had* to be enough time.

–

By English class word had spread about the sophomore who had drank too much at a homecoming party. Apparently, his liver couldn't get the toxins out fast enough and he had choked on his own vomit while his friend slept nearby.

Vic suspected the soul of the friend could be an easy Take. The willing often gave their souls up easily. But she decided she wouldn't press her luck with one student in a coma and another dead in the matter of a weekend.

She felt particularly guilty about this Taking. It had been a bit hurried due to Asher's visit and her father's demand that she return home sooner, but Vic had tried to ensure the boy had a chance by calling for help. But she couldn't have known how much he had drank, or that his liver was already damaged, or that he would end up choking on his own vomit. Just because Vic Took the soul, didn't mean a person necessarily died. It just meant they became a hollow shell of who they once were. A vessel. A vessel could be emptied, but it could also be refilled. At least that's what helped her sleep at night.

When she entered English class, she slipped into her seat and gave Cal a tentative smile. Luckily, before he could ask her anything, the bell rang and Mrs. Williamson was announcing that she was giving them a pop quiz on diagramming sentences.

Nick and—what sounded like Elaine—groaned. *It was just homecoming weekend! How could Mrs. Williamson expect them to take a quiz!?* To which, Mrs. Williamson had responded that the festivities that occurred over the weekend should have no impact on whether or not they understood sentence diagramming unless they'd engaged in illicit behaviors and killed too many brain cells in the process.

Vic was more than happy to diagram sentences. The process was tedious, but a welcome distraction allotting her time to gather her thoughts about what she could say to Cal. She had to seem like everything was fine. That she'd had a nice visit with her mother over the weekend.

Vic chewed on the eraser of her pencil. Contrary to her father's nature, Vic hated to lie. Even small white lies. Each one was like a tiny needle in her gut.

As the end of class neared, she noticed that Cal had already finished his quiz and was reading a book. She discreetly tilted her head to try and catch the title, but the book was old and worn and missing the dust jacket.

Finally, with three minutes left in the period, she placed her quiz face down on the corner of Mrs. Williamson's desk. Usually, Vic was meticulous with assignments, so finishing only just before the bell wasn't uncommon for her.

She returned to her seat and saw a folded up piece of notebook paper in the shape of a triangle laying on her desk. Her heart beat just a little quicker. She glanced at Cal, whose face was buried in his book, but whose lips were curled in a small smile. Sliding into her seat, she carefully unfolded the note.

Skip 7th period ?

Vic's head shot up, but Cal wasn't paying her any attention. Well, if he was, he was doing an excellent job of hiding it. Cal didn't seem like the type to skip class. Unlike herself, despite being an excellent student grade-wise. However, it was easy to make up excuses when you were the daughter of the King and Queen of the Under World.

Before she could write out a reply, the bell rang signaling the end of fifth period. Nick let out a loud groan, his quiz unfinished. Clearly, he had killed too many brain cells over the weekend. As the class spilled out into the hallway her shoulder bumped against Cal's.

"Meet me at the first floor stairwell after sixth period."

It wasn't a question as much as a consent.

Cal only smiled, the dimple in his right cheek making Vic's stomach do a little somersault. His amber eyes were lit up as if he had a secret he couldn't wait to tell her and, despite what her father wanted and what Asher suspected, Vic felt herself inexplicably wanting to know all of those secrets, not for anyone else, but for herself.

–

The first floor stairwell was home to an often unlocked door that led through the school's maintenance area and to a door that opened onto the school dumpsters. If you happened to stumble upon some of the janitorial staff out for a smoke break behind the dumpsters, they often pretended they didn't even see you. It was a sort of silent understanding because they weren't supposed to be smoking on school grounds. So if you kept your mouth closed, they kept their mouths closed.

Vic and Cal slipped passed the green dumpsters that reeked of days' old food and stale cigarettes, then slipped through the gated entry. They came out on the far side of the parking lot. Vic couldn't control the bounce in her step as she tossed her book bag into the bed of the truck and slid into the driver's seat. Cal climbed in and placed his book bag on the floor by his feet as Vic pulled out of the school lot.

"That was kind of exhilarating."

He used the shiny silver crank to wind the passenger window down.

She hung a right onto the main road, suddenly having an idea. "Your first time skipping?"

A pink flush rose up Cal's neck. "Yeah, maybe. But that definitely wasn't your first time."

Vic chuckled and shook her head. "Not by a longshot. So did you have something in mind?"

Crimson, orange, and gold leaves spun across the road. The sun was bright and the heat still persistent. In between housing developments, long stretches of dried out grasses blurred past. Vic inhaled deeply. The smell of falling leaves and the crisp air, despite the unseasonable warmth, was one of her favorite things. It was like Vic was autumn itself, the intermingling of life and death—the Above World and the Below World. Perhaps that's why she found it so appealing.

Cal gave her a sheepish grin. "Actually, that note was as far as I'd gotten. You know being a novice and all. I really just wanted to see you—er, how your weekend was. But you seem to have a place in mind."

His eyes caught the green sign with one arrow pointing back the way they came, toward Olympia High and another arrow pointing the way they were now headed, toward the city. City was a loose term in Olympia.

To some people a city meant sky scrapers, yellow taxicabs, and suits in a hurry. But to Olympians, city meant an actual grocery store, a coffee shop, a post office, a small bookstore only open a few hours a day and run by an elderly couple, a mechanic, and several mom and pop stores specializing in items varying from hardware to secondhand dresses and even a cobbler. Somehow with so few choices, one could still find anything they needed.

They were headed north in the general direction of the looming purple mountains. Normally, Olympia would have had at least one snow fall by now, but with the weather in its homeostasis, everything seemed in a sort of limbo. Vic thought of her mother and how she'd gotten sick right before the spring season. At first it hadn't seemed like anything serious.

An immortal could get sick—it was unlikely, but it wasn't unheard of. But then she couldn't make the trip to the Above World. So she had stayed below during the spring and early summer months. It was in mid-summer—according to the harvest calendar—that Hades had intervened, sending Vic to the Above World.

Demeter was devastated. She couldn't go to the Under

World, if she did the lack of sunlight and fresh air would quickly cause her to wither. The Under World was made for no one but Hades and his kind, with the exception of Persephone, who out of her love, had eaten six pomegranate seeds as a compromise between her mother and the man she loved. This perpetual autumn was the result of Demeter's grief and helplessness in her daughter's plight. It was possible she could blame Hades—think it was his fault—but everyone knew how much Hades cherished Persephone. It was unthinkable.

Tucked in the front pocket of Vic's t-shirt was the Russian Snowdrop that had bloomed on her forehead. Not that she needed a token, but it was a reminder of how little time she had left.

"I have something in mind," she smiled.

Downtown Olympia was a thirty minute car ride from the school. Olympia itself was rather large, at least in acreage if not in population.

They passed the time talking about their weekends. Cal's family—all six kids, his parents, his maternal grandparents, and several sets of aunts, uncles, and cousins came up from California. They had decided to have a last minute housewarming party since the weather was so mild. He chased around his younger siblings and cousins until everyone had collapsed around a bonfire in the back yard.

The mention of the bonfire caused an image of drunk teenagers to unexpectedly pop into Vic's head, but she quickly shoved the thought away, burying it deep in the cobwebbed corners of her mind where she liked to leave things she'd rather forget about.

"Do you feel like you missed out by not going to the homecoming dance?" Vic asked before she could stop herself. It was stupid to ask since he'd basically asked her and she'd told him no. It's not like she could go back and change her mind if he said yes.

"Nah. I've been to dances before at my old school, and besides you, I wouldn't have known anyone." He shrugged, absent-mindedly fingering the silver watch on his right wrist. "Plus, I know you'll find this hard to believe, but I'm not really all that great of a dancer."

Vic feigned shock. "Now, that I find nearly impossible to believe."

The sun caught his freckles and Vic felt a pleasant flutter in the pit of her stomach. In the course of the car ride and the easy conversation that flowed between them, Vic couldn't imagine that Cal was anyone other than who he said he was. Asher could be mistaken—it wouldn't be the first time, and it could be as simple as Cal's soul was young and kind which made it so pure and light.

"How was your visit to your mom's?" Cal glanced at her, then his eyes flicked toward the windshield and the approaching town.

Rows of small houses were coming into view as they neared downtown Olympia. They lined both sides of the street. Pumpkins sat out on front stoops and on porches, smiling scarecrows were nailed to Sycamore and Oak trees, and stalks of dried cornhusks were tied to telephone poles.

"It was good. It always goes by too quickly, you know?"

"Have your parents been divorced long?" he asked.

His left hand was on the white leather between them and Vic felt the sudden urge to intertwine her fingers with his. Instead, she kept both hands on the large steering wheel of her truck.

She hadn't realized by saying to visit her mom, that it implied her parents were divorced. Obviously, Cal assumed she lived with her father. It wasn't likely a teenage girl lived all alone in a large estate. And with a groundskeeper no less. So the logical conclusion would be that her parents were divorced. As a kid, with her mother gone half the year, it had sometimes seemed that way. Vic decided to not correct the assumption.

"Since I was little."

She didn't elaborate and felt a twinge of guilt as the speed limit slowed and they approached downtown—a double-sided street with one direction headed north and then looping around to head south. In the center, acting as a divide between the one way sections of highway, was a small park with a few mature trees ablaze in orange and red, along with a few benches, and a manicured garden maintained by the Wives of Olympia. Vic knew there was a small plaque placed in the garden dedicating it to Demeter and thanking her for the harvest they used each year to hold the Apple Festival at the end of October. Olympia was known for its apples and they were sent across the country and sold in stores all over, but the best ones were kept right here.

Parking spots surrounded the park, so that when Vic parked, the street behind them continued north toward the mountains. The shops and cafes ran along the opposite side of the street and then in a mirror image on the west side of the street, except the one-way road on that side headed south.

"This is it," Vic smiled as she pulled the keys out of the ignition.

Cal stepped out of the truck with a humble look of awe on his face. Barrels of flower arrangements and small pumpkins lined the streets and American flags flapped at regular intervals. Downtown Olympia was old-fashioned Americana at its finest. Benches and decorative iron railings lined the streets. In the summer kids could chain their bikes to the railings, but currently a large chestnut colored horse was tied to one of the railings just outside the hardware store.

"This is for real?" Cal asked.

"Yep. Definitely for real. A bit different than surfing after school."

"A lot different," he spun in a slow circle. "But it's beautiful."

Feeling a burst of pride and courage, Vic looped her arm through Cal's and tugged.

"Come on, there's someone I want you to meet."

She pulled him along to a shop squeezed in between the coffee shop and a secondhand store that sold 1940s dresses and knitted berets. The door to the shop was wooden and carved with a giant twisted serpent—a python—inside a circle. The sign above the door was old and gnarled, carved in knotted wood: *The House of Snakes.*

Cal paused, glancing into the street side window which showcased various crystals with little signs describing their healing properties, as well as a giant golden statue of the Buddha wearing a white rosary, and a large, leafy green fern plant. A hand-painted sign was propped up and read:

Charms, Curses, and Tarot Readings

Vic caught his expression and couldn't help her laugh.

"Don't worry there aren't any snakes inside. It's just a really old name. Like, super old. Kind of a tribute to Greek mythology. It's kind of a thing around here."

Cal gave her a disbelieving look. "Are you going to get a Tarot reading?"

"Something like that. Come on. You can trust me," she

coaxed pulling open the heavy wooden door.

Immediately the earthiness of patchouli and the sweetness of incense flooded her nostrils. She held out her hand and Cal wrapped his long, warm fingers in between her own, allowing her to lead him into The House of Snakes.

Chapter Ten

Contrary to the name, The House of Snakes was actually quite cozy. There were glass dishes full of various crystals: smooth gray hematite for grounding, jagged purple amethyst for healing, crystal quartz for amplifying. Soft, rhythmic chanting music wafted through the small shop.

The floor was old, worn wood and decorated with hand-woven runners and rugs. Shelves of incense, incense holders, and small statues of Buddha, Vishnu, and Krishna were intermixed with figurines of Jesus and the Virgin Mary. Rosaries were stored next to elaborate Celtic crosses which were placed beside bundles of sage to clear out negative energy. There were bookcases full of spiritual and religious books spanning the gamut and baskets full of Tarot and Oracle cards. A rainbow of colorful silk scarves hung from the ceiling.

When they'd entered, a small bell above the door had signaled their presence, and now a black and white cat with piercing yellow eyes jumped onto the counter and stared at them. Beneath the glass of the counter top, various charms, pendants, and rings were showcased in black velvet-lined boxes.

Vic went up to the cat and scratched between its ears. It purred contentedly, flicking its tail. Cal inspected a row of incense holders, but Vic was pretty sure he had no clue what they were. Before she could inform him, a familiar voice called.

"Fortune and mystery await! Welcome to the House of Snakes!"

Cal looked up as a beautiful woman emerged from a doorway at the back of the store that was lined with a multi-colored beaded curtain. She was dark-skinned and her hair was in dreads that were piled on top of her head. Her eyes were a light gray and her full lips a contrasting violet shade. A magenta colored silk scarf was tied around her curvy hips and on top of the patchwork dress she wore. Her shoulders were covered by a lacy shawl and her bare feet were in a pair of Birkenstocks. The toenails of her feet matched the vibrant shade of her lips and rows of silver and gold bangles lined both of her arms from her wrist to her elbow. A pair of rectangular, Dumbledoresque silver spectacles sat on the tip of her wide nose.

Those startling eyes fell on Vic and the woman broke into the biggest smile Cal thought he'd ever seen.

"Victoriana Haden!" The woman's voice was deep and rich as she sashayed toward the front of the store. She grabbed Vic in a big embrace, practically pulling her up so that only the toes of her Chucks skimmed the floor.

"Pythia. It's been a while." Vic gasped as Pythia let her go and she could reassure herself that all of her ribs were still intact.

Pythia moved onto Cal, inspecting him like he was a moth pinned beneath glass.

"You've brought a friend." She leaned in closer and seemed to be smelling him. Incense and violets wafted over him. He realized he should introduce himself, but it was as if he were suddenly struck dumb and couldn't remember who he was or what he was called.

Vic slid an arm across his shoulders, shattering the haze that had momentarily held him.

"This is Cal. He's a friend from school."

Pythia arched an eyebrow in response. The cat jumped down from the counter and began to twine itself in and around Pythia's legs. She cocked her head, regarding him with a sharp eye. Trying to assess just how much this newcomer did and did not know.

"I assume you're here for a reading then?"

Vic nodded, dropping her arm from Cal's shoulders and fingering a set of rosewood meditation beads that hung from the fingers of a large Buddha statue.

"Yeah. Just the usual."

The way she said it, Cal had a feeling it was anything but the usual. But Vic was right. The shop was cozy and welcoming, and although Pythia seemed a bit on the distrusting side, she also responded to Vic with such familial kindness that Cal couldn't help but follow when Pythia said, "This way then."

"Apollo, you mind the store?" she added and the seemingly docile cat hissed in response. "And mind your manners."

Pythia led them past the rear of the store where there were large pillow cushions scattered about, and back through the beaded entry way.

The light was dimmer in this back hallway than it was in the store, and as their eyes adjusted Cal could see that the hallway was lined with stacks of boxes. A red EXIT sign shone above a door at the end of the hallway. Pythia paused in front of a door. She pulled a keyring from her skirt's pocket and unlocked it.

It opened onto a winding stairwell that led them to the floor above the store and to a second door. This door also had the mark of the serpent, but instead of carved wood, it was a beautiful painting of teals, emeralds, black, and white. Pythia used a different key and pushed open the door.

"*Mi casa es su casa.*" Cal recognized the phrase even though he'd spent the last four years taking French instead of Spanish. He'd thought it a great way to get some culture and meet cute girls. He'd been mistaken on the latter.

Vic stepped over the threshold into a small studio apartment. The entire wall to the right was lined with windows, flooding the apartment with the golden October light. To the left was a small kitchenette with a well-used stove that already had a pot simmering with what looked like water and herbs. A hammock was strung from the ceiling and the wood floor was covered in a half dozen different rugs atop which sat several more of the pillow cushions that Cal had noticed in the shop.

Spiraling green plants grew from pots and in the corner was a bamboo water fountain that trickled soothingly. The air smelled like sage, lavender, and incense.

"Go and make yourselves comfortable. Would you like a cup of tea?" Pythia asked heading toward the stove.

"Uh, yeah, that would be great," Cal responded, not one to turn down hospitality.

"Sure. No sugar in mine." Vic said as she moved some

cushions around a low dark wood table.

It reminded Cal of the time his parents had taken them on a family trip to Japan. Cool vacations were a perk to his father's busy work schedule.

Vic gestured to the cushion beside her and Cal fell into its crimson-colored plushness. When his gaze went upward he noticed the ceiling was covered in hooks with hanging baskets of herbs and flowers spilling out of them in some sort of elaborate hanging garden. He'd never seen anything like this place in his entire life.

"Isn't it great?" Vic asked giving voice to Cal's unspoken thoughts.

"I've never seen anything like it," Cal admitted.

Vic flopped back onto two cushions and gazed up at the garden ceiling. Soft guitar music started to play as Pythia banged around in the kitchen, filtering and pouring tea. Moments later she swayed into the living area and placed a round, golden tray onto the small table. The mugs containing the tea were mismatched, a chipped blue stoneware mug was placed closest to where Cal sat.

The steaming mug smelled like chamomile, tea his mother often gave him when he was having trouble sleeping.

Vic sat up and leaned her shoulder into his and smiled, her fingers wrapped around a small yellow mug with a smiley face. "If you finish it, Pythia will read your tea leaves."

Pythia chuckled and waved her hand at Vic. "You insult me so, tea leaves are the least of my talents." She picked up a steaming mug (that read *tea leaving and psychic readings* on the side) and inhaled deeply before taking a sip.

"Are you a Tarot card reader?" Cal said, then added quickly. "The sign said…"

"I am many things. Some call me a Tarot card reader,

others use the word Seer or Oracle. No matter what they choose to call me, I cannot guarantee that the results are always happy." She said the words easily, as if it didn't matter much to her whether what she told her customers was good or bad.

"Guess I won't be asking for my money back." Cal choked uneasily on his laughter.

"Don't let her scare you. Pythia has been doing this…forever. She's just being dramatic." Vic swirled her fingers in Pythia's direction. "It's part of the persona."

"As long as man has needed fortunes told. If I do say so myself, I *am* uncannily accurate."

Vic grinned over her mug. "That's true."

"And while I may not be able to guarantee the results are always happy, I can guarantee that they are always correct. But the future isn't always so easy. It's constantly changing, not a thing that's set in stone. But in the moment, it's one-hundred-percent accurate."

"How can the future always be changing?" Cal asked taking another warm sip of tea.

"People's feelings and choices are always changing the outcome. It's the gift of free will. Basically, Pythia can give you a recommendation for a course of action. But it's more like a prescription then a prediction," Vic replied.

"That's a lovely way to put it," Pythia replied, her eyes were closed and she was swaying slightly to the music, a small smile on her lips.

Vic took another sip of tea, peering into the inky water and swirling leaves as she drank and wondered just what they might have to say about her future.

–

Pythia took Cal's empty mug, and then drained the

lingering liquid into a small orange bowl. From what Vic could see in the mug, the leaves just looked like goops of wet herbs, but Vic knew that Pythia's eye for Tasseomancy would find meaning in the randomness.

Her large hands turned the mug this way and that, inspecting the leftover contents. Cal squirmed on his floor cushion.

"What exactly is she looking for?" he whispered out of the corner of his mouth to Vic.

"Symbols and shapes that might appear out of the remaining leaves."

"Ah." Cal didn't look convinced. Vic sipped her tea which was now almost cold. The soft guitar music permeated the air and the sun's light coming in through the windows was turning a darker shade of amber.

"It's rather peculiar," Pythia finally said setting the blue mug back onto the table. "But there are several clouds in your leaves."

"Clouds?" Vic and Cal asked at the same time. Vic was hoping a visit to Pythia would give her—or at least lead her to—answers about Cal. But clouds didn't sound very promising.

"Don't doubt the Oracle." Pythia cut a glare to Vic, who bit her bottom lip to silence herself. "Clouds represent air. They are a symbol of our higher consciousness and intellect."

"Well, that sounds okay. Right?" Cal peered into the mug, his expression showing that he clearly saw no clouds inside the black contents stuck to the bottom and sides.

Pythia continued in her deep voice. "However, they can also symbolize gloom and disaster. The clouds can obscure our vision. If they come in the form of fog, for example, they can confuse you. Many people have found their deaths lost in a foggy forest or on a foggy road. I would heed the symbol with caution. Perhaps something—or someone—is clouding your vision and preventing you from accomplishing something that you set out to do."

The color drained from Cal's face, his freckles standing out like constellations against his pale skin.

"But then again, if you heed your inner wisdom, perhaps you will overcome this fog." Pythia leveled him with a gaze that was all business and no nonsense. She took her readings very seriously. And she was good at them…thousands of years of practice will do that. "Remember. Prescription. Not a prediction. Heed the wisdom of the leaves."

She turned toward Vic who had grown slightly nervous during Cal's reading. Filing away the information to review later.

"And now yours, my dear." Vic drained the remaining tea in her mug and handed it to Pythia. She quickly emptied any lingering liquid into the same orange bowl from before, then began to inspect the remaining leaves hanging to the sides and bottom of Vic's mug.

Maybe it was a bad idea to bring Cal here after all. Vic had thought it could be fun, but also a way to help him. What she hadn't thought of, is what if her reading revealed something about herself that she wasn't yet ready to share with Cal? She knew it wasn't fair to keep secrets, especially if she wanted to know Cal's secrets, but she wasn't just a regular girl. Nor would she ever be. Her blood pounded in her ears, drowning out the acoustic guitar. She nervously fingered the chain of her necklace.

Cal's fingers found hers and he gave her a reassuring squeeze, noticing the furrowed expression on her face. He didn't know, but the Oracle did. She knew what was at stake if she revealed too much about who Vic truly was and what she was tasked with doing. Vic squeezed Cal's fingers back. He didn't let go.

"Interesting. It's not often I come across more than one or two symbols in one reading. There is a sword. The sword, in Tarot anyway, is associated with the Air element." She raised her eyes briefly and Vic registered the meaning in them. It was a connection to Cal's reading. "Swords also symbolize courage, power, and conflict. But I suspect that diligence will be rewarded with success. On the opposite side of the mug is a flower. Typically, flowers symbolize growth and regeneration. Out of the conflict—or out of the darkness, depending on how you look at it—comes new life."

Vic felt her heart thumping against her ribcage. Flowers also meant Persephone, maybe at the end of all this her mother would be saved after all. Vic's mind quickly chided her: this was not a prediction. It was a prescription.

"And yet, most peculiar, at the bottom of your mug, is a heart. Unfortunately, it has a jagged line across it. A broken heart. I think that one may explain itself. The leaves do not name names, of course. But sometimes risk and power come with new life and change, but not without loss." Pythia's eyes seemed to lose focus as she regarded the remnants, her plump lips forming a frown. Suddenly, as if snapping out of it, her voice changed into a more cheerful cadence.

"Would you two like some scones? I just baked some raspberry-orange ones yesterday afternoon."

Vic's palms felt sweaty and she carefully slipped her fingers from Cal's.

"Oh, no, Pythia. Your hospitality has been more than enough. I, uh, think we should get going. It's a school night after all. Homework and all." She cut a pointed glance to Cal.

"Oh, yeah. Yeah. I have calculus homework that I'm sure will take me a while to get through." He stood abruptly. "It was nice to meet you, Miss Pythia."

Vic scrambled to her feet as Pythia stood. The space suddenly seemed too small for all three of them and Vic wasn't sure if it was a result of the ominous reading or Pythia's millennia old personality. She pulled Cal toward the door.

"We can see our way out."

Cal opened the door and stepped into the coolness of the stairwell, but before Vic could follow him, a strong, firm hand grasped her forearm.

She turned and Pythia's gray eyes had gone vacant once more—as if she were seeing from a very far-off place. Her voice once again took a deep resonance that over the years Vic had come to associate with the moments when Pythia didn't use Tarot or Tessomancy, but was channeling something else from beyond. It was the same as when she had told Hades and Vic how to best help Persephone.

"The air is the sword and the sword is the air. The broken pieces shall be scattered. Old is new and new is old. The beginning is the end and the end is the beginning. It is all for nothing and yet nothing at all. Heed the words of the Oracle, spoken for millennia, originated in Delphi. The House of Snakes has risen and will not be slayed."

Every hair on the back of Vic's neck stood up as Pythia's grip loosened. The vibrancy returned to her eyes and she shook her head, a thick dread falling from the pile on top of her head.

"Crazy things." She shook her head again as if she could shake out whatever being she had just channeled. "I better go lie down. Apollo can mind the store a little while longer. Do give your mother my best when you get the chance." And with that she shut the door, pushing Vic into the stairwell with Cal.

Pythia's words had only lasted seconds, but they cut deep into Vic. Words could make you bleed. They were only words. Until they weren't.

"Are you okay?" Cal asked, his forehead wrinkling.

"Yeah. Yeah I'm fine. Come on let's go home."

She headed down the spiral staircase and could feel Cal behind her. Instead of returning through the shop, Vic turned left and headed out the door with the glowing red EXIT sign. The air was still much too warm for early October, but Vic inhaled deep gulps of it. Letting it fill her lungs and her head.

Cal had his hands in his jeans pockets and had rolled back onto his heels as he stood beside her on the sidewalk.

"So, that was pretty weird. Enlightening, but weird."

His voice wasn't accusatory or mean, simply amused. Maybe he had found it all to be a game or a show. For all Vic knew, he could think Pythia was a crackpot. He had no idea who she was or where she came from. How she had predicted the fall of Sparta and the death of Nero in old times, and the modern wars and rises of power in modern times.

Vic laughed, releasing some of the pent up energy that churned inside her, spurred by Pythia's words.

"Yeah. It was, wasn't it?"

She felt Cal's hand fall on her shoulder. She could feel its reassuring weight through her t-shirt. "You're sure, you're okay?"

"Yeah, yeah. I've known Pythia a while, she can just be intense…I'm fine. Really."

And she realized that she really was. If she narrowed in on this exact moment and ignored the extraneous junk: Asher's out of character behavior, her mother's illness, Hades' demands of her, and Pythia's portentous words—then yes, she was fine. Crimson colored leaves floated past in the autumnal light of early evening. Several people passed by as they made their way in and out of the shops, the crunch of leaves beneath their footsteps. The scent of coffee from the little café permeated the air, mixing with the scent of sage and incense that still clung to her shirt.

Cal looked at her with concern in his amber eyes, peering at her from behind feathery black lashes. She wanted to press herself into his cinnamon-honey scented softness and let its comfort envelop her.

"Come on, let me show you something."

She quirked her head at him. "You show me something? Aren't you the new guy?"

"Trust me," he replied tossing her words back to her on the wind. She flung her keys at him and he caught them in his left-hand.

With each step away from the House of Snakes, Vic felt a little bit lighter. It didn't mean that she wouldn't heed the warning, as the Princess of the Under World she'd be foolish not to, but right now in this moment, she was choosing to just be a high school girl on a sort of date with a definitely cute guy, regardless of his soul.

She hopped into the passenger side of her truck, feeling its peculiarity and relishing in the oddness of it. Cal carefully turned through the square so that they were headed back south. A comforting silence fell over them as Cal gently maneuvered Vic's mint baby onto a side road. He slowed down his speed as the paved road turned to gravel.

The surrounding woods grew thinner and Vic knew what lie ahead. When they reached the metal railing the road dead ended. Out the windshield Vic could see a vast lake illuminated in the fire of the setting sun. Cal had brought them to Aphrodite's Ledge.

He turned the ignition off and his hand slid across the white leather seat to find hers. Feeling bold, she scooted a little closer, so that their relaxed hands sat in between them. The sun was hovering just over the horizon and in that moment, she truly was fine.

Chapter Eleven

Nothing was making any sense.

Vic hated when stuff didn't make any sense.

Two more days had passed and Vic still wasn't any closer to finding answers. Short, of peeping in the Bishop's windows, Vic wasn't exactly sure how she could learn more about who Cal was and where he came from.

Granted, Vic strongly believed he was *exactly* who he said he was. A nice, mortal guy from California whose father was transferred from Pacifica to Olympia. It seemed the most likely answer. His reaction to Pythia was unsurprising. He seemed like a pretty relaxed guy, open to different things. Vic could still feel the warmth of his hand over hers, his face half cast in shadow and half illuminated in amber light.

She chewed on a peanut butter-chocolate chip cookie, laying on her stomach with school textbooks spread on the bed in front of her. It wasn't helping her save Cal, nor was it helping her save Persephone. But for the time being it made her feel better. Normal.

The strange prophecy from Pythia had unnerved Vic, which was part of the reason she was cramming cookies in her mouth. The sugary sweetness calmed her nerves. In typical Oracle fashion, the prophecy had been riddled with, well, riddles. Vic cracked a smile at her own joke, tapping a pencil on the physics textbook laid out in front of her. To her left was a lined piece of notebook paper with the prophecy scribbled out in her sloppy, half-print, half-script handwriting.

Most of what Pythia had said seemed to go along with the Tessomancy reading. Obviously, some sort of conflict was happening. That much was clear. What wasn't clear was between who.

Vic felt it was something bigger than just her and her little nuclear family. Things had been calm for a couple centuries now, but maybe there was something Hades wasn't telling her. Her mind continued its wandering as she brushed crumbs off her textbook.

If Cal was the air, since in his tea leaf reading Pythia had seen clouds, then Vic was clearly the sword. Did it mean Cal's vision was obscured from his own conflict? And that Vic could help him overcome it? Her brain was beginning to hurt just from trying to piece it all together.

She heard the back door open and quickly yanked her onyx dagger from beneath the bed, sending peanut butter crumbs flying across the bedspread. She cursed.

"Such a pretty face to speak such ugly words"

Asher. He appeared in the doorway that led into the kitchen, a smirk on his pouty lips and a stack of books in his arms. Irritated at the unexpected intrusion, Vic skillfully flung her dagger at him, embedding it in the doorframe beside his right ear. The jerk didn't even flinch.

"It's called knocking. You know, it's what normal people do."

Ignoring the dagger, Asher entered the room and dropped the stack of books onto the bed. The physics book flipped closed.

"We're hardly normal," Asher replied. He picked up the remaining cookie from the plate on Vic's bed and took a bite.

"Obviously. Since when have you even ever opened a book?" Vic asked waving a hand at the pile. "And you're eating my cookie."

Asher inspected the cookie. "I don't see your name on it. And that's a lie, I've read a book before. Do you want my help or not?"

Vic pretended she was in deep thought. "Let's go with not."

Asher moved toward the bed and Vic's stomach tightened. But he took her pillows and propped them against her elaborate headboard, so that he could sit against them. The books sat in between them.

"Do you want to save your new boyfriend or not?"

Vic scowled at him. Asher was so irritating. Part of her, the part she would never ever admit to, was glad that he was there. It was easier to bounce ideas off of someone else and she very well couldn't do that with Cal since he didn't even know who she actually was and what it was she was in Olympia to do. Her past with Asher may be rocky, but there were few secrets between them.

"First of all, he's not my new boyfriend." She used air quotes around the last two words. "And second, of course I want to save him."

Asher raised a dark eyebrow, using two tattooed fingers to brush crumbs from his lips. "If he's not your boyfriend then why do you want to spare him? You didn't spare any of the others."

Vic's stomach coiled. He had her there. It was true. She hadn't spared the others whose souls she had Taken. When she could, she tried to get help to the scene. But it was more for her own conscience than a matter of sparing a life or the lives of the victims' friends and families. *Gods, she was a rotten person.* Maybe Vic *was* a sword, one that stabbed and Took without remorse. A blade so sharp that it couldn't be trusted.

"Okay, then. Let's settle on a truth. You do like this Cal person. I know you do, Tor. I've known you a long time—your whole life more or less—and I know the expression you wear on your face when you're into someone."

He kindly didn't add, that it was probably the same expression she used to wear around him.

"Fine. You're annoying you know that?" She picked up a Converse from the floor and threw it at him. It banked off the headboard, causing him to duck and it *thunked* to the floor on the other side of the bed.

"I do my best." He glanced at the floor. "You know that could have hurt. Shoes are not weapons."

Frustrated with the course of events, Vic flopped onto her back so that her feet were near the headboard, and her head was near Asher's still booted feet. He caught her glance, rolled his eyes, and immediately began unlacing them. He kicked them off to the floor.

"Better? You've gotten so much more civilized since being in the Above World."

"Maybe you should try it sometime," Vic shot back.

"Again, you wound me so with your words, Princess." He pressed a large hand to his heart. Today he was wearing black jeans and a white t-shirt with an abstract, paint splattered black design.

"I still have another shoe, you know."

"Noted. So, aren't you going to ask me why I brought all these books with me?" Asher coaxed, toeing the pile with his charcoal gray-socked foot.

Vic glanced at the pile that had now slid over and across the watercolor printed bedspread. Books on Greek and Roman mythology made up the majority of the pile, but a book called *Prophets of the Ages* caught Vic's eye. It was a black book with no dust jacket and gold foiling on the spine.

"You do realize that we're part of mythology right? The Above World is just blind to it. They think it's made up."

She picked up *Prophets of the Ages* and flipped to the title page. The smell of must and sawdust washed over her. There was an underlying hint of fresh cut grass and vanilla. She inhaled deeply. It was one of her favorite smells.

Asher nudged her shoulder. "You're such a weirdo, you know that right?"

She gave him the finger.

"If your father only knew how atrocious your manners have gotten since living in the Above World," he chided. "I know *they* don't know, but do you know?"

It was actually a valid question. How much did Vic actually know about her own lineage, the stories and tales that made up her own family, her own history? Admittedly, she took much of the knowledge for granted. Sure, she'd had a tutor in the Under World when she was younger, but after age twelve, she was pretty much left to her own devices. Her father wasn't easy to work for and, at the time, Vic wasn't an easy student. She had an insatiable desire for knowledge and would barrage her tutors—whoever it was for the moment—with impossible questions. She loved to challenge the status quo and, much like Hades, was quite stubborn.

"I know…stuff." Her voice sounded like a petulant child even to her own ears.

"That's what I thought. What if the answers are as simple as studying our—your—past? These books could have the solution that we need. Maybe we can save your friend Cal—" the name sounded annoyed on Asher's lips—"and save Persephone as well. It doesn't have to be one or the other."

Vic stared at the ceiling. It would be amazing if she didn't have to choose, because really there was no choice. Even if Cal was someone with who she could fall in love, she would choose to save her mother every single time. But if there was a way to save both of them…Vic liked that option much better.

Asher saw the change in her eyes from an annoyed gray to a curious gold. He smiled. She still wasn't sure what was in this for him. Asher *always* had an ulterior motive, but she temporarily pushed the thought aside.

She plucked a book from the pile and tossed it to him. It landed on his stomach.

"Then let's get reading."

–

After two hours, Vic and Asher were not any nearer to any answers. Asher had eaten the last remnants of the peanut butter-chocolate chip cookies and Vic was tired. She had a test in Latin the next day and her physics homework still sat unfinished.

Asher yawned and stood up, stretching his arms over his head and revealing a sliver of tanned skin above his waistband. It wasn't fair that someone could eat so many sugary things and be so trim and fit. Vic began to pile the books on the floor beside her bed as Asher pulled on his boots.

"Thanks for this," she said, shoving her physics book back into her book bag.

Asher didn't look up. "I've told you, Tor. I love Persephone, maybe not as much as you because she's your mother, but besides River, she's the closest I've known to a mother of my own."

He finished tying his boots and stood up. Asher was not the type to share his feelings, and although Persephone was usually gone half the year, she'd also taught Vic many things. She'd taught her the rhythm of the seasons and was actually the one who taught a small Vic how to read one long winter, igniting a life-long love of books and the written word. Persephone also taught Vic about being kind to all creatures, which made the Takings that much more difficult. What would her mother say if she knew of the sacrifices and violations against the natural order Vic had committed in order to save her life?

Vic felt a well of emotion inside her. And yet, there was something nagging at the corners of her mind. Something she had been trying to grasp at for the last week, but kept coming up empty.

Now, something in Asher's expression—the curve of his mouth or the arch of his eyebrow, maybe even how he casually leaned against the doorframe leading into the kitchen—made her stomp over to where he stood and yank her dagger out of the wooden frame, from where it had gotten lodged earlier.

She fingered the onyx blade, her voice soft when she asked, "Tell me, Asher. Is that the only reason that you're helping me?"

"What gave me away?" he gave her a crooked smile.

"Everything," she replied simply. "Showing up announced. The pomegranate orchard, showing up with all these books.

You're up to something." She didn't sheath the blade, and instead pointed it at him as if it were her finger.

"Maybe I just like spending time with you," he said smoothly. But he still didn't move. His arm was pressed against the door frame, his hand falling lazily above his hair. He lowered his voice. "Maybe I just want to help you."

Vic snorted. "We both know you aren't that virtuous." Her mind was reeling and she wanted to dive for her bag and pull out the scrap of paper on which she'd written Pythia's prophecy. Did it mention Asher? Were there hints of a deception?

He shrugged and ran his hand through his long, brown hair. "Or maybe I just want to protect you."

Her hand holding the dagger dropped to her side. She hadn't been expecting that. It was perhaps one of the worst replies he could have given because it implied her father.

"Hades put you up to this? To helping me? *Watching* me?"

Asher noticed the change in her eyes, from golden and warm to cold and gray. He put up both hands.

"It's not only his interests that are at heart."

She took a menacing step toward him, the dagger raised between them, the tip nearly pressing into his chest. He took a step back.

"Be careful with that thing. I'm just saying, maybe your father asked that I watch over you a little bit, but did you ever stop to think it was possible that I *wanted* to watch over you too?"

"That's what stalkers and creeps say," Vic said jabbing out with the dagger. She was sick of being treated like a child, like a pawn in her father's plans.

In one swift movement, Asher twisted Vic's arm up and behind her, releasing the dagger which he swept up in his free hand, before pulling her into him so that her back was pressed against his chest. He took the dagger and pressed it against her neck, behind her left ear.

"Don't forget who trained with you. I know all of your tells. How your body moves."

The words seemed both flirtatious and threatening. Vic knew he wouldn't hurt her, but she could feel his breath warm on her skin. The smell of incense and the distinct smell that was simply Asher pressed against her. She hadn't been this close to him since she pounded her fists into him and then cried in his arms. Her chest heaved against his tattooed arm.

"I know your vulnerabilities." He twirled her around so she faced him and handed her the dagger, bronze handle out. "And that's why I agreed to watch over you."

"I don't need a baby-sitter," Vic replied through gritted teeth, sheathing the blade.

"No, but you don't know what you're up against. That's why I was trying to help you figure it out. To protect you."

"I don't need protecting!" she growled. She stalked to the back door and pulled it open. The warm night air danced into the kitchen, it only stoked the already hot embers of Vic's temper. "Out."

Asher strode toward her. "You're frustrating, you know that? You're arrogant and stubborn."

"And you're obnoxious and a liar. So I suppose we're even." She placed a hand on her hip, the other still on the doorknob.

He closed the space between them and for the briefest of seconds, Vic feared her might try to kiss her. And she feared even more that she might kiss him back. Vic was all fire and Asher was like gasoline. It was not a recommended combination. They'd consume each other from the inside out.

She could see that now.

But he didn't kiss her. Instead, he tucked a strand of hair that had fallen out of her braid, behind her ear.

"You don't know who he is. You know nothing about him." Cal. He was referring to Cal. So that's what this was. She was right, he was jealous and her father wanting him to spy on her was also the perfect reason to keep his eye on her and possibly meddle in her affairs.

Asher's fingers hovered in the air near her ear, so she took a small step back.

"Maybe I take him at his word. That he is exactly who he says he is. Some guy from California whose father got transferred to another state because of his job!"

His hand fell to his side. "Or maybe he's a threat. Maybe he's the one who is poisoning your mother, killing her! Did you ever stop to question the timing of his arrival? You just take him at his word? Just like that?"

He was clearly irritated and Vic couldn't truly understand it. It explained why he was willing to help her figure out who Cal could possibly be, but for right now Vic had no reason to suspect Cal was anyone else than who he said he was. Her heart—the same one that told her Asher was not a good match for her and that any relationship with him would just lead to a broken heart — hadn't given her a reason to believe otherwise.

"Yes. Just like that. It's called trust, Asher." She bit her lip to prevent herself from adding, *something we never had.*

Asher took a step toward the door and stood on the threshold. "He's not like us you know. When he finds out, how could he possibly understand you? Once he knows who you are—what you are, how could he ever love you?"

Coming from Asher, the words were meant to jab and

needle. To get her to retaliate and stoke the flames. It was a manipulation of her feelings because she'd lost control when she had been home, he had honed in on her weak spots. Just like a predator.

"I suppose that's all the reasons why, Asher. Because he isn't like us. Good night."

She began to shut the door as Asher backed away. Before she closed the door all the way, she called out to him. "And if you come near me again, I'll slash the tires on your bike."

–

That night, she laid restlessly in bed. She'd stripped the sheets and the bedspread and threw them in the laundry to wash the smell of Asher from them. The rhythmic sound of the tumble cycle made her doze, but then she'd hear a sound—the crack of a twig, the hoot of an owl—and she'd snap awake. Her dagger was beneath her pillow and she knew Asher wouldn't be returning.

But something he'd said kept playing in her mind, over and over like a song on repeat. *He's not like us.* And Vic had agreed. Cal wasn't like them. What she had meant was that he was a kind and good person, not violent and manipulative. But as she lay in bed staring at the ceiling and listening to the sounds of the dryer, she realized that Asher had actually meant something very different. He had been implying that Cal wasn't privy to their secret world that bled into the regular lives of the citizens of Olympia, that Cal wasn't immortal. And the thought that had Vic's mind reeling was just the opposite: *But what if he was?*

Chapter Twelve

Vic was up before the sun the next day.

She made some oatmeal dumped with brown sugar and maple syrup and brought the bowl back to her bed. Leaning against the headboard, she pulled two of the books from the pile on the floor onto the bed.

First, she pulled *Prophets of the Ages* into her lap. She'd thought something had seemed familiar about it, but had forgotten because, as usual, Asher made her lose her mind. Shoving a spoonful of sugary sweet oatmeal into her mouth, she turned to the title page. The author wasn't a name that she recognized. No Plato or Socrates, or some other philosophical name. She carefully turned to the table of contents. The pages of the book were yellowed with age and were more like onion skin than modern book pages.

Her eyes scanned the names which were listed alphabetically: *Moses, Nostradamus…Oracle of Delphi.* Curiosity aroused, Vic flipped to page eighty-seven. The head of the chapter had an ink illustration of a beautiful woman writhing on a rock-altar-type of thing. She was half-nude, her eyes rolled back in her head and Vic had to laugh because she couldn't imagine Pythia in this role. Nevertheless, she began to read as she ate.

There was nothing there that she didn't already know. That the Oracle originated in the Temple of Apollo and that she used to enter a trance-like state using the vapors from a chasm in the rock. Vic noted that the book was mistaken in saying that the Oracle was replaced upon death. Because Pythia herself was millennia old. She simply changed every few hundred years. They all did. It was how they survived.

Disappointed, Vic sat her now empty bowl on top of the book and picked up the second one, *The Dynasties of the Greek Gods*. It sounded like a textbook. The cover was leather bound and dyed a navy color. In the center was an embossed gold circle with a lightning bolt across it. She knew these were most likely her father's books and that Asher probably had taken them without permission. There was a slight pang of guilt for how she'd treated him, but her ire still snaked through her veins. Two things Vic did not like were being used or being betrayed.

She glanced at the clock and saw that she had an hour before she had to leave to get to school on time. Flopping over, so she was on her back and her legs were up the wall, pajama pants falling around her knees, one sock slouched down the other still hugging her calf, she looked through the book. She wasn't completely sure what she was looking for. More than anything it was simply a feeling. A feeling that Asher wasn't completely wrong—that Cal may not be who he said he was—but that it wasn't as simple as that.

She hated not having something more concrete to go off of. Feelings were flimsy things, like gossamer that hung from the eaves of the barn, shining in the autumn sun.

The book was divided into three sections. The first section was about *The Primordial Deities*. Vic had never even heard of such a group. She knew her father and his brothers and sisters, were not the first generation of gods, even though they'd lasted the longest. But she had believed—apparently erroneously—that the lineage had started with the Titans when Cronus and Rhea gave birth to Zeus, Poseidon, Hades, Hestia, Hera, and Demeter. And she knew that the siblings later overthrew the Titans in the Battle of the Gods. The battle sealed the Olympian gods' fates as rulers of the Universe.

And yet, this book was telling her something slightly different. That the Titans were not the first. Why had she never been told? She supposed she could blame the tutors that couldn't withstand her ire, but isn't it something her father or mother should have mentioned?

According to the text, the primordial deities were the very first gods and goddesses born from the void simply known as Chaos. From Chaos came Darkness and Night, or according to the genealogical chart that was on the opposing page from the text, Erebus and Nyx. Erebus and Nyx then gave birth to Light and Day, also known as Aether and Hemera. Later, Light and Day would give birth to Heaven (Uranus) and Ocean (Pontus). And eventually, according to the text, Uranus would later pair up with Gaia, and together they would give birth to the Titans. The rest Vic more or less knew.

But she read on, fascinated, as the text explained how things like misery, compulsion, eternity, fate, doom, and time came to be. A simple line chart hardly did it justice. The gods were not simple lines and branches, their history did not form a tree, but a complicated web of lovers, heroes, and villains.

She knew of Cronus, the first Titan, but she, like so many

others, had mistakenly believed he was the master of time. In fact, it was the Chronus of the primordial deities who was the true father time.

Time. The flash of a silver watch with a dark mother-of-pearl face, a watch that seemed just slightly out of place on a surfer boy from California. She didn't know why, but she felt that it was significant. It couldn't be a coincidence there were two Chronuses, the only difference being a single letter, the letter *h*, and yet somehow time had turned one into antiquity.

Biting her knuckle, she skipped ahead to the passage about Cronus, the one who led the Titans and who the modern Olympian gods had overthrown. Each god and goddess had an ink drawing and a list of their lineage and symbols. Vic scanned the image of Cronus and her eyes dropped to the box containing the words she was afraid she'd find. Cronus was the Titan of Harvest. How had she missed something so obvious? Under the list of symbols she found the words: scythe and sickle, but her heart froze in her chest on the last one: snake.

The House of Snakes has risen and will not be slain.

Energy surged inside her and she leapt from the bed, knocking over the empty bowl, and began pacing around the living room. She had the pieces, she just had to put them together. Grabbing her book bag she pulled out a spiral notebook and tore out a fresh sheet of paper. She grabbed a Sharpie from her pencil pouch and began making a list of the things that she knew:

-CHRONUS AND CRONUS

-CRONUS=TIME=CAL'S WATCH???

-CRONUS=TITAN GOD OF HARVEST=BATTLE OF THE GODS=SNAKE

-PYTHIA=HOUSE OF SNAKES

-PERSEPHONE=GODDESS OF THE HARVEST=COINCIDENCE?

When she was finished, she read the list twice. Chewing on the cap of the Sharpie marker. It wasn't much to go on, but it was a start.

Somehow she knew all of these things were connected, she just didn't know how. She glanced at the clock and practically tore out of her pajamas to hop into the shower.

As she stood under the hot stream of water, her brain kept trying to put the pieces of the puzzle together, but it was as if she was missing all the center pieces and just had the outside ones. She cursed as shampoo ran into her eyes.

Cal was part of this. She didn't know how—she wasn't even sure he knew how—but he was part of Persephone's illness and, gods, help her, he was going to be part of the solution. She towel-dried her hair and decided it would have to be good enough, even if it meant that it would be a crazy frizzy mess by second period.

Vic didn't believe in coincidences. She believed that everything happened for a reason. Pythia's words rang in her mind: *The beginning is the end and the end is the beginning.* If the primordial gods were the beginning and the Olympians were the end, was someone trying to kill off the modern day gods one by one? What exactly had happened to the Titans after they were overthrown?

Vic tried to rack her memory but couldn't remember, so she shoved *The Dynasties of the Greek Gods* into her book bag beside her unfinished physics homework. Maybe she'd be able to finish it at lunch.

Cursing Asher for eating the last of her cookies, she

dashed out the back door and to her truck. As she pulled out of the driveway, images of her mother drowning in hyacinth popped into her mind, the syrupy black veins beneath her butterfly skin. The thought that someone could do this to her mother on purpose set Vic's blood on fire. She supposed a part of her—the naïve, optimist part—had hoped that it was some kind of never-before-seen-illness or even an accident, but the evidence was beginning to prove otherwise. She could—no, she *would*—save Persephone and she wouldn't Take another soul to do it either.

In fact, she was going to create an ally of the very soul her father had asked her to Take. Cal may or may not know what he signed up for by befriending her, but Vic knew, just as Asher had, that there was something innately good about Cal. Something that she liked, but also envied. Something that she wished she had inside herself.

It wasn't going to be easy, she was going to have to be honest with him and lay it all out on the line. Most people didn't respond well to the whole, "Hey, I'm the Princess of the Under World!" thing, but she was out of options. She needed an ally—no, she needed a partner. Someone who could help her to figure this all out and someone who she could trust to do the right thing.

And that someone was Callum Bishop.

She sped down the street toward the school, the warm breeze drying her wavy hair and the smell of bonfires and falling leaves hanging heavy in the air. For the first time that morning, Vic smiled.

Chapter Thirteen

MEET ME AFTER SCHOOL?

This time it was Vic's turn to pass the note in English. Cal looked up from his copy of *The Grapes of Wrath,* and grinned. He gave Vic a nod and slipped the scrap of lined paper into his book as a bookmark.

After that the day seemed to drag on. Vic sat through sixth period and then seventh period, wondering how she was even going to broach the subject. Assuming, *"Hey, are you immortal? Because I think you might be!"* could seem a little bit strange.

The paper with her notes from the morning stuck out of her physics book. Carefully, she pulled it out, folded it into a neat square, and slipped it into her jeans pocket. She'd had a chance during lunch to finish the assignment that Asher had interrupted, but it wasn't her best work. She'd be lucky if she got a B on it. Definitely, not Vic standards. But sometimes one had bigger fish to fry.

When the seventh period bell rang, Vic nearly jumped out of her skin. Cal gave her a strange look then fell into step beside her as the hall flooded with people. The weekend was nearing, not to mention the Apple Festival was only another week away, so the hall was abuzz with excitement. Any solemnness about the incidents around the homecoming weekend long forgotten.

As Vic changed out her books for the ones she'd need for homework that night, Cal leaned against the locker next to hers. He was wearing a red flannel with the sleeves rolled up to the elbow, torn jeans, and red Chucks. He caught her eye and Vic felt her cheeks flush. She really, really hoped she was right about all this.

"What's this Apple Festival I keep hearing about? It seems like all anyone is talking about today."

Vic zipped up her book bag and shut her locker, heading toward the stairs. She glanced at Cal and he shook his head, letting her know he already had all the books he'd need for later. He'd brought his book bag to last period. So, Vic headed down the stairs and out one of the side doors and into the warm autumn air.

"It's a festival of apples!" she said grandly, pulling a pair of oversized aviators from a compartment on her book bag. She jingled her keys as they walked. It would have seemed out of excitement, but really it was because of her nerves.

Cal chuckled. He ran a hand through his dark hair and the sunlight caught the face of his watch. "I gathered that much."

"Well," said Vic as she unlocked the truck and climbed in. She reached over and unlocked Cal's door and once he was in the truck, continued. "It's a harvest celebration. And basically, it's apple everything. Apple pie, apple bread, apple butter, apple honey, apple cake, apple cheese, apple beer..."

"Did you say apple cheese?" Cal asked, his mouth curled in disgust.

Vic cranked the engine. "Don't knock it until you've tried it. But, yeah, there's a parade and an Apple Blossom Queen—"

"A queen?"

Vic was beginning to suspect that they didn't have Apple Festivals in California.

"Yeah. Usually, one of the PTA moms who won the apple pie bake-off the previous year."

She pulled out of the parking lot, unsure which way to turn. It would be a little strange to invite herself over to Cal's house. Then there was the whole issue of his family. She could take him to the manor. There was no rule saying that she couldn't have friends over. Richard would probably still be there and he may or may not tell her father.

And that was another thing. Her father. Cal thought she lived with her father, if he came over it would be very clear that she lived alone in the manor, considering she lived in about one-sixth of the house.

No, it was too risky. So, she decided to go to the town library. It was near the convenience store and maybe they could grab sandwiches or something too. At least the library was an excuse to try and find more information on the Greek dynasties.

"An apple pie bake-off sounds delicious," Cal said, breaking into her thoughts. She hadn't even realized a period of companionable silence had stretched between them.

"It really is. The festival is fun. There's bobbing for apples and they usually rent a dunk tank and you can pay to dunk

Mr. Beckerman. Besides the typical carnival games, the festival usually ends with a firework show."

"It's surprising that there's a festival like that so close to Halloween."

She shrugged. "Actually, I'd say the festival is kind of a bigger deal than Halloween around here. Apples are what Olympia is known for. It's our bread and butter."

She said *our* like she was an actual part of the town. Like the place belonged to her and her to it. It didn't, but at times it felt like it did. Like she was a regular citizen of Olympia, and not that outsider always looking in.

She turned onto a gravel driveway that led to the parking lot of the little library. The library was less building or institution, and more someone's house. It had a small front porch lined with rocking chairs so that when the weather was nice, you could read outside—or like today some older Olympian women were knitting scarves and beanies for whenever the weather did decide to turn. The sole library in Olympia was a little forest green-sided building. Vic had visited many times and knew its layout by heart.

The attic area housed the children's and teen books. Two of the upstairs bedrooms contained non-fiction books and a third contained adult fiction works. The back entrance led into what was probably once the house's main floor and contained a small circulation desk, two computers, the reference section, and a few displays with the newest books the library had obtained for circulation. Audiovisual materials were available upon request, and usually stored in the basement.

"This is the library?" Cal asked shutting the truck door and placing his hands in his pockets.

"Let me guess, libraries are a little different where you're from?" she smiled. Cal may have a small town heart, but he had big town expectations. "Trust me. It's marvelous."

Instinctively, she reached for his hand and was relieved when he didn't pull away. Instead, he intertwined his fingers with hers and she led him into the little library.

A corkboard outside the entrance greeted patrons and had fliers pinned to it advertising dog-walking, baby-sitting, and tutoring services.

An older man and a middle-aged woman were the only two workers, both sitting in high-backed chairs at the circulation desk. Vic knew the library only had a handful of employees, but she didn't know any of them particularly well since she tended to keep to herself, so she gave a little wave with her free hand before leading Cal to the staircase.

"What we're here for is upstairs."

"And just what exactly are we here for?"

Vic gave him a surreptitious grin. "Spoilers."

She pulled him up the steps. The library had worn wooden floors in a faded shade of brown. They were scratched and scuffed and dented. Vic loved them. The doors and hinges had been removed from the bedrooms, and instead each room had a small plaque beside it indicating the treasures it held. She headed toward the bedroom on the far left, which was painted a pleasant shade of acorn brown. This room contained the two-hundreds, which is where Vic knew the religion and mythology books were located. She possibly could have memorized the Dewey Decimal System at one point in time.

"No. Not non-fiction!" Cal hissed, keeping his voice low even though it appeared there were no other patrons in this room.

"And just what is wrong with non-fiction?"

"It's so boring! We just spent all day in class!"

"*Grapes of Wrath* isn't non-fiction. And it's plenty boring."

"It's realistic fiction which is basically borderline non-fiction," he protested.

But he continued to let her pull him. Without furniture and with narrow aisles, it was surprising just how many books would fit inside a standard bedroom.

Vic continued toward the back left corner of the room where she knew the two-hundreds were shelved. The numbers started on a shelf about eye-level and went to the bottom. She dropped Cal's hand and scanned the spines, pulling out anything with the words Greek, Greek mythology, ancient Greece, gods, goddesses, or dynasties. As she gathered them she piled them into Cal's arms until he was weighted down with about forty pounds worth of books.

"I strongly suspect that you're making me do homework that isn't even worth a letter grade," he grunted as he followed her to the room's opposite corner where a nook with a small table and two frayed leather armchairs sat. She relieved him of the top of his pile and placed it on the table. Cal then placed the rest next to her pile. His forearms were indented with thin lines from the weight of the books.

"We're going to do some research. But first, I need you to tell me about your watch."

–

"My watch?" Cal gave Vic a puzzled expression as she plopped into the seat across from him.

She nodded. "I mean it's beautiful, but I've just been wondering where you got it. I've never seen anything like it before."

She knew it was both an odd and abrupt question. But so far Cal had played along with all of her strange suggestions, even though parts of her regretted taking him to see Pythia. Granted, it was hard to ever be prepared enough for something of that caliber. She was going solely on the assumption that if he could handle that, he could handle nearly anything.

"It was a gift from my father before we moved. For my eighteenth birthday." He admired the watch as he spoke, the afternoon light from the small round window catching the dark mother of pearl face, a kaleidoscope of colors. "I'd never really been a watch guy before, but the gesture meant more than the watch itself. Which is why I wear it. When there's six kids in a family, material gifts can be a rare and special treat."

The wheels of Vic's mind were slowly turning. She lightly drummed her fingers on the pile of books as she tried to put together the pieces of the puzzle.

"Yeah, that must be difficult." She couldn't really relate, being the only child of the King and Queen of the Under World, so instead she asked, "What's your dad like?"

Cal's face went thoughtful. "He's a decent guy. Supportive of his family, but also kind of a workaholic."

"You moved here because of his job, didn't you?"

"Yeah. It was kind of unexpected."

"What is it that he does? For work?" The wheels were spinning faster and faster, so fast that Vic almost couldn't keep up with the amount of questions that kept bubbling to the surface.

"He works in agricultural technology. Actually, I don't know much about it." He chuckled and ran a hand nervously through his hair.

The realization struck her that she was maybe interrogating him a bit. She wasn't very good at playing detective, but the fact that his father worked in agricultural technology contributed to the mounting evidence that Cronus—the Titan one—was somehow tied to this.

But how could Cal be so oblivious? How could he not know his own identity? Vic tried to imagine if she hadn't grown up in the Under World, if all her life up until now had been spent in the Above World. If she had lived with Persephone year round and if her mother had chosen to hide her gifts from her daughter, would Vic ever have realized that she herself was immortal? That she too had gifts?

The air is the sword and the sword is the air.

Vic decided it was now or never. This awkward dance couldn't continue. She'd either gain an ally or would lose a friend, but either way she was running out of time to save Persephone. She needed help and there was only one way to get it.

"Listen, I haven't been completely honest with you. About my parents. It's going to be hard to believe, but I'd really like for you to hear me out, because I'm in a situation and I can't do it alone anymore. And I think you could help me."

Surprisingly, she didn't stumble over the words. They felt right. Like she was on the brink of learning something important. You had to give trust to gain trust.

Cal's eyes widened but before he could say anything, Vic pressed on, her courage growing. Cal was the first person in the Above World—besides Richard and his wife—who would know her actual identity. The thought of telling someone the truth was like a heavy burden being lifted from her shoulders.

"My name is Victoriana Haden. I don't live with my dad. In fact, I live alone in a huge manor off Styx Hill. My father hired a groundskeeper named Richard, and while I'm living there he helps me out and takes care of the house. My mother is really ill, in fact she's dying, and my father sent me here to try and save her, but nothing is working. I'm running out of time and out of allies. I feel like this is much bigger than me or even my family. I think someone poisoned my mother on purpose. I just don't know who and I don't know why."

The words tumbled out in a rush and when she paused to catch her breath, she gestured to the stack of books.

"It's not a coincidence that this town is called Olympia and it's even less of a coincidence that my last name is Haden. My father is Hades, the god of the Under World, and my mother is Persephone, the harvest goddess. This strangely warm autumn is the result of her illness. She's been sick nearly a year now and is too weak to return to the Above World and be with her mother, Demeter. So the seasons are in homeostasis. When I went home this past weekend, it was to the Under World to see my mom. She's getting worse every day, instead of better, despite the tasks that have been given to me to try and save her."

Vic cast her eyes downward at the pile of books. Anything to distract her from catching the look on Cal's face. To distract herself from his amber eyes and spattering of freckles.

"I know it all sounds crazy, and you have no reason to believe me. But it's the truth. And I'm trying to find a way to save my mom. I can't do it alone anymore."

Finally, she glanced up at him through several strands of frizzy black hair. Her heart sang with relief when she noticed that his eyes contained no judgment. Instead they were clouded with thoughts, as if he was trying to sort the fact from any possible fiction, and find the evidence that would contradict or validate the truth.

"Pythia?" he asked, scratching at his chin.

Vic sighed. "The Oracle of Delphi."

"Anybody else?"

She shook her head. "Not that you've met, but I'm beginning to realize there's a lot I've been unaware of."

She laughed bitterly and Cal reached out a hand and placed it on her knee. His warmth felt like a reassuring weight. Maybe he believed her after all.

"And what is it that you think that I have to do with all this? With your mother's illness or with this other world which you say coincides with my normal one?"

Vic cringed at the word *normal.* It was an isolating word, the word that made her feel like she was a spectator and could never have what everyone else had. That she'd never fit in living in the Above World, and would forever have a fate in the darkness of Below.

"Honestly? I'm not sure. I was kind of hoping you'd help me to figure it out."

Cal gave her knee a reassuring pat before pulling his hand away. Suddenly, she felt cold without his protective warmth. He looked out the window, unable to meet her gaze. Her heart began to beat just a little bit faster in her chest.

"I'll help you figure it out. That's what friends do for each other. And somehow, despite the illogic of it, your words seem to ring true. The things Pythia said…your questions about my father. There are things I need answers to that I think only you could help me find." He glanced at her and smiled, but it was laced with sadness.

Or was it regret? Her heart beat faster.

"But if we're going to move forward, you're right. We need to be completely honest with each other. I've told you—truthfully—that my father is a busy guy and I actually don't know much about him. Yeah, we moved here for him. But is it a coincidence then that we moved to a small town called Olympia where the daughter of the Under World just happens to be a student at my new high school? I don't know. I'm not a big believer in coincidences. To me it all happens for a reason, sometimes it just takes a while to figure it out. And like you said, maybe by helping you, I can help myself too. I'm sorry your mother is sick and that she's dying. I can't imagine how that must feel."

He stumbled over the last words, imagining his own mother—the pillar of the Bishop family in his father's frequent absences.

Vic felt frozen. She wasn't good at sympathy. She didn't know how to properly receive it nor did she know how to give it, so she sat silently and waited for Cal to say something else, something more that could press them forward and out of this awkward conversation.

She wanted to put the pieces of the puzzle together—figure out Cal's role in all of this and give them both some answers before Persephone died and was lost to Vic forever. After their trip to the House of Snakes, Vic had already resolved to not Take Cal's soul. He didn't deserve it and she didn't truly believe that it could save her mother. There was something else at play here and it was much larger than Cal or Vic, but she felt sure that together, they'd be able to tackle it. They were a team.

Cal continued, "But I have a secret I need to share with you. And I think I'm going to need an answer."

She felt her heart stutter. He looked her straight in the eyes, his amber eyes were warm, but ringed with confusion and some sadness. The autumnal light from the window fell across his hair, bringing out shades of cocoa, pomegranate, and honey. Perhaps her heart knew before her head the words he would say next, because fate was a fickle creature. Still, it didn't prepare her for the irreparable cracks to their friendship. Because deep down Vic knew she was a monster, and who could ever love a monster?

"I saw you that morning. Before school, on my first day here. The car accident. I saw what you did to that girl. To Lauren. And I need to know why."

Chapter Fourteen

Vic's heart plummeted to her stomach.

This couldn't be happening. She'd had enchanted protection. How could he have seen? Her fingers instinctively went to the silver bat charm that hung at her throat. Had she been so careless that morning?

Cal's expression held no judgment, but his eyes showed conflicted emotion. He wanted to believe Vic wasn't capable of the unspeakable. But she could no longer continue lying to him.

"You won't find the reason acceptable," Vic said slowly, her voice nearly breaking on the last words.

She had to look anywhere but at him, looking at him felt painful. She didn't deserve his calm demeanor. He should be terrified of her. He should know what a monster she had become, all to save her mother.

"Try me." Cal's lips were turned down into a frown.

Vic averted her eyes to the shelves of books to the right. The four hundreds, languages. One of her favorite sections. She had studied Latin, Greek, and French and found comfort in the way her tongue formed the unfamiliar sounds and the way her hand scribed the new combinations of letters.

"When my mother was taken ill and we realized her illness wasn't going away, my father and I went to see Pythia. It wasn't for a tea reading, but an Oracle reading where Pythia inhales ancient vapors and channels, for lack of a better word, the beyond." Vic paused, reciting the sections of the four hundreds in her head as she spoke: *Language*, *Linguistics*, *English* and *Old Languages...*

"The recommendation was an elixir. Soul of the living, blood of a lover, fruit of the dead. My mother was to drink the concoction every few weeks or so, but now...It's no longer doing anything. It's not helping."

Tears welled up behind her eyes, but she stubbornly refused to release them. A monster does not deserve sympathy.

"And what you did to Lauren...that golden shimmering thing? That was her soul?"

Oh, gods! How much did he see? Vic cringed and gave a small nod. She could only imagine to unknowing eyes what it would look like to see her removing the glowing orb and cutting its tendrils before placing it in her pouch.

"But Lauren's not dead."

Vic's reply was automatic. "Just because the soul is Taken from the body doesn't mean that one dies."

Cal nodded thoughtfully. "The soul is what gives us our essence. It's who we are."

Again, Vic nodded. Surprised that Cal grasped concepts that even took Asher—who saw the dead on a daily basis—two decades to understand.

"The soul is the life force, our heart can beat without it, but essentially you become a pale shadow of who you were or who you could be."

"I've heard of studies that try to capture the soul as it leaves the body. Even some that have tried to measure its weight by weighing a body before and after the moment of death." Cal paused as if realizing something. "And that sophomore? That was you too?"

Vic bit her knuckle to keep the tears at bay. *German and Related Languages…French and Related Languages.* "I called for help. But I guess they weren't fast enough."

Cal shook his head, a lock of dark hair falling across his forehead. "But that wasn't your fault. I overheard some guys talking about it in my French class. He drank too much and passed out, then choked on his own vomit. Essentially, he asphyxiated."

Vic shook her head. "My mother needed it." A frustrated tear rolled down her cheek and she brushed it away. She felt Cal's hands rest on either of her knees, sending a shock of comforting warmth through her.

"Listen, Vic. I don't really know you. And I don't know your family. But what I do know is that if my mother was dying, I would do just about anything to save her."

She continued to avoid his gaze. "Even steal someone's soul?"

His voice was unwavering. "I can't answer that in good faith, never having been in the situation. But if I was desperate and scared, and my father told me it was the only way to save her, then I believe that yes, I would."

Vic's ears couldn't comprehend what Cal was saying. This acceptance defied logic. It defied everything she'd come to believe about herself. Therefore, her brain couldn't seem to register the actuality of the words.

"You don't think I'm a monster? A killer?" More tears escaped and this time Cal carefully brushed them away before grasping her chin so she had no choice but to look into his eyes.

They were clear and focused. And she was surprised to find that they didn't contain any sympathy. Instead, she found something more akin to understanding.

"No. I do not think you are a monster and I definitely do not think you are a killer. For one, what happened to that kid is not an anomaly. And there's no way to prove that you are responsible for his death. Two, I think that you did what you thought you had to do to save your mother. I imagine you were frightened and appalled by what was asked of you, and yet, at the same time, determined to do it. So no, I do not see you as any less. If anything I see you as more."

Her heart thudded in her chest and more tears slipped down her cheeks. She didn't know what to say because she'd never thought of herself in this way. Her mind went back to the image of two Vics. The Above World Vic who was a good student and had goals for herself. The one who really liked Cal and wanted to go on dates and maybe secretly wanted to go to homecoming dances. And then there was the Under World Vic. The one who was sent on a mission that asked too much of a seventeen-year-old girl and that made her feel like she was forever an outsider, and would inevitably be inextricably involved with manipulative guys like Asher. Part of her believed she deserved it. A monster got what they deserved. But what if someone decided to take the time to see the monster with new eyes? What if doing what you think is right doesn't mean you are a monster after all? Maybe right and wrong aren't always as clear cut as Vic had once believed.

Finally, Vic sniffed. "Thank you."

Cal touched the corner of her mouth with his thumb and smiled before pulling away.

"We can save your mother. I'll help you find a way. Just tell me where to start."

–

Vic was not used to such kindness. Perhaps, that was one thing that Asher had gotten right about Cal. His soul was indeed different.

They poured over the stack of books until it grew dark and the librarian quietly let them know that they'd be closing, and that they could place any unwanted books on the cart in the hallway. Outside, the air was warm as they walked to Vic's truck.

They hadn't found much in the way of new information.

She'd shared her notes with Cal about the Greek dynasties, but not Pythia's prophecy. It was nice to have an ally and she didn't want to scare him off with so much doom and gloom, if it wasn't absolutely necessary. Cal had used the copier in the basement of the library to photocopy some of the dynastic family trees and he promised her he'd see if he could find anything more on his father or his paternal lineage.

Interestingly, he didn't seem to know much. He wasn't in touch with his paternal grandparents; and as far as he knew they lived in Estonia, a small country in Europe so he'd actually never even met them. When pressed, he wasn't even sure at what age his father had come to America. His father had simply never discussed his past. Cal being the oldest and, out of respect for his father, had never pressed his father for more information about his paternal family. But now Vic could see the light behind Cal's eyes and the puzzle pieces that were laid out before him.

They grabbed sandwiches to go from the convenience store, and when Vic pulled into Cal's driveway, they said good-night amidst promises that she'd look through some more of the books and see if she could access any archives online that might help them.

Before he slipped out of the truck, Cal reached a hand across the bench seat and found her fingers. The moonlight filtered through the trees in his front yard and streaked across his face in pale lines.

"I meant what I said earlier."

She nodded, words knotting up in her throat once again. Her feelings toward Cal were becoming stronger quickly. She'd never quite felt this way before and didn't know what to do with the influx of new emotion, so they just seemed to lodge in her throat.

Finally, she managed an, "I know." But it was inadequate for all she really wanted to say. Instead, she held Cal's gaze in the moonlight and it seemed to be enough for him. "Thank you. For helping me."

This time Cal grinned, his teeth reminded Vic of the Cheshire Cat, the way they seemed to float in the moonlight.

"You'd do the same for me."

He gave her fingers a gentle squeeze, then slid the rest of the way out of the truck.

The house glowed with warm light and Vic wondered if their research would somehow shatter this pleasant façade. If perhaps beneath, there lurked something that once they figured it out and the wheels were set in motion, they couldn't undo it.

Cal stopped in the doorway, nothing but a shadow against

the house's light and held up a hand in a wave. The way the light fell around him made him look as though he were an angel. Vic felt her heart tingle as she reversed down the driveway, her palms sweaty on the steering wheel, and her stomach filled with millions of butterfly wings.

She realized Cal was right. She would do the same for him. The truck turned onto the main road and Vic headed home with a heart that was just a little bit lighter than it had been before.

Chapter Fifteen

Time was running out.

Every minute without any answers was also a minute closer to Persephone's demise. Vic poured over books until one in the morning, when she finally gave up and decided to enlist the help of the internet.

Sleep found her a couple of hours later. She woke with her face pressed into the keyboard, several keys indented into her cheek. She rubbed the sleep from her eyes and glanced at the clock. It was twenty minutes before the start of school. At this point, there were simply more pressing matters to attend to. Ones that she couldn't attend to alone.

Pulling her hair into a bun, she shoved her feet into a pair of white Chucks and grabbed her truck keys. As she drove in the direction of the school, she ran her fingers over her bat charm and used the speed dial of her cell to call the school office. In a voice matching her father's, Vic told the school that she wasn't feeling well that day and was running a fever, so she'd be staying home and that, yes, if it was more than two days he'd be sure to send in a doctor's note.

It didn't take her long to find Cal pedaling along the shoulder of the road. His backpack slung across his shoulders. She slowed down beside him, keeping an eye on the road as she reached across the bench seat and frantically rolled down the passenger side window.

"Going my way?" she called out.

Cal glanced over his shoulder and nearly crashed his bicycle into the ditch. She pulled over several paces in front of him and he pedaled over to the truck and heaved his bike into the truck bed. Once he'd climbed in, she made a U-turn in the middle of the road.

"I know it's early and, no offense, but you certainly look tired, but I think school is in the opposite direction."

Vic grimaced. "No offense taken. Here, take out your cell phone."

Cal reached into his pocket. He was wearing a light weight, white waffle-knit Henley shirt that accentuated his tanned skin and faded blue jeans. Vic instructed him to call the school office and as he did, she brushed her fingers over her bat charm. She could hear the secretary answer on the other line. Cal gave her a strange look, but Vic nodded encouraging him to speak.

"Hello," said Cal in a deep, aged voice. His eyes grew round in surprise. "Uh, yes, I'll be calling off my son, Callum Bishop, today. Seems he has some sort of stomach bug. Bad sushi, I think." There was a pause. "Yes, of course. Thank you."

Cal ended the call and when he spoke to Vic his voice had returned to its normal cadence. "How did you do that? Magic powers?"

Vic shrugged and half-smiled. "Something like that. But really, let's address your fibbing skills. Bad sushi?"

Cal shrugged. "It was the first thing that came to mind!"

They drove in silence for a few minutes before Vic turned into the manor's long driveway. She didn't bother parking the truck in the barn, instead she parked near the back door. Richard's black Jeep was already in the driveway.

"I thought you lived alone?" Cal asked as he slung his book bag over his shoulder.

"I do. That's Richard's car. He's the groundskeeper. Basically, he's the closest thing I have to a father in the Above World."

As they approached the back door, Richard was already raking the copious amounts of leaves out of the back flower beds and mumbling about excessive weather. He looked up at their approach, his eyes a wizened blue behind wire framed glasses. His hair was completely white and a bit too long and his face was lined with wrinkles. He stood slightly hunched over and wore an oversized sweater, shorts with about a dozen pockets, and a floppy hat on his head. He wore hunter green wellies on his feet and dirty gardening gloves on his hands.

"Well, good morning, Victoriana. I wasn't expecting you home today," he smiled kindly but his eyes were questioning. "And I see you've finally made a friend."

Vic's cheeks flushed with embarrassment.

"Yeah, we have a project to work on and, uh, school was cancelled due to a water leak," Vic brushed her fingers against the bat charm and knew that speaking the words would make it so. Lying to Richard sent a pang of guilt to her abdomen.

School would be evacuated and students sent home as water flooded the halls. At least now, she wouldn't have to worry about a doctor's note and the absence wouldn't count against either her or Cal. She'd only wished she'd thought of it sooner.

"Oh, that's nice. Not the leak, I mean. But the project."

"Richard, this is Cal. Cal, this is Richard. His wife, Anastasia, makes the best peanut butter-chocolate chip cookies."

Richard nodded in polite greeting before gesturing to all the leaves.

"Your mother has made my work cut out for me, Victoriana." He shook his head as the leaves he'd just raked into a neat pile seemed to dwarf in size compared to the leaves that kept falling. But then he smiled. "At least it keeps these old bones busy!"

Vic took it as a dismissal as she led Cal to the back door.

"It was nice to meet you, Sir," Cal said as he followed Vic. Then in a lower voice he asked, "Is he an immortal?"

Vic pushed open the kitchen door and closed it behind her, leaving it unlocked in case Richard needed to come inside for anything.

"Gods, no. The Olympians are fairly modernized, practically assimilated. But they sometimes make bargains with mortals. In this case, Richard had the unfortunate happenstance to make a bargain with my father."

"Not his soul?" Cal asked dropping his book bag to the floor.

"No, no. Nothing like that. My father has grown very fond of Richard over the years. He's more like a helper, or even a family friend."

Cal spun in a slow circle, taking in Vic's little habitat. Clothes were strewn about and she was still wearing the sweatpants and fitted t-shirt, she'd thrown on when she got home the previous night. Luckily, nothing embarrassing was laying around. But her bed was still made, clearly unslept in. The pile of books was spilled across the floor and her book bag sat on the fancy-backed settee. The large brocade curtains were still tied back and letting in copious amounts of morning sunlight.

"This is your house?" he asked.

"Yeah, I guess." She kicked off her shoes and pushed them beneath the bed. "I mostly just live in this space though. I'm just one girl, so I don't need an entire house to myself."

Cal sunk onto the edge of her bed. "So let me get this straight. You have this entire house to yourself?"

She wrapped her arms around herself, suddenly self-conscious. Things had changed so rapidly between them and she found herself feeling shy and unsure, and wanting his approval.

"Yeah."

"Aren't you lonely?"

She thought of the ambient light of the white colonial house and of Cal with his five other brothers and sisters, all younger, noisy and running around.

She sank into her desk chair. Her laptop was still open and a screensaver of brightly colored fish swam across the screen.

"Sometimes, I am. But I also enjoy the solitude. You get used to it after a while."

Cal nodded and fidgeted with the clasp of his watch. "So what's the big plan?"

"I was hoping you had one."

"Hey, you're the one who kidnapped me!"

Vic rolled her eyes. "I didn't kidnap you. You came willingly."

"You enticed me."

"Only with my sparkling personality. So this is what I've

found so far. It's not much but it's a start."

She pulled out a notebook from beneath her laptop where she had been charting a family tree that was comprised of the primordial deities, the Titans, and the Olympians based on what she'd found online, before she'd fallen asleep. Cal took it from her and looked it over, biting on his bottom lip.

"Of course, any mortal relations aren't listed. The gods and goddesses are always consorting with mortals all throughout history, so it's kind of difficult to keep track of the lineage."

Cal handed the notebook back to her as he stood up. He unzipped his book bag and pulled out something oversized with a dark brown, leather cover.

"I found this. This is our family scrapbook. My brothers and sisters, my parents, my maternal grandparents. And there isn't a single thing in there about my paternal side of the family. You really got me thinking last night." He handed the book to her.

Vic flipped through the pages. There were birth announcements, and photos of a young amber-eyed Cal with dark hair so long it practically obscured his eyes. Always wearing a dimpled smile. A few pages later were other siblings, shades of brown and dark blonde hair. But Cal was almost always a full head taller than the rest. She caught sight of a family portrait. His mother to the right and his father to the left, with the children spread through the middle.

His mother had kind, light eyes and brown shoulder-length hair. She didn't appear remarkable in anyway, but her smile seemed genuine. A hand was rested on Cal's shoulder in the photo. On the other hand, his father wore a smile that didn't quite reach his eyes. His dark hair was longer and curled beneath his ears. He didn't look angry or mean, he simply looked tired. Like a man who lived to work instead of the other way around. Cal was maybe eight or ten in the photograph.

Vic flipped through the rest of the book, stopping on a hand drawn family tree. It started with Cal's maternal great-great-grandparents, but when she got to his mother, Rachel, there was only a single line connecting to Cal's father, Christopher, and to their children. No other names were listed connecting anyone to Christopher. It gave the lineage an incomplete feeling.

Cal had gotten up and was pacing the floor in front of the bed.

"I started piecing together the things that you said. And I can't believe the number of things that you're right about. My dad is a total workaholic. Yeah, he's there for the major things and when it counts, but he's absent a lot. Travels on business. My mom pretty much holds down the fort, with my help." He wrung his hands as he spoke.

"We know nothing about my father's parents, or any relatives on that side of the family. It kind of was an unspoken assumption that he was estranged from them. I never even overheard my parents talking about it or anything. All our family events were with my mom's family." He paused and held up his wrist. "And this watch—it was an odd gift. I'd never worn anything like this before. It's way fancier than my usual style."

He gestured toward his Henley and chucks. "Honestly, you've made me question everything I've ever known about myself."

A pang of guilt shuddered through Vic. She didn't want Cal to have an existential crisis because of her own suspicions which she wasn't even a hundred percent sure were true.

She pulled out the folded over scrap of paper on which she'd written the Oracle's prophecy.

"I didn't want to overwhelm you—or scare you—but this is something Pythia told me right before we left."

She handed the paper over to Cal and she watched as he read it. He read it over twice before handing it back to her.

"The House of Snakes. It's the name of Pythia's store…but is it more than that?"

Vic pulled out the book on prophets and flipped to the section on the Oracle of Delphi. She pointed out a passage and handed the book to Cal.

"Kind of. Pythia is the name of the High Priestess. History is mistaken, in that there is and always will be only one. Her name is a derivative of a word meaning to rot and has to do with a python that was slain by Apollo. As far as I know the House of Snakes *is* Pythia and vice versa."

"I thought Apollo was a cat," Cal looked up and handed the book back to Vic.

"The cat is named after Apollo." Vic shrugged. "Although, one of the symbols of Apollo is a python."

"Do you think Apollo is the one who made your mother ill?"

Vic shook her head doubtfully. "It's been centuries since there was contention between the Olympians. I can't imagine why someone would start something now. And poisoning is not something to be taken lightly. Nobody wants to feel my father's wrath."

"Hades."

She stood up and swept an arm up over her head and bowed. "The God of the Underworld and his daughter at your service."

Cal grabbed a pen off her desk and added the words

snake/python to her paper with notes on it. He continuously clicked the pen top lost in thought.

"There's something about the snakes. I feel like it's an important piece of the puzzle that we're missing."

He began pacing again. Click and pace. Click and pace.

Vic grabbed her laptop and began searching snakes and their symbolic meanings.

"The House of Snakes has risen and will not be slayed." Cal muttered. His watch face caught the sunlight from the window and Vic looked up.

"Wait a second!" She practically threw her lap top to the floor before leaping back to her feet and grabbing Cal's wrist. Her heart pounded at their closeness. She dragged him closer to the window and moved his wrist so that his watch face captured the sunlight. "There's an engraving. On the six of the watch face."

The watch didn't have numerals, just tiny silver bars for hands. When the dark mother of pearl face was in the full direct light of the sun, a small silver snake appeared as the number six. But when Cal moved his wrist out of the direct light it disappeared.

"I've never noticed before." Cal sounded astounded as he moved his wrist back and forth in the window's light. Vic's fingers were still curled around his wrist.

"The primordial god, Chronus. He's known as father time. Some say he's actually the one who gave birth to light and dark. Even to the seasons themselves and to…the void."

"The void?" Cal asked, he dropped his wrist and Vic's fingers fell away, already missing the warmth of his skin against her own.

"Yeah. The void…or as some stories refer to it, Chaos."

The watch had given her an idea. She wasn't completely

sure, but she grabbed her laptop. "Chronus—the time one—is later often confused with Cronus. The Titan god."

"The one who your father and the rest of the Olympians defeated?"

Vic nodded. "In the Battle of the Gods. Maybe we've been approaching this all wrong. Honestly, the watch confused me until just now. I knew it was important, but not why. I think it has to do with the snake."

She pulled up an online encyclopedia and showed Cal the entry for Cronus, the Titan. He leaned over her shoulder, his breath warm against her cheek. Excited, she pointed.

"It was right in front of me this whole time. Cronus has some of the same symbols as Demeter, involving the harvest. But the snake is also one of his symbols."

"Do you think it's possible that the House of Snakes in the Oracle's prophecy has to do with Cronus?" Cal asked.

Vic nodded. "I think it might. When the Olympians defeated the Titans, Cronus was cast into the Cave of Nyx by his own children."

"Nyx is the night, isn't it?"

Vic nodded again. Cal was scribbling down their new findings.

"What if the House of Snakes has to do with Cronus? *Old is new and new is old. The beginning is the end and the end is the beginning.* The Titans were the beginning and their end was the beginning of the reign of the Olympians."

Cal clicked his pen thoughtfully. "And you think that maybe after all this time the Titans have decided it was time to exact some kind of revenge?"

"Maybe. Except the one thing I can't figure out is the significance of your watch. Is it coincidence that it's both a symbol of keeping time and of Cronus, who was born of

Chaos? My mother is the changer of the seasons, and since she's been ill the seasons have been stuck in a sort of homeostasis. Like time has stopped."

Vic's heart was once again pounding in her chest. The number of puzzle pieces were overwhelming, but it would seem not a detail had been overlooked by whoever created the puzzle.

The broken pieces shall be scattered.

"Vic?" Cal's voice sliced through her thoughts. He'd stopped clicking his pen. "If we're actually right, and my father could be this Cronus, this Titan god, then that would mean, well, wouldn't that mean that I'm immortal too?"

She turned to him, as if seeing him for the first time. He was right. If his father was Cronus, he was indeed immortal. More importantly to Vic, it meant that he was like her. At least in some small way.

"It would."

"So that means I could, like, jump off the roof of your barn and nothing would happen to me?"

Vic shook her head. It was such a typical mortal misconception about immortality.

"Well, first off, we're still going by a theory. And secondly, being immortal does not mean that you cannot still break every single bone in your body. Think of it more as extended life than indefinite."

Cal's face was pale with shock. He sunk onto the edge of the bed and ran a hand through his hair.

"All this time…my father…" His amber eyes grew wide. "But Vic, say this theory is true. Then that means…if my father is part of this new House of Snakes…then he most likely wasn't transferred here like he told us. If that wasn't the reason, then why did we move here? Of all the towns, we moved here. To small town, USA. To Olympia."

"I don't believe in coincidences," Vic responded quietly, echoing Cal's words from earlier.

"Me neither."

They sat in silence for a moment before Vic nervously blurt out the one thing still nagging at her. "My father wanted me to Take your soul."

Cal's face grew even whiter. "Wait, what?"

She groaned. "When I went home he said he needed a soul that was purer, more light-filled. And he told me it had to be yours. My ex-boyfriend, this hellhound, Asher. He'd been following me and he saw you…"

Cal held up a hand. "Let's back up a second there. Your ex-boyfriend is a *hellhound*."

She waved a hand dismissively. "It sounds way cooler than it actually is. But you're missing the point! If we're right, if your father is Cronus, then everything that's happened…*is* happening is his doing! My mother's illness would be the exact thing that would enrage my dad so much that it would prod him into battle….into another war even. My father would tear apart Hell itself if anything happened to my mother. No pun intended."

"None taken."

Vic's mind was spinning. She was on a roll now.

"And then, my father tells me to Take your soul…and if your father really *is* Cronus…then that means…" Now it was Vic's turn to have all the color drain from her face. "Oh, gods."

Understanding dawned on Cal's face at the same time. "Your father knows who my father is and wanted to get revenge."

Vic's hands trembled as she carefully closed her lap top

and turned toward Cal, who had resumed his pacing.

"It means my father knows who poisoned Persephone. It means our fathers want a reason to start another Titanomachy."

Cal paused and gestured. "But all this…it's…it's still a theory though. We haven't proved that my father is actually Cronus."

"No, we haven't."

"But we can." His voice shook ever so slightly.

She had to admire his courage. His insatiable desire to learn the truth. It was a feeling with which she was intimately familiar.

She stood up and put a hand on his arm. "Yes. We can. But, Cal, this is so much bigger than us. Another war between the Titans and the Olympians could tear apart the world as we know it. Both the immortal one and the mortal one."

A look of determination washed over Cal's angular features and in that moment, with the sunlight illuminating his eyes in a fiery glow, he indeed looked like he could be every bit the immortal they suspected he was. He placed a warm, gentle hand over Vic's still trembling fingers.

"Then I say we find out the truth. Save Persephone. And end this war before it even starts."

Chapter Sixteen

As Vic saw it, there were two ways that she and Cal could prove or disprove that his father was Cronus. One way would be to simply ask. Vic wasn't sure that would go over really well.

She imagined sitting down at the Bishop's kitchen table along with Cal and his parents, steaming cups of tea in front of them, and asking point-blank if Mr. Bishop was indeed the Titan Cronus. If he wasn't they'd simply think she was some looney person that Cal had somehow taken under his wing at school. If he was Cronus, then there were a myriad of possibilities and none of them, in Vic's humble opinion, were very good. Mainly, Vic was afraid of becoming collateral and in the process unable to save her mother. Also, his daughter becoming collateral would most likely ignite Hades' temper and, to put it in the words of a comic hero, you wouldn't like him when he's angry.

No, it just wouldn't do.

The second, possibly less volatile option, although not by much, was to take Cal home with her and confront Hades. She had the sneaking suspicion that her father already knew and could simply confirm or deny Cal's identity. However, this plan also ran the risk of Hades being furious at Vic for bringing Cal to the Under World. It also ran the risk that Hades himself may try and Take Cal's soul. But Vic highly doubted it would help Persephone at this point. Not that her mother was beyond saving, but because the more she thought about it, the more she considered it a power play on both her father's and Asher's behalf. Which simply infuriated her even more.

If Cal's father received wind of his son being in the Under World, maybe he would fear a betrayal, or worse that his son was now in danger. It could be the catalyst to end this nonsense, or it could be the gasoline to fuel it.

Either way, Vic knew she was more than capable of protecting Cal on a visit to the Under World, and Cal, having placed his unwavering faith in Vic, had agreed it was probably the best option. He admitted if he could spare his younger siblings the knowledge that their life was possibly a sham, then this was the best route until he could act with absolute certainty to protect them.

And so it was, that Vic and Cal concocted a lie that there was a group of friends heading on a camping trip upstate over the weekend. Cal assured Vic his parents—at least his mother—would be so overjoyed that he'd made some new friends, that there was no doubt he'd have permission to go.

Vic resigned to the fact that she'd have to summon Asher and another hellhound in order to transport them into the Under World. Asher was more or less assigned to her even though her father employed him, and so if she summoned him he would come.

She was most definitely not excited for Cal to meet Asher. As she laid in bed that night, she realized she was anxious for Cal to visit the Under World and to meet her father. The more she thought about it, the more she realized how much she truly liked him and didn't want him to be scared of her family. Or of her.

That night she dreamed that winged swords flew through the red haze of the Under World. The sky of the Under World had opened and was raining pomegranate seeds that withered and died as soon as they hit the scorched crimson earth. Vic bent over and when she picked up one of the blackened seeds, a pale blue eye blinked back at her. She picked up another and it contained a lock of pale blonde hair. Horrified, Vic gathered the scattered pieces of her mother as quickly as she could.

–

The plan was to leave after school. (Turns out the leak wasn't nearly as bad as initially thought.) Vic and Cal would go to the manor where Vic would summon Asher. Cal's parents weren't expecting him to be home, since he'd said the drive upstate was three hours and they wanted to arrive before dark. He'd already left a book bag of camping supplies in Vic's truck for when they'd met in the parking lot, his mom having dropped him off at school so he wouldn't have to worry about his bike.

Vic spent the day imagining all the things that could go wrong and replaying them in her head over and over on a constant loop. Her mind was completely distracted and she was pretty sure she'd be lucky if she skated by with a C on her physics exam. Despite the continuous rapid fire of Vic's mind, the day seemed to drag by impossibly slow.

Everyone was abuzz about the Apple Festival, which was happening the following weekend. Throughout the school, the marching band could be heard in full swing practicing the fight song and girls leaned against one another's lockers talking about which floats they were on and what they were going to wear. In some ways, it was more exciting than the homecoming dance. School dances could be isolating. The Apple Festival was inclusive, something that the entire town participated in, and was held in Downtown Olympia.

Lost in her own mind, Vic had nearly forgotten about it. The Apple Festival reminded Vic once again of how the townspeople had no clue about the layered world that existed around them. Pythia would have a stand outside of her shop selling hot apple cinnamon tea. People would stop for a steaming cup and have no clue that they were being served by the Oracle of Delphi.

They would have no idea that the world intertwined with their own was on the brink of the biggest war in millennia.

Finally, the school day ended. Vic and Cal tore down the road in the direction of the manor. The day was overcast, but still uncomfortably warm. Cal had the navy sleeves of his long-sleeved t-shirt pushed up to his elbows and for the first time that day Vic noticed he wasn't wearing his watch.

He caught her glance and shrugged.

"It just didn't feel right anymore. After all this…it's made me question everything. Who my dad is…who I am…"

Guilt laced Vic's heart. It truly wasn't fair. But, she reminded herself, she wasn't the one who had lied to Cal. If anything, she was the one determined to help him figure out the truth and get the answers he needed.

She pulled into the barn. They got out of the truck. Hay and kerosene of another time lingered in the air. Cal dragged over his backpack, unzipped it and took out a few items: a lantern, a jacket, and some s'mores supplies. He left them in a pile on the dirt floor before slipping the pack back over his shoulders.

"Actually, hand me that." Vic pointed at the bag of marshmallows from the s'mores ingredients.

Cal gave her a curious look, but tossed her the bag anyways. She tore it open and shoved an entire jumbo-sized white puff of sugary corn syrup goodness into her mouth. The overly sweet processed treat immediately soothed her nerves.

"Now that's impressive," Cal reached into the bag and stuffed two marshmallows into his own mouth. "Fluffy bunny," he said, the marshmallows slightly obscuring the words.

Vic recognized the challenge. She crammed two more marshmallows into her mouth.

"Fluffy bunny," she repeated trying her best to annunciate around the chewy mounds.

They kept cramming marshmallows into their mouths until Vic reached seven and Cal couldn't get any more into his mouth and still say the words properly. Part of that was probably due to the tears streaming down either one's cheeks. Vic pulled out several marshmallows, ate the ones in her mouth, then finished off the rest and licked her sticky fingers with a flourish.

"I win."

She wiped a tear from the corner of her eye.

Cal finished off his own marshmallows and smiled. "I'm not sure whether I should be horrified or impressed."

Vic laughed. "Maybe a little bit of both."

Cal tied a knot in the now half-full bag of marshmallows and stuck it in his backpack.

"You have a mean sweet tooth, my dear."

Caught in a moment of vulnerability, Vic replied honestly. "The sugar helps subdue my emotions. My father likes sweets as well. It's as if the sugar somehow tempers our feelings. Whenever I'm feeling anxious, sad, scared, happy, excited, or angry…pretty much any emotion, I end up scarfing down bags of cookies or two orders of ice cream at Molly's." She felt her cheeks flush at the admission.

"Who would have thought the devil and his daughter would have a sweet tooth?"

Cal playfully bumped his shoulder into hers.

"Don't be anxious. Or afraid. Or whatever it is you're feeling. Don't be, because I'm not."

Vic looked up at him. He was only a little bit taller than her, but her forehead was level with his lips. When she turned a bit they were suddenly standing very close.

"You should be afraid. My father…even me…we aren't always nice people." She was staring at his lips, which shone with sugar from the marshmallows.

"I don't define someone's goodness by how nice they are, Vic." He carefully pushed a strand of hair away from her mouth where it had been stuck to her lip from the marshmallows. But he didn't move his hand away, instead he rested it on her cheek. His fingers sent a jolt of warmth through her. "I define them by how they treat others when they think no one is watching and by their courage to do what's right even when the odds are stacked against them."

His amber eyes looked down at her and Vic felt the sincerity of his words and the assuredness in his gentle touch. Anticipation, exhilaration, and other feelings she hadn't let herself feel in well over a year swirled in her gut, and she couldn't help but think that there wasn't a guy more worthy of stirring up those emotions. Before she could quell her fears,

Cal leaned forward and his lips found hers.

The kiss was filled with overcast skies, unspoken promises, and marshmallows.

–

Summoning Asher was fairly easy.

Vic and Cal stood in the driveway, the sun setting and the sky turning to shades of velvety dusk. Her fingers grasped the bat charm at her throat. She placed its head—just between the ears—in between her lips and blew.

Cal arched an eyebrow when no sound emitted from the charm.

Vic shrugged. "It's kind of like a dog whistle. Only the hounds can hear it."

It was a lame joke, but in essence it was the same principle. The sound of the whistle was at such a frequency that it could pass through the worlds and reach Asher's ears. Normally, she would text him, but cell service wasn't the greatest between the Under World and the Above World.

Suddenly, there was the familiar roar of a Harley-Davidson Sportster Iron 883 coming up the road. Cal gave Vic a wary glance and slung his backpack over his shoulders. She blew the whistle again and almost instantaneously the sound of another motorcycle filled the early evening air.

In true Asher fashion, the all-black motorcycle tore down the driveway going much too fast before sliding to a stop in front of Vic. Asher was wearing his mirrored aviators and a black button down shirt, rolled to mid-forearm but still showing ample ink. He pushed his aviators back onto his forehead. His green eyes darted from Vic to Cal and back to Vic.

But before he could open his mouth to say something, the second motorcycle came tearing up the driveway. It was another Sportster Iron 883, but where Asher's was all black, this one had every inch in red. The guy sitting atop it had blonde hair in a buzz cut and red Oakley wraparounds. Piercings lined his ears all the way up and down and he had round gauged piercings in each lobe that were the size of a quarter.

Whereas Asher was all lean muscle, this second hellhound was stocky and solid. Built like a linebacker. His black t-shirt hugged his biceps revealing intricate tribal tattoos and when he removed his sunglasses, Cal saw that one of the tattoos traveled up the side of his neck and around the side of his face, stopping at his temple. If a man could be carved out of rock, he'd probably look like this guy. Cal was slightly speechless.

"You summoned, Princess Victoriana?" the rock asked.

Despite the hard façade, Vic knew that Brim harbored a special soft spot for her. He was older than Asher, but younger than her father and had played with her as a child and accompanied her on any diplomatic trips around the Under World.

Cal turned to Vic. "Princess?" he mouthed, his eyes wide. Vic could only imagine what must be going through his mind.

"I did. Thanks, Brim. I need you to accompany Cal home with me." She bit her tongue and smiled, but it didn't reach her eyes which had taken a slightly gray cast. "I'll ride with Asher."

"No problem. Hop on, little buddy."

Cal looked at Vic, his expression unsure.

"It's fine. I've known Brim almost my entire life."

"Not to sound uncool, but we don't need helmets or anything like that? Sunglasses? Is that a mandatory accessory?" he asked as he awkwardly climbed onto the back seat of Brim's red bike.

"No helmets needed. Hellhounds don't crash. Protective enchantments and what not. We are responsible for the safe passage of the King and Queen of the Under World after all." Brim slid his sunglasses over his eyes as Cal placed a hand on either of his large shoulders. "As for the sunglasses. They just make us look cool."

"As if being a hellhound by itself wasn't cool enough," Cal mumbled.

Brim let out a loud laugh. "Ready when you are." He hit the starter and the motorcycle roared back to life.

Asher gave Vic a long, cool glance. Their fight was only several days before, but really she had no choice. She could have had Cal ride with Asher, but she didn't want Asher trying to talk to him or trying to kidnap him or worse, kill him.

So without a word, she climbed onto the back of the black bike, slipping her fingers beneath the rim of the seat so that she wouldn't have to hold onto Asher. She saw his posture stiffen at the slight, but regardless, he put his aviators back on and the motorcycle thrummed in rhythm to Brim's bike. They tore down the winding driveway. A hellhound symphony of its own making.

Chapter Seventeen

Surprisingly, Cal handled the drive into the gates of hell better than Vic would have expected.

They had waited behind, just in case Cal freaked out right before the impact. But Vic knew Brim was the best person with whom to experience a first trip to the Under World. He was careful and age made him less reckless. Asher gunned it for the trunk of the tree and Vic instinctively closed her eyes. When Asher rode up behind the red bike, Brim was waiting idle on the other side.

Cal's face had gone pale, his freckles standing out across his cheeks like a constellation. His amber eyes were wide with amazement as he looked back at the nothingness from which they'd come—simply a hazy sort of blackness, like a gauzy curtain—and then to what lie ahead which was gnarled, burnt-out looking trees and scorched crimson earth. He coughed as brimstone swirled in the air around them.

The expanse of bruised sky stretched over them as they followed along the river. Brim rode alongside Asher now, and Vic watched Cal as if she could somehow see her world through his eyes. What it would look like to someone not cast in damnation to see the world in which she had grown up for the very first time.

Vic watched the look of confusion that appeared on his face when they zoomed past the hunched figures, the Mendax, as they picked her father's enchanted berries. She was ashamed to admit that the berries were the main ingredient in the favorite of her mother's pies.

Sweat dripped along Vic's hair line and she could see that Cal's long-sleeved shirt was damp and pressed against the small of his back, just beneath his backpack. They passed the black cauldrons of lime green flames, the Abutens continuously stoking the flames. She wished she could see this place through the wonder with which Cal now looked on, somewhere between being stuck in a nightmare and some sort of fantasy video game.

Vic tensed as they neared the domain of the Interemptor. She turned away as the tower of cages came into view, with their demonic bodies repeatedly released into the River Styx to die and die again.

Instead, she focused her attention on the icy blackness of the rushing river. For this she didn't want to see Cal's expression, which she was sure would be riddled with horror at what he saw.

Vic wouldn't know until sometime later that Cal had simply wondered how a creature as magnificent as the one he had kissed only a short while before had come from a place of such darkness.

Both hellhounds stopped just before the bone bridge.

River was there leaning on her staff, a vision in crow black with her blood-red lips.

"Two hellhounds in one day. And…what's this?" she sniffed the air. "The princess and another?" She walked, red dust clouding around her bare feet, toward Brim's bike. Her black cloak swished around her legs, the slits revealing bare, dark skin.

"Not yet dead. Perhaps never to be. Strange boy." She focused her black eyes on Cal and he stiffened slightly as she leaned toward him.

"And what do you call yourself?" She tapped his cheek lightly with her wooden staff as if it were an extension of her body.

"Cal, ma'am."

"Cal ma'am?"

"No, I mean…"

His cheeks flushed and Vic wished she could slap River's staff out of her hand. River was often bored and her teasing was an endless source of amusement for her. Fresh blood was also rare in these parts.

River chuckled. "No, no. I know. Apologies, Your Highness. Just a little fun. I am the River Styx."

"But I thought…" It was as if Cal could barely get out a complete sentence.

"Yes, I'm afraid all those Above World writers infrequently give credit where credit is due. The woman was first, the river itself second. The river is named after me and I am the guardian separating the domains from the inner sanctum. I grant passage to those who are worthy."

Cal's face paled again.

River smiled wickedly. "And to guests of the Princess, of course."

Vic rolled her eyes, but only so Cal could see.

"Thank you, River. Let's go Brim. Asher."

"Your Highness."

The bone bridge rattled slightly as they drove across and onto the long drive leading up to Vic's childhood home. Pomegranate trees lined the rotunda, their fruit juicy and red. Ripe for the taking. Cal's eyes widened first at the onyx fountain of Hades and Persephone and then once more at the sight of the black castle looming before them, the tallest spires obscured by indigo clouds.

Asher pulled up next to Brim in a long line of hellhound transport waiting to be used. This time, Vic climbed off the back before Asher could try and offer her his hand, her sweaty legs and bum still vibrating from the long ride. Cal looked just as awkward as he adjusted his backpack and thanked Brim for safe passage. Even in the Under World, Cal still clung to his manners. She could only hope that her father saw the goodness that she saw.

Without a second glance at her, Asher became intensely focused on fiddling with something on his bike. Vic refused to give in to his wounded pride. He'd lied to her more than once and shame on her for letting her walls down to let it happen a second time.

A person like Asher was a user, a manipulator, there was always a bigger agenda at play. And he so reminded her of her father that it made her want to kick over the motorcycles like a set of dominoes. If Asher was the accelerant to her fire, then Cal was the inhibitor.

She came to stand beside Cal, so that she could feel the heat rippling from his body. His dark hair clung to his forehead. He craned his neck to stare up at the huge, onyx castle that was all sleek and metallic lines. Black glass staring back onto the orchard of lush pomegranate trees.

"So the story is true?" he finally asked.

"What story's that?" Vic asked. Her heart pounded in her chest, knowing it was on the brink of so many answers and that once they crossed that threshold, there was no going back.

"The one about the pomegranate and Persephone?" he glanced over his shoulder at the orchard.

"Yeah, that one they actually got right. I can't blame her though. They're not like the ones you buy at the grocery in the Above World."

They stood on the doorstep. Brim and Asher had disappeared. They were alone.

"It's hard to imagine you come from a place like this." Cal gestured, indicating everything around them.

Vic tilted her head. "Is it?" She looked around, at the familiarity of the place she called home, but that wasn't the place for which her heart longed.

"I suppose we carry a part of where we come from inside us, always. A piece of the past that reminds you where your story began." She turned back toward Cal, whose brow had furrowed. "You don't know all parts of me yet. You may not like them all."

He reached for her hand and she let him take it. Despite the heat, his hand felt cool in hers.

"I may not know all the parts and I may not like them all, Vic." Her heart trilled at her name on his lips. Something so simple set her all a-flutter, like a crow's wings. "But I want to know all of the parts of you, regardless."

–

Vic knew without a doubt that her father was aware of her return home. There was very little that occurred in the Under

World of which Hades was not aware. But before she introduced Cal—her sole Above World friend—to the King of the Under World, she wanted him to meet the softer side of it. The life that meant so much to Vic that she would Take from others.

He followed her up the stairs, eyes glazed over in wonder at the sleek black floors and elaborate bone chandelier with its enchanted neon green flame. The glassy onyx walls reflected distorted images back to them. Cal's footsteps echoed throughout the hallways, but Vic's were silent as a cat's on the prowl.

Cal startled at the abrupt change as they entered the separate wing of the castle. Vic ran her finger along the familiar sand-colored walls and trailed them along clumps of velvety clematis. It was as though they'd entered a garden but were still indoors.

Yellow, white and blue flowers poured out of wooden boxes that hung from the walls. Cal's steps crunched across a rug made of some kind of woven seagrass. It was bright and airy, and he realized the scent was something that lingered in Vic's hair. Not the raining brimstone they'd traveled through, but the scent of roses, crocuses, and daffodils. If he hadn't known better, he'd have thought they'd entered a different world.

Vic stopped at a door and gave a soft knock, but didn't wait for an answer. She pushed the white-washed door open and Cal was shocked at the sight on the other side.

Every single inch of space was covered in pastel shades of hyacinth. He recognized the flower as it was one his mother happened to enjoy. The floor was a blanket of springtime and, although the flowers seemed to part around their steps, there were so many that they crushed delicate petals as they waded through the ankle deep hyacinth. The flowers' sharp scent twitched at his nose. They covered the walls and lined the window sill. Pale purple and blue hyacinth cascaded down the curtains and across the curtain rod. Peach, yellow, white and pink covered what Cal suddenly realized was a bed. In which lay the delicate form of a woman.

She had the palest blonde hair—almost white—that looked dull and lifeless. It was spread like a halo across the pillow upon which her head rested. Her eyes were closed and she appeared asleep—if Cal didn't know the story, his first impression would have been that she was dead. Long-fingered hands were clasped across her belly, which was covered in a calf-length, silky white dress. Her feet were bare and Cal could see that her veins were not blue, but an inky black. The black snaked up her legs and down her arms, a garish mark against her almost translucent skin.

Very carefully, Vic sloshed her way through the flowers and to her mother's bedside. Where she climbed in like a small child and curled up beside her. It took a moment for Cal to realize that Vic's body was trembling with silent sobs. She clasped at her mother's dress, gripping the fabric between her desperate fingers.

And in that moment of total vulnerability, Cal understood.

He understood Vic's softness. He understood where she got the delicate slope of her cheekbones and the cupid's bow of her lips. He understood why the Above World was in perpetual homeostasis, while an eternal spring bloomed in this small bedroom. He understood that Persephone was dying and that the frail woman before him was an immortal, a goddess who was millennia old and yet on the brink of death.

Part of him hoped this could not be the work of his father. That perhaps they were wrong. And another part of him wanted to wreck the man who had done this to someone so majestic even in the face of death. He could not yet fully understand why his own heart crumbled as he watched Vic's heart shattering into tiny, irreparable pieces. Revenge licked at his insides and it was an emotion Cal wasn't used to feeling. It felt twisted and ugly.

He moved as if through water, reaching out a hand and placing it on Vic's back, which was curved toward him. She was cold to the touch and Cal made the connection then that Vic's emotions were intrinsically linked to her body's physiological responses. The despair she felt was literally leaching the fire from within her.

Persephone's eyes fluttered, long, damp black lashes caressing her cheeks and when she finally opened her eyes an icy pale blue looked around wildly, before comprehension set in.

"*Filia mea*, I drown in your tears. *Amica mea*, please do not cry. It weakens my heart so." Her voice was like the rustle of fabric, soft as a butterfly's wings flapping on the wind.

Vic sniffled, trying to stop the flow of tears. "Maman, I've missed you."

She knew this was a rare moment of clarity for her mother. And she wasn't sure if it was her copious amount of tears or that she somehow sensed the presence of an unknown person, but Vic wanted to cling to these threads before they completely unraveled.

"And I you, *filia mea*." Her eyes fell onto Cal, his hand still placed reassuringly on Vic's shoulder like a stake that would keep her grounded. "You have brought a friend."

Cal didn't know what to say. Your Highness? Your Majesty? So he simply said, "Hello."

He quietly slipped his hand from Vic's shoulder and

placed it awkwardly in his pocket.

Silent tears still slipped down Vic's cheeks and Cal wanted to brush them away, but wasn't sure if the intimacy would be crossing the line in what he perceived was a much-needed tender moment between daughter and mother. He took a slight step back, careful to crush as few hyacinths as possible beneath his tread.

"Maman, this is Callum Bishop. He's a friend that I made while I've been…away." She tenderly brushed the locks of hair from her mother's fevered brow.

"Well, it is a pleasure to meet you, Callum Bishop." The cracked corners of her lips turned up in a small smile. Her eyes slid closed. Vic held her mother, fully prepared to lose this rare lucid moment.

"Likewise, ma'am. Your daughter is…unlike anyone I've ever met before." He could feel his cheeks flushing at the admission.

Persephone's eyes opened to small slits, a sliver of cornflower. "*Filia mea, Amica mea.* She is a force unlike any other. She has her father's brains and her mother's heart." Her eyes slowly slid closed once more.

"No, Maman," Vic whispered. "You are mistaken. I have my father's rage and cruelty, but I have my mother's capacity for love and hope. I am the worst of my father, but the best of my mother."

Cal swallowed the lump in his throat.

Eyes still closed, Persephone slowly untangled Vic's hand that had been clutching the silk of her dress and raised it to her lips. She unfurled her fingers and very gently placed a kiss on the inside of Vic's palm. Where her lips touched, bloomed a small white flower with a tiny blue stripe running across each petal.

A Russian Snowdrop.

Vic curled her fingers around the tiny flower as her mother's hand slipped away and her breathing slowed until it was nearly imperceptible. Persephone was returning to the fevered sleep of the creeping sickness that flooded her veins.

Wiping the tears from her cheeks, Vic pushed herself up from the bed with great effort. There was nothing more that she wanted than to stay pressed against her mother's side forever. Nothing more, except revenge on whoever did this. Black spots marked Vic's vision, as she grasped Cal's hand, pressing the snowdrop into his palm.

"Come. Let's go find my father."

–

Vic knew Hades couldn't be avoided forever. As Cal pulled Persephone's door closed behind them she noticed the change in the blackness that ringed his amber eyes and she knew that he understood the pain that she was feeling. And that he would do anything he could to take it away from her.

Cal curled his fingers around Vic's, which were still cold, and she led him back into the darker parts of the castle. Sconces of bone leapt with lime green flames and cast eerie reflections against the black walls.

Usually, her father tended to reside in the library or in his study. But Vic could feel that something was different. The hairs on the back of her neck stood up. She knew that Hades was aware of their arrival and probably also aware that she had taken Cal to see Persephone. He wouldn't like it. Not even Asher knew the full extent of Persephone's illness.

The way the syrupy blackness now coated her body, covered her arms, legs, and chest. A thin line ran up her neck and behind her ear. And the flowers. Vic assumed her father had them swept away each morning, only for the room to become covered again once more. Persephone was dying and along with it her magic.

Her senses were hyper aware. Vic paused outside her father's study, but shook her head. She didn't hear his familiar movements behind the closed door. The rustle of his shirt sleeves or the open and closing of a book. Instead, she led Cal into another wing of the castle.

At the end of a short hallway was a sleek set of stainless steel double doors with large rivets. Unlike much of the castle's rooms which had normal locking mechanisms, this one had a sleek LCD device embedded in the door. Vic pressed the screen and it lit up with an image of a rotating golden key. A small panel with a padded portion ejected out of the device.

With a smooth movement, Vic produced her blade and pricked the thumb of her right hand. She pressed it into the pad and sensing the pressure and then relief of pressure, the device pulled the panel back inside itself. There was a click and then *Access Granted* flashed across the LCD screen.

The locks of the door tumbled and the doors slid to either side much like the doors of an elevator. Vic sheathed her knife and they entered into a large, hexagonal chamber. Each side of the hexagon had a stainless steel door. Enchanted flames leapt, bone sconces flanking each door. In the center of the ceiling was an elaborate chandelier made of white bone and twisted black tree branches like the ones Cal first noticed when they'd arrived in the Under World. Green flames flickered, casting the room in a sickly glow. It felt like he was trapped inside of a video game.

Beneath the chandelier was a hexagon shaped table with six onyx high-backed chairs. All were empty except one. Hades sat at the head of the table, facing the entrance from which Vic and Cal had just entered.

He was strikingly handsome, Cal noticed, with olive-toned skin and deep, bottomless eyes. His hair was black and curled beneath his ears. He was clean-shaven and impeccably dressed in what Cal guessed was an Armani suit all lean lines and expensive looking black fabric. His tie was narrow and blood red and the light glinted off a silver pin which was in the shape of a pomegranate. A circlet of black feathers crowned his head. Hades looked like the villain in any one of Cal's comic books. He felt his breath freeze in his chest and words sought flight.

It took a moment for either Vic or Cal to notice Asher, huddled in the corner. His face impassive, arms crossed, back pressed up against one of the walls like a soldier standing sentinel. Vic knew the room in which they now stood was her father's war room.

Hades was preparing for battle.

Chapter Eighteen

"Hello, Daughter."

Hades' voice was smooth as the black silk shirt he wore. But Vic was not having any of it. Black dots still riddled her vision and if it wasn't for Cal's hand now resting on the small of her back, she was fairly certain she'd have gone blind in rage minutes ago. At the moment, she was not inclined toward pleasantries.

"You lied to me," she accused, taking a step forward.

"An omission perhaps. But not a lie." Hades placed his hands together so that they formed a temple beneath his chin.

"You wanted me to Take his soul, but not so that it could help Maman. No, it was so it could help *you*, wasn't it?"

"Has he filled your head with this?" Hades cut a glance to Cal, who was standing slightly behind Vic trying his best not to show the tremor of his hand. Whereas Persephone was soft edges and kind smiles, Hades was hard planes and sardonic grins.

"*He* has no idea! Whoever you think he is, he has no idea!"

Vic's vision was starting to soften around the edges, her father coming into clear focus in the center of her sight—like a crosshairs in a hunting rifle. She wouldn't be able to control her rage for much longer. She needed answers and she needed them now. Her father may be stronger, but Vic was so much angrier than his strength. It would be an ugly battle of wills.

"Impossible! How can he not know who his father is! It's ludicrous!" Hades placed both palms onto the table in front of him and pushed to a standing position. It was a power move if Cal had ever seen one.

"Maybe his father keeps secrets too!" The words came out a growl and Cal could feel Vic's muscles tensing beneath his palm.

"*He* is standing right here," Cal softly interjected. And then louder, as he sensed the shift in Vic like a ship captain can sense the change in tides. "Until Vic told me, I never knew…never suspected. Sir, if my father is…is this Cronus. And if he's looking for a war…then I want to help. I want to fight."

Asher flashed a small smile, ridiculing Cal's words and Hades sighed pacing along the side of the table.

"Why would a boy such as yourself want to fight a battle for which he has no idea?"

"Because if all this is true—if you can confirm that indeed my father is not Christopher Bishop, but is this Cronus, the Titan god, then he is guilty of treason for poisoning Persephone. The father I know, he would never be capable of such a thing. And if it is so, then my life has been a lie. It is not my own. I have been living someone else's story." Cal glanced at Vic, the rise and fall of her chest as her body battled its own fighting instinct. "If that's the case, then I want to make my own story. A new one."

Hades eyes lightened and he looked from his furious daughter, hair slipping out of her ponytail and framing her face, to the boy who was holding her back without a single restraint. This was perhaps more curious to him than anything. He looked at his daughter.

"Why did you bring him here?"

Vic straightened, thrusting her shoulders back. "Because we want to know the truth."

Hades arched a perfectly groomed black eyebrow.

"Fine, *I* want to know the truth. I want to know how long you've known it was Cronus behind mother's illness. I want to know why you didn't bother to tell me and, more importantly, I want to know why you sought revenge on Cal—my *only* friend in either the Under or Above Worlds—who, by the way, is an innocent in a matter between two men who are millennia old, but who are acting like reckless children. And that—not Cronus escaping the Cave of Nyx—is what will surely bring about the second Battle of the Gods. I want to know what this is all about. The truth. From your lips to my ears."

It was the most Vic had spoken since her arrival to the Under World. Words died on her lips when she spoke to Persephone as her heart shattered into tinier and tinier fragments at the sight of her mother's decaying body, a mere shadow of the Maman that she adored.

But standing here, in her father's war room, she felt Cal's steady and familiar presence. Her reminder of all that she had to lose in the Above World. All of the dreams she had for herself which her father wrote off as a teenager's fleeting fantasies. To her, this was about two things and two things only: her mother and the world that she had come to know and love. It was this conviction, deep inside her and breaking her heart, that made her demand answers from her father instead of succumbing to her childish rage—a rage which roared, unbridled inside her and in which she often barely managed to keep tempered—as she stood before him in the devil's war room.

Hades stroked his chin, deep in thought. Maybe he had misjudged the boy. He had been, after all, relying on Asher's word and his emotions had long been entangled with his daughter's. Instead of Taking from him or killing him, perhaps it would be much more effective to have him as an ally.

"It's the truth that you want? Fine then. I will show you—both of you—the truth."

–

One of the doors on the hexagonal wall slid open revealing a darkened tunnel. Hades motioned for them to follow and Cal and Vic hurried to keep up. The tunnel walls were rounded and the walls were made of stainless steel and were more about practicality than appearance. There were lights periodically lined up across the top of either side of the tunnel. Hade's dress shoes snapped across the tunnel's floor like mini firecrackers.

Vic knew the tunnels led to different places. There was a tunnel that led to each of the Under World's domains and one that led to the cavern where the River Styx was rumored to empty into a black waterfall that was considered the point of no return in the Under World. She wasn't sure about the other two tunnels as she'd never had reason to explore them.

This was one of the tunnels in which she'd never been in before.

She wasn't sure what to make of this change in her father. Why he would suddenly seem to take to heart whatever it was that she had to say. She was used to his lies—only Persephone ever seemed apt at seeing through them—and his manipulations, but this sudden change of heart...well, a sudden change of heart didn't usually come easily to someone who most saw as heartless. Vic knew her father wasn't really heartless of course, but with her mother's deteriorating health she wondered if her father's heart was deteriorating right along with it.

Finally, the tunnel ended at a very old-looking door. It was made of blackened wood and after all this time, Vic could still smell the sharp edge of cedar that had been charred to make it better withstand time. Most of the castle was either enchanted or high-tech, but here her father pulled out a large metal key ring. It made her think of the caretaker in a scary, teen horror flick. He chose a key and placed it into the lock. As he turned it, Vic and Cal could hear numerous mechanisms tumbling on the other side. They glanced at each other, unsure what exactly to expect.

Hades wasn't exactly known to be full of surprises. He was fairly predictable, but he did have a flare for the dramatic. Especially, if he felt that he needed to prove a point. The door swung open onto a blackened room. Hades clapped his hands—two sharp explosions in the silence that made Vic's ears ring.

A pit in the center of the room blazed to life with lime green flames. The room itself was gigantic. It was circular and carved from the red earth so that it was smooth—not a single edge. And along the walls were numerous glass cases containing objects, artifacts. Vic had never even known a room like this existed. She took a hesitant step forward and when her father didn't stop her she stepped fully into the room, Cal at her heels.

"Take a look around. Tell me what you see."

Hades waved a hand. It was much the same attitude he'd held when it came to Vic's education. He would take her places that she'd never been and ask her to explain the things that she saw. She didn't know then, but it was a valuable lesson in noticing one's surroundings and using deductive reasoning. Ironically, the same skill that led her to suspect her father had somehow orchestrated some of the events in which she and Cal now found themselves.

Hades stood in the center of the room, his olive face cast in green flame, making him look even more sinister.

She walked over to the left and inspected the first glass case. Inside it were what appeared to be white crab claws, mounted to black velvet and held in place with small metal pins. Beneath the case was a plaque that simply read: Oceanus.

She moved on to the next case, Cal following slowly behind her, warily inspecting the crab claws.

The next case was larger—long and rectangular—and it held a weathered looking wooden oar. The plaque beneath it read Tethys.

Vic moved onto the third case, which was a large cube containing a tarnished and slightly chipped cymbal. Beneath it the plaque read: Rhea. Some of the names sounded familiar and Vic looked over her shoulder at her father, who was rubbing his chin and watching her intently, his expression blank.

She looked back over her other shoulder, and saw that Cal

had realized something that she had not. His face had gone slightly pale, even in the green light that danced off his skin, and he was working his jaw, thinking. Calculating. Trying to get one step ahead.

Vic didn't have the heart to tell him that with Hades, the effort was usually futile.

When she reached the next case, it was empty. The plaque beneath read: Cronus.

Vic turned toward her father. "It's empty."

Hades confirmed, "It is."

"But I don't understand."

She fingered the plaque and turned toward Cal with an expression of confusion. The puzzle had somehow grown larger and she'd reached the point where she couldn't see the forest for the trees.

"I do." Cal stepped forward and turned toward Hades, who truly cut an intimidating figure in his suit and tie, lit in lime green light.

"These cases contain objects from the Titans. There were twelve of them and there are twelve boxes. But this one here—" he pointed to the empty case. "This one belonged to Cronus. And the item is gone. The items are linked to the god or goddess somehow, aren't they?"

"Indeed." Hades nodded approvingly. "Go on."

Cal began to pace, immediately lost in thought, his head bowed.

"Cronus was cast into the Nyx Cave, but he escaped. And if he escaped he must have had help." His head shot up and a look of dawning crossed his face. "The objects are linked to the Titan it belongs to. But you have this room under lock and key." He turned to Vic. "And your mother has been ill." He turned back to Hades. "That means you had some sort of security breach. Whoever did this was someone on the inside. A traitor."

Vic's heart froze. A traitor? Was it possible? Someone they knew—who knew Persephone—did this to her? To her family? The thought made her knees go weak. Vic stumbled and Cal caught her arm, pulling her gently upright. Who would dare risk the wrath of the King of the Under World? Whoever it was, the person they pledged allegiance to must be infinitely more powerful. Cronus. Was Cal's father that powerful?

Hades clapped slowly. "Very good, Callum. I must say I am impressed. Your deductive reasoning far surpasses even that of my daughter. Cronus raised you well."

But Cal shook his head. "Not my father. He wasn't around. My mother, Rachel, more or less raised my siblings and me."

Hades tilted his head and Vic could see the shift in his dark eyes as he re-evaluated what he'd assumed he knew about Cal. To Vic, that was at least a relief. If her father saw an ally in Cal and not an enemy, then his life would be spared as long as he didn't outlive his usefulness. Her gut twisted. Thinking like her father bothered her in more ways than one.

Cal's hand still rested on her elbow, a reassuring reminder that this was something they were in together. "A traitor. Who is it?"

Hades' shoulders sagged. "I still haven't figured it out. It's something Asher's been assigned to investigate."

"And he conveniently thought Cal had something to do with it?" Vic gritted her teeth.

Her father gave a small smile. "To be fair, your friend does have something to do with it. At the time it just wasn't known how much."

"So Taking his soul would have helped you figure it out? No, that was simply going to be a power move. You were using me as a pawn in this mess of yours instead of trusting me to help you. Instead of trusting your *daughter*, you trusted Asher—who by the way has proven numerous times that he cannot be trusted—and sent me on a wild goose chase. Tell me, Dad, did you send me to the Above World to help Maman? Or did you send me up there so Asher would have a good reason to spy?"

Hades angular face twisted in what could best be described as anguish—if it were an emotion he felt regularly. Only when it came to Persephone did he feel other emotions besides rage or indifference.

"I never said I was a perfect father."

Vic took a step forward. "I'm not asking you to be perfect. I'm just asking you to trust me. To trust me and my judgment and to realize that I'm quite capable. I've always done what you asked." She glanced at Cal. "Well, almost always. And it's because I trust you. Why can't you do the same for me?"

Hades bowed his head and scratched at his neck, the crow feather circlet tilting so that it rested against the top of his left ear. Cal had never imagined that he would see the god of the Under World cowed by a seventeen-year-old girl.

It was true that she hadn't told her father about the Oracle's prophecy and that somehow the prophecy linked her and Cal together—the sword and the air. But she figured such things would arise in due course. Right now, she needed to know who had helped Cronus and just what it was he was planning.

"You're right. I was wrong. This time. Cal seems unaware of his father's transgressions. It would seem that Cronus has gone deep into the Above World, possibly recruiting other Olympians to his cause. I'll send Asher to notify Zeus, Poseidon, Ares, and Athena. Perhaps they already have some insight on the situation. We will need allies if Cronus plans to take his attack on us further. The poisoning of Persephone is an act of war in and of itself. In the meanwhile, we need to find that artifact. If we can find the artifact, we can tether it back to the Cave of Nyx and Cronus can then be contained. Again."

Vic already had a sneaking suspicion, but she asked her father anyways. "What's the missing artifact?"

Hades looked up, his expression one of renewed vigor.

"A watch."

Chapter Nineteen

And yet Persephone was still dying.

Vic knew that she had been manipulated. Still, the Oracle had said that Taking the souls would buy Persephone more time. Perhaps it had. Maybe if Persephone hadn't drank the concoction she'd already be dead. There was no way to really know.

Her stomach roiled with the possibility that someone among their own had done this to her mother. Sure, people for the most part hated Hades—fear and not taking the time to understand someone often led to hate—but everyone loved Persephone. Whoever had done this to her, Cronus had to have been very persuasive.

"Will you sit down already? I'm afraid you're going to wear through the floor." Cal's voice interrupted her rapid-fire thoughts. He was seated in an opulent chair that had a high back and a piece from which thin tulle curtains hung. It was Vic's reading chair and very much fit for a princess.

She'd been pacing—a habit the two of them shared—and

pulling on the end of her ponytail. Irritated—but not at the interruption—she flopped onto her bed and stared at the ceiling which was enchanted to look like the night sky of the Above World. Her obsession had started long before she'd ever even actually been up there.

"I have so many questions!"

Cal gave her a sympathetic look. "Yeah, me too. Do you really think my watch is the missing one? From that artifact room?"

Vic turned her head so she was staring at Cal instead of the ceiling. His amber eyes were worried and his brow was furrowed creating a little, wrinkled eleven between his brows.

"Yeah. I do." She propped herself up on her elbow. "Do you?"

Cal looked at the floor as if the white fluffy rug was suddenly the most interesting thing in the world.

"I don't want to believe it. I want this to just be a really cool experience and then to go back home and things to just be normal. But when your dad said that the missing artifact was a watch, every hair on the back of my neck stood up."

Vic frowned. "But I don't understand why all the other items were super old looking and Cronus's is some super fancy watch. It doesn't make any sense."

Cal toed the carpet with his Chucks. "Maybe it's not the watch itself, but a component of the watch. Like a jewel-encrusted snake in the watch face."

Vic sat up excitedly. "Or there could even be something stored inside the watch! Between the face and the back of it. Have you ever opened it?"

Cal shook his head. "I never really started wearing it until we moved to Olympia. My eighteenth birthday was a month or so before we moved. My surfer friends would have made fun of me if I'd worn a watch like that." He grinned. "Things are so different now."

Vic frowned.

"Good different," Cal corrected. Vic frowned deeper. "Okay, you're really the only good different thing. But I'm sure once this is resolved there will be other good things."

Satisfied, Vic laid her head down on her arm, but remained on her side so that she was still facing Cal.

"I wish I knew who did this. I wish I knew how to fix Maman."

"If wishes were fishes we'd all swim in riches," Cal agreed. "You don't think Asher…"

But Vic shook her head.

"No. He's manipulative and mostly a jerk, but he has a soft side."

Her mind went to the scene not long ago in the orchard. He definitely was someone who brought out the worst in her.

"And Persephone is like his own mother. He adores her. I'm not sure it could be any of the hellhounds. They take a blood oath. If they violate it, they're sentenced to death."

"How does one kill an immortal?" Cal asked.

If Cronus was so horrible then why did they banish him to the Cave of Nyx instead of killing him outright? Then again, if they had, Cal surely wouldn't be sitting here in the Under World in the enigmatic Vic's bedroom.

Vic picked at the bedspread which was frayed and in swirled shades of amethyst, ruby, and black. "There are a few ways. One is poisoning, like with Maman. But it takes much longer. It's a slow, painful death." Her breath hitched on the last word and Cal was moving before he could stop himself.

He sat on the bed and gently pulled Vic into his arms, cradling her so that her left ear was pressed against his heart.

A silent tear rolled down her cheek and then another. She felt Cal rest his chin on the top of her head, her arm wrapped around the solidness of his waist. She cried silent tears for a few moments and then when her breathing stopped hiccupping and the tears were just wet spots in her shirt collar, she continued.

"The second way is to throw them into the Waterfall to Nowhere." The black waterfall that leads beyond. Vic had never seen it, but she'd heard talk of it.

"Well, that sounds pleasant."

Vic cracked a smile and leaned back so she could see the small dimpled smile on Cal's face.

"Immortals aren't easy to kill. It can be done. We can still get injured and whatnot. We just heal significantly faster than those with limited life expectancy."

Cal's arm was still around her shoulders, her legs curled up beneath her, so that she was still pressed in snuggly to his side. She could smell the soft, baked scent that seemed to follow him.

"And what about me?" he asked after a comfortable silence.

Vic wrapped her fingers around a navy blue loose thread that hung from the sleeve of Cal's shirt. "Well, if your mother is a mortal and your father is Cronus. Then I'd say your half-mortal and half-immortal. A Halver is what we call them."

"A Halver, huh?"

"Yeah, half-a this and half-a that." Vic laughed.

"Well, I guess there are worse things that I could be called."

There was the sound of opening and closing doors. Footsteps in the hallway. A horn sounded, announcing the arrival of Zeus—the King of the Gods and the Above World.

Then silence.

Vic's heart sank. Part of her had hoped that her father would summon her. They hadn't yet told him about the watch, Vic was still distrusting of her father. It wasn't in his way to be one-hundred percent truthful, but even a little truthfulness was a much needed improvement. She hated thinking that she was just as guilty as her father when it came to omission, then again she had learned from the best.

"I wish we could hear what they were discussing…"

"If wishes were—"

"Yeah, yeah. If fishes were wishes…actually. That just gave me an idea."

Vic grinned wickedly.

–

The River Styx—the river not the woman—ran in front of the palace, but it also ran beneath it. Vic led Cal deep into the bowels of the castle, into a wing that seemed not often used. The furniture was older, more archaic and coated with a layer of dust, forgotten with time. Some pieces were even covered by a draped velvet cloth. Dust motes floated in the air. The walls turned from the sleek mirror-like granite, to something like sandstone or limestone.

"Do you have a flashlight in that backpack of yours?"

There were no bone sconces containing enchanted lime green flames in this part of the castle.

Cal slipped off his pack, unzipped it, and produced a Maglite. He really did pride himself on being as prepared as possible. Although, nothing could have prepared him for the knowledge that the Olympians were real and lived among them, his father was a banished Titan, and that some sort of second Titanomachy was imminent.

Vic turned on the flashlight and continued down the

winding corridor which led to a set of stone steps. She motioned for him to follow.

"This part of the castle was the original. Being immortal, tastes change with the times eventually. We don't use it for anything anymore, but as a kid I loved to explore. This staircase leads to a tunnel and in that tunnel flows the river. Guess where it comes out?"

Cal rubbed a hand over the back of his neck. This part of the palace was extremely creepy. It was ancient and it reminded him of the myths they'd read in English class at his old school. Of a time long ago. But to Hades and Persephone it wasn't really all that long ago. All the mortals who'd lived then were long gone. And yet they lived on. Cal took a shaky breath. And so would he. Maybe not forever, but he'd most likely outlive his loved ones. All of his siblings would too. The thought was like a fist clenching his heart.

"Cal?"

Vic had stopped and he'd nearly ran into her. She shone the flashlight so that it illuminated his face.

"It's a lot to take in at once. I know. I'm sorry. I wish I could say that it was all going to be over soon. But I don't want to lie to you. Never to you."

Her expression was so fierce that Cal had no choice but to believe her. He followed her down the stairwell that wound along, as if they were in one of the castle's many turrets. Finally, they reached the bottom.

They could hear the sound of rushing water.

"Like I was saying. The river runs right beneath the castle. This tunnel begins here, the river is a way out of the castle if it were to be under attack. We've never had to use it for something like that, but Asher and I used to play down here. Now that I think about it, I'm thinking my childhood was much stranger than I ever realized."

Vic shone the flashlight a little off to the left and Cal peered into the water. It was black with gray foaming froth. Not a calm river. An angry one. Not that he'd come to expect anything less in the Under World.

"It leads to your father's war room doesn't it?"

Vic nodded. "It does. If you were to paddle upstream it leads out and back past the Bone Bridge. But if we follow the flow, there's an additional tunnel that leads to the War Room."

"And if you were to follow the course of the river beyond that point?"

Cal absent-mindedly rubbed his wrist where his watch usually sat—at least for the past couple of months that he'd worn it. Vic noticed he had a slight tan line, like a faded bracelet.

"It goes to the point of no return. The end of the line." She glanced over her shoulder at him. "I've never personally been to look, but I've been told there's no coming back."

Cal shuddered. Despite what his father was doing—and whatever he had done—he didn't want to think of his father suffering a fate such as that. He pushed the thought aside.

"How do we get there? To the war room?"

Vic grinned again and handed him the Maglite. He watched, fascinated, as she kissed the bat charm that hung at the hollow of her throat in between her collar bones—a spot he found his eyes always drawn toward, a spot he wanted to press his lips to because on Vic it seemed both beautiful and vulnerable.

She mumbled something unintelligible and then let the bat charm fall back to its resting place. She knelt beside the river. She held her hands out above it, fingers twitching. It rushed past, ignoring her and sending up spray that coated her fingers and her palms.

Cal watched as the river shifted beneath her hovering hands. It twisted and turned, and as it did Vic used her hands as if she were shaping something invisible, continuing to mutter under her breath. She urged the river to take shape—to obey her.

It wasn't something easy to do and it often exhausted her, but she held both her father's and her mother's power within her blood. As she called to the river and manipulated its form, she remembered how she had shown Asher this ability. Naturally, he'd been fascinated, but he'd also been jealous. For as long as she'd known him, Asher always desired being special and Vic was somehow always showing him just how unspecial he was.

Cal's reaction was quite the opposite. His expression was one of child-like awe and he nearly dropped the Maglite as Vic molded the unruly river like an artist molding clay. A long, snakish shape took form. It bucked and writhed beneath her hands, but the water molded into something that appeared solid. So solid, that it turned and glared at Cal with bright yellow eyes. He was looking into the face of a sea serpent.

A sea serpent completely conjured by water and magic. Vic rested a hand on its neck and threw a leg over its body so that she straddled it like a horse. Her ponytail had fallen out long ago and her black hair rippled behind her. Cheeks flushed from the effort of conjuring something from nothing. Cal felt his mouth slide open and for the second time he nearly dropped the Maglite.

She looked like a warrior and she was beckoning to him.

Vic didn't understand Cal's hesitation—at least not in the way Cal experienced it. She thought maybe he was scared. She remembered—and was embarrassed of—how he'd seen her cause the accident and Take Lauren's soul, what seemed like months ago now, but was only a couple weeks past. She reminded herself that once Persephone was safe again, she would make Lauren's life right as best as she could. She'd find a way to somehow undo some of what she had done.

But Cal wasn't scared; he was enamored.

He handed Vic the Maglite and with one hand she held it and with the other she helped Cal climb up behind her. Once he was settled, she squeezed her heels into the side of the slimy black sea serpent, made from the River Styx, and urged it onward downstream.

Unsure what to do, Cal placed his hands on Vic's hips, sending shooting sensations of warmth through her, his cinnamon honey scent mixing with the dewy mist of the river.

They tore through the tunnel, gliding along the water. The beam of light in Vic's hand bouncing along and off the limestone walls that surrounded them. Her hair whipped around her face and since the creature was her own creation, it obeyed only her. They sliced through the water spraying gray foam in their wake. It was akin to flying and it had been so long since Vic had conjured a creature that she couldn't help but smile despite the dire circumstances.

Cal gripped her hips for dear life as the serpent bucked and twisted its way down the river. While, Vic was clearly enjoying herself, he was taking deep breaths in through his nose and out through his mouth. The combination of speed and height—which gave some people like Vic an adrenaline rush—made him feel a bit queasy.

Naturally, he would never tell Vic that. He was thankful when they pulled to a stop in front of a non-descript looking door.

Vic slid off the serpent gracefully and watched with a bemused expression as Cal fumbled his way off. His jeans were soaked from the spray and he looked discombobulated. Once he seemed to regain his land legs, Vic snapped her fingers and the creature instantly dissolved into tiny black droplets that plinked softly back into the river as if it had never existed at all.

"Come on. We need to hurry. I'm sure we've already missed some important information," she said grabbing his hand and leading him up to the door. It had a numeric dial lock built into it—not the complex technology that had been upstairs. Vic dropped his hand and spun the dial left, then right and the lock clicked open.

"He always chooses my birthday," she shrugged.

She pushed the door open and they entered into a tunnel that began as limestone and then abruptly changed to granite. Sleek and smooth, slippery beneath the damp soles of their shoes.

The tunnels had a ventilation system. She just had to remember where the hatch was. Cal tripped behind her, grunting as his knees hit the granite. Vic turned, shining the flashlight on his grimacing face. He'd tripped on the lip of the hatch she was looking for.

"Are you okay?"

"Peachy," Cal grunted. He shoved himself back onto his butt and inspected the damage. Nothing appeared to be broken or bleeding, but his ego was surely bruised.

"It's this damn granite, it's like running on ice. But luckily, you found the hatch I was looking for." She grinned at him and handed him the Maglite.

She pulled open the hatch, dropped her legs in and immediately disappeared from sight.

"Vic?" He scurried over and shone the flashlight down onto her. She was standing in a stainless steel tunnel, her gold eyes like cat eyes peering up at him.

"Jump down! But land softly if you can. There's a grate a few paces from here and we can see into the war room from there."

Cal tossed her the flashlight and then hopped down behind her, landing gently on his feet and ignoring the jolt of pain his still-recovering knees gave him.

Eerie voices drifted down the tunnel and Vic picked up the pace. Cal hurried behind her, trying to make as little noise as possible. Vic was silent as a panther on the prowl.

All the voices drifting through the grate were male. But Vic was sure Athena would have shown up. She wasn't one who liked to be overlooked. A grid of chartreuse light fell onto the floor of the tunnel and Vic put out an arm to stop Cal from continuing. She turned off the flashlight and gestured to the grate, then silently made her way to the other side so they could both peer into the war room.

Five of the six sides of the hexagonal table were now occupied. Hades faced the doorway, the right side of his face to the air vent. Across from them was a man who appeared slightly older than Hades, with silvery blonde hair worn long to his collarbone. His eyes were a piercing blue and he shared the same angular features as Hades, but had a jagged lightning bolt scar down his left cheek.

"Zeus," Vic mouthed to him in the dim light.

At a slight angle from where they watched, was another man. He had curly blonde hair and blue eyes as well, but his eyes were playful and more the color of sea foam. Of the three brothers, he looked the youngest despite a full beard. His skin was tanned and there was a slightly bored air about him. Cal assumed this was Poseidon.

The last male at the table had his left side to the grate. His skin was dark and his black hair was shaped into a Mohawk with red tips. He had gold hoop earrings up and down his ear and in his eyebrow. He was built like a mountain and wearing a cut-off sleeved heavy metal band t-shirt with black spandex pants and motorcycle boots. Colorful tattoos snaked up and down his arms from his wrists and up into his shirt sleeves, or lack thereof.

"Ares," Vic mouthed.

Cal wracked his brain for Greek mythology and recalled vaguely that Ares was the god of war, although in this instance he looked more like the lead singer of a rock band that yelled their music rather than sang it.

The last person at the table could only be partially seen. Despite mostly seeing the back of the person and a small portion of her face, it was clearly a woman. Her tawny brown hair was in a long braid that was coiled around her head in a large bun. On the back of her neck was a tattoo of an owl in flight carrying a snake in its beak. She had the same angular cheekbones as Hades and Zeus. Unlike Persephone, there was little softness about her. She wore a black leather corset and a short denim skirt with over the knee black leather boots.

"Athena," Vic mouthed.

To Cal, she looked more like a witch or a vampire than the goddess of war and wisdom. He could hardly believe that only a few days ago, he'd have believed none of this. Now, he was living it. He was half-immortal, his father was the Titan Cronus escaped from the Cave of Nyx and trying to overthrow the Olympians.

Now he was about to eavesdrop on a conversation between five of the gods and goddesses of Olympia. While sitting in an air vent with the daughter of Hades in the Under World after having ridden a magic sea serpent and earlier being escorted by an actual hellhound. If he hadn't experienced it for himself, he'd have thought it was all a dream.

His sore knees and pounding heart told him otherwise.

Hades' stern voice floated over to them from where he sat. "I've brought you here for a most urgent matter."

"It better be urgent, I left in the middle of band practice."

Vic could see that Hades was trying very hard not to roll his eyes at the younger god, Ares.

"I assure you. It is a most pressing matter. I won't mince words. It would seem we have been betrayed. Persephone has been poisoned and death is not far. I regret to inform you all that the Cronus artifact is missing and he has escaped the Cave of Nyx. It would seem that war is imminent."

The last word was drowned out as the war room erupted into chaos.

Chapter Twenty

"Impossible!" cried Athena slamming her hands onto the table.

"After all these years? Surely, you're mistaken, Brother," said Poseidon calmly.

"I told you the Cave of Nyx was not strong enough to hold the Titans!" exclaimed Ares sulking in his high-backed chair.

Only Zeus remained silent, his pale blue eyes observant

Hades jaw worked and Vic could see her father trying to pull in as much calm as he could. It wasn't wise to be on the receiving end of Hades' wrath. Immortal or not.

"I assure you. It's quite possible, Athena. The artifact is gone. Someone—someone who we trusted—has betrayed us."

"Who would be foolish enough to cross the Olympians?" sneered Athena.

Vic admired her ferocity and fearlessness, but even Vic

knew it was naïve to think that the Olympians did not have those who opposed them.

The general human population didn't even know they actually existed, so long brainwashed into believing they were nothing more than ancient myths and legends. But some, beings and creatures not necessarily aligned to the rules and whims of the Olympian gods and goddesses, were kept under a careful watch.

"Someone loyal to Cronus. Someone who would know what the artifacts meant and how to get around any security measures in place. Someone who wants to see us fall." Hades' voice was measured.

Vic felt a little bit bad for him. In a way, the admission of the stolen artifact was the equivalent of admitting he was bested under his own roof. If anything, Hades didn't like to be wrong and he definitely didn't like to be bested.

"How is Persephone?"

It was the first words Zeus had spoken. Vic hadn't encountered him often. He was an intimidating figure and he kept to himself for the most part, living high up in the mountains at an altitude that would seize even the strongest climber's lungs and leave him in an icy grave.

Truth be told, he frightened Vic just a bit.

Hades turned. He bowed his head and a lock of black hair swooped out of the circlet and across his forehead. His expression was pained and Vic had never seen him look as miserable as he did now.

"She is not well. The Oracle suggested a tincture that would slow the spread of the poison, but it has not been working as planned. She is…dying."

Vic knew the last word cost him. He turned what she knew was an agonized sob into a cough and then spread his hands across the smooth surface of the table before taking a steadying breath to regain his composure.

"This doesn't sound like an attack on us, as much as an attack on *you*," Ares accused pointing a gnarled finger, like a boxer who'd broken his fingers after too many punches.

Hades glared at Ares. "Is an attack on one of us, not an attack on all of us?"

"He's right," Poseidon spoke again. His voice was soft and calming, like a whispering lullaby. Vic had always liked him. He was kind, but also had a temper. Unlike her father though, it took a lot to anger Poseidon. Mostly, mistreatment of the sea or its creatures was the quickest way to flare his tempest. "Who is to say one of us is not next? Perhaps Persephone was an easy target as she travels between worlds so often."

There was silence around the table as the others thought on Poseidon's words. Despite Athena and Ares' outbursts, no one spoke ill of Persephone. She was well-loved by the Olympians and known for her sweet temper and child-like wonder.

"What are our next steps?" Athena finally asked. She'd leaned back in her chair. "If this is an attack, a call to war, are we not playing into exactly what Cronus wants? I say we find the traitor and make an example. Perhaps it will remind Cronus just what the Olympians are capable of."

Cal leaned toward Vic and whispered. "Didn't Cronus once eat his own children? Is there really anything worse than that?"

Vic smiled. "Actually, much worse."

She knew the Cave of Nyx was one step away from the waterfall that led to the Beyond World. It was complete darkness and not just turn-off-the-lights dark, but complete and utter blackness. A night so palpable that one had no sense of the passage of time. Whether one was coming or going, living or dead. In a manner of speaking, it was much like a living death. Complete awareness, slowly creeping into madness, and not a damn thing to stop it. Cronus had been trapped in the Cave of Nyx for millennia.

That said a lot about his possible mental state.

"I have no knowledge of who the traitor could be. My hellhounds have been searching for months. The security footage of the artifact room had been disabled prior to the artifact's disappearance. I had no idea the artifact was even missing until I began investigating Persephone's illness. I suspect it has been gone for eighteen years, give or take." Hades said the words thoughtfully, but Vic could see how much it cost her father to say them. He looked old and tired. And very sad.

"Eighteen years!" exclaimed Athena.

"What makes you say such a number?" asked Zeus at the same time. His voice was gravelly from infrequent use. The lightning shaped scar down the side of his face crinkled as he spoke, pulling at the side of his mouth so it looked as if he were snarling.

Vic knew where this was going and she could feel her heartbeat speed up. She looked across the square of light at Cal and saw the recognition in his eyes. He was about to be outted. Once this happened there was no going back. Everyone would know. Vic just had to hope that he wouldn't become a target for any displaced anger and frustrations.

"We found a boy."

"A boy?" asked Poseidon.

"A boy eighteen years of age who recently enrolled in the high school Victoriana has been attending in the Above World."

"How do we know he is connected to Cronus?" Athena asked. "He could just be a regular boy."

"My hellhound told me his soul was very pure and bright. Closer to the souls of the Aether."

"The Primordials?" Athena stroked her cheek thoughtfully. "What if the boy isn't actually a son to Cronus?"

"What do you mean, Ath?" Hades asked, dark eyes narrowed. "What are you suggesting?"

Vic could see that Athena's mind was whirling. She knew she had a laser-sharp mind. She was not only the goddess of war after all, but also of wisdom.

"What if he is a Primordial son and Cronus simply raised him as his own?"

Cal's eyes grew wide and panicked. Vic knew it was too much too soon, but they had to take one thing at a time. The more information they had the better off they'd all be. They could make sense of it all later.

"I suppose that is possible, but—"

Hades' words were cut off as Brim burst through the doorway, out of breath, a look of sheer panic across his stone-like features.

"Brim, what is it?" Hades stood, alarmed at his hellhound's abrupt entrance.

"She's gone, my King!"

The words came out choked with fear. Vic wasn't sure if it was fear for himself for having interrupted an important meeting or fear for what he was about to tell Hades.

"Who is gone?" Hades' voice was all clipped patience.

Brim looked pained to say it, his face twisted in anguish. "Persephone."

Chapter Twenty-One

Vic couldn't hear anything after that.

Her body broke out into a cold sweat and everything seemed to slow down as if time itself was wrapping its arms around her. She jumped to her feet, not caring if she was heard, and broke into a sprint down the tunnel.

Not Persephone. Her mother couldn't be gone.

Kidnapped.

Vic's heart tripped over the word. She sprinted down the tunnel, hearing Cal's steps echoing after her own.

Her mind rushed with information. Things about the meeting had surprised her.

She was surprised by the suggestion that Cal could be a Primordial son, but it also fit with why Asher kept insisting that Cal's soul was bright and untainted. If he was a descendant of Aether, then that would be true because Aether is pure light.

This was much bigger—and much more dangerous—than Vic had ever anticipated. Her heart was split in two—pained for Cal and this latest revelation that once again would rock his world—and broken for the possibility that her mother was missing and most likely being held captive.

Persephone was dying and she hadn't anticipated her earlier visit as her last one. This was someone she was not yet ready to let go, and whom she would die fighting to protect, regardless of who tried to stop her.

The Maglite's beam bounced along the tunnel until Vic reached a grate at the end of the tunnel which she knew opened up onto the sub-basement of the palace. She knocked the grate out with a flying front kick and it bounced along the stone floor like cymbals clashing. Cal was right behind her as she scrambled out of the ventilation system and dashed down the hallway to a winding staircase.

She took them two at a time and her lungs felt like they would burst with the effort, and she cursed the time she spent faking cramps to avoid sprints in gym class. When she reached the top, an old wooden door opened onto a hallway that led directly to Persephone's wing of the palace. Vic sprinted down the woven carpet and slid to a stop in front of her mother's door.

The door was cast open and without her presence, the piles of hyacinth that littered the floor were already beginning to wilt. Asher stood at the foot of the bed with a bewildered expression on his face. In his hand was a wilted lavender-colored hyacinth. He heard Vic's approach and turned toward her.

"She's gone."

The words were rimmed with disbelief.

Vic stepped into the room and slowly turned toward the bed which was still covered in hyacinth. In its center was a woman-shaped space of white linens, where Persephone had lain only hours before. Now empty. The space mimicked the Maman-shaped hole that now carved itself into Vic's heart.

–

She knew it wasn't Asher's fault. And yet she couldn't stop herself.

Vic's vision filled with black spots of despair and rage. Her muscles tensed and her heart pounded. An animal whose body was surging into fight mode. She launched herself at Asher, knocking him to the floor. Unlike the last time—the time where he consoled her and didn't fight back—he tried to shove her away as she clawed at his bare arms.

Sobs wracked her body and she couldn't even make out his features.

Anonymous.

He tried to pin her arms to her sides, but then she kicked—making contact with his knee joint—and he lost his grip. All the energy she kept inside, all the feelings, just built up with nowhere to go until something made her explode. She was a ticking time bomb and was honestly surprised she hadn't imploded thus far.

She kicked, punched, and pulled. Her mouth emitted guttural sounds that did not sound like a normal teenage girl. But Vic was not a normal teenage girl. She was an immortal, the daughter of the God of the Under World. Her power was much untapped and she had no idea the impact the disappearance of Persephone would have on her.

Rage and frustration boiled over inside of her. Despair coursed through her veins. She felt the surge of heat inside of herself, a white-hot pinprick in the pads of her fingers. She grabbed for anything on Asher's person—someone needed to pay for this. She would make them all pay.

Asher howled in pain. "Tor! You're burning me! Please!"

Her nostrils caught the smell of singed hair. And she gagged as strong hands pulled her back by the torso. They wrapped around her waist, not trapping her, but as if the pressure could calm her down. She was panting and sweating, but she could feel the coldness of the arms wrapped around her.

The black dots began to fade and she could see a pale, white light—like fog—rising off the arms that held her. Familiar arms. Cal. Asher pushed himself to his feet and said nothing.

Her temper wasn't new and he couldn't completely blame her for her reaction to her mother's disappearance. And yet, something had changed. He regarded her with frightened eyes. Her nails had made scratches near his temple that bled into his eyes. Dark hair was singed at his neck and there was a red burn beneath his ear that oddly took the shape of her fingers.

Vic's stomach twisted at what her lack of control had done. The marks it had left. But worse, at the look that Asher now gave her that was a combination of both fear and pity.

Feet pounded in the hallway, the sharp click of wingtips. Hades appeared in the doorway and took in the scene of Asher bloodied and burned, a bruise blossoming on his left cheek, and of his daughter, drenched in sweat held in Cal's arms that still were emitting a soft foggy essence.

The sword is the air. The air is the sword.

"Come. Explain," Hades commanded and without looking at Vic, Asher followed her father out into the hallway.

Adrenaline still coursed through her and Vic could smell

Cal's spicy-sweet scent. It filled her head, pushing out the dark with something light and warm. His breath was cool on the back of her neck. The scent coalesced with the familiar incense of Asher, and the sharp scent of hyacinth, now hinted with decay.

Footsteps faded away in the hallway along with murmured voices.

Vic's breath slowed and once it was even, Cal slowly loosened his grip. It was enough to let her know she was welcome to stay there, or she could break free. She wanted to stay there, shrouded in his embrace, but instead she stumbled forward.

Hyacinth crushed beneath her sneakers as she made her way to the bed. She crawled across the white linens. It still smelled like roses and sunshine. Vic started to cry, softly this time. All the rage was drained from her in that one explosive outburst. Instead, despair and the twin flames of guilt and shame took over.

She knew she was a dangerous creature. Unsure what things someone as kind as Cal saw in her. Her mother wasn't like this—why couldn't she be more like Persephone? Calm, sweet, and good-natured? Instead she was fire and brimstone, rage and frustration. Being home—being below—it brought out the worst in her. As above, so below just didn't seem to hold true for Victoriana Haden.

She inhaled her mother's scent, hyacinth petals pressed into her cheek, and cried herself into a dreamless sleep.

Chapter Twenty-Two

When she woke, Cal was sitting on the floor near the door, a mound of pastel hyacinth pushed to the side to make room.

Vic sat up, rubbing at her eyes. They were tender and swollen. Her chin was tender where Asher must have accidentally hit her in his attempt to get away when she attacked him. Heat rose to her cheeks at the memory of her uncontrollable rage.

She glanced at Cal. His expression was impassive, but his amber eyes held concern. He abruptly stood up and disappeared out the door and into the hallway. Vic felt her chest hitch and the gritty burn of tears behind her eyeballs.

Her temper had scared him away. The one person who seemed inextricably linked to her—to her life—the only one who could calm her down in her worst rage yet, and even he was too disgusted to talk to her. But he'd stayed while she slept. To make sure she didn't harm anyone else? Or to make sure she didn't harm herself?

When she heard his now familiar tread return, Cal entered the room holding a glass of water. He didn't hesitate as he sat at the foot of the bed and handed it to her. She took a drink and downed nearly the entire glass. The heat that had burned her up from the inside out had apparently made her thirsty.

Cal watched her and where Vic had expected judgment she saw none. She saw no fear, no pity. Only concern. She felt like she needed to say something, to explain her wrath, as if words could somehow undo what she'd done.

"I lose control sometimes. Mainly, when I'm home. Something about this place…the Under World. It's like all my negative emotions are bottled up and then something happens that causes them to explode, like a match thrown into a room full of natural gas. I don't know why. But it's been getting worse." Her voice dropped. "I wish you hadn't seen that."

Cal waited a moment before replying, his fingers worrying at the edge of his sleeve. "Did I not tell you I wanted to know all of you? That includes the bad parts, Vic."

She rambled on. "I know it isn't Asher's fault. Often he's the target of my rages—at least it seems so lately. I don't know if it's because I've known him my whole life or what. It's almost like he expects it. But this time. It was different." She bowed her head. "I think he was afraid of me."

Again, Cal didn't say anything for a long while.

"What's it like for you?"

Vic was confused. That wasn't the question she'd been expecting him to ask. Maybe *what's wrong with you* or *how could you do that?* But not something less than accusatory.

"What?"

"When you're in a fit. A rage. An episode. Whatever word you use to call it. What happens? What are you feeling?"

She searched his face for hidden meaning, but there was still only concern and perhaps thinly-veiled curiosity.

"It's like I'm not myself."

Cal nodded, encouraging her to go on.

"My vision gets clouded with black dots and I can't see straight. Blood rushes through my head and I can't hear right. I feel like I'm invincible, like I'm wrath incarnate. It's almost as if all the bad emotions hijack my body," she chuckled. "That's kind of Dr. Jekyll and Mr. Hyde."

"And it's always been like this? These rages."

Vic was still holding the nearly empty glass of water. No, no it hadn't always been like this. Sure, when she was younger she'd had temper-tantrums. What kid didn't? But nothing like this. It had only started more recently.

"No. Not always. I think that Maman's illness somehow triggered them. Don't get me wrong I've kind of always been quick to temper, but not like this." She swallowed. "Not violent like this."

She looked up from the glass and back to Cal's calm, studied expression. How he could have witnessed her acting as she had, and still seem so placid was a bit beyond Vic's realm of understanding. He had stopped her. Not even Asher could have stopped her rage. Not this time. But why Cal?

"That thing you did…with the white misty stuff…"

Cal raised an eyebrow at her. "I don't know myself. You were upset and not acting like yourself. Even Asher—I mean come on the guy's a freaking hellhound—couldn't seem to get you off him. I didn't know what you were capable of—"

"*I* don't know what I'm capable of."

"I just knew I had to stop you if I could. I didn't think it would work. But as soon as I wrapped my arms around you, I just tried to funnel good thoughts into you. Positive thoughts."

"Positive thoughts?"

"Yeah. Like kissing you with the taste of marshmallow on your lips. Or the way your hair falls into your face when you're diagramming sentences in English. My brothers and sisters laughing as I chase them around the backyard. The ocean lapping at my surfboard as the sun crests the horizon."

Vic was startled by these revelations. All she could think of was Asher's betrayals, the regret of the Takings, and despair over Persephone and frustration at her father. Sadness and jealousy that she couldn't be normal and live an Above World life like any other seventeen year old girl could. All these emotions simmered and percolated inside her until they boiled over and to the surface.

But maybe. If she'd thought of other things instead, like Persephone's musical voice, her classmates laughing as crimson leaves flooded into the classroom, the smell of must and old books as she entered a library, or Cal's eyes aglow as the sun set reflected in them, his hand warm and reassuring in her own. Even her mint green truck. Or Anastasia's peanut butter-chocolate chip cookies.

Once Vic had stumbled upon what her father referred to as 'New Age Junk'. There was a spattering of books in the library—acquired who knows how or when—and one had caught her attention. It was called the *Tao Te Ching* and had footnotes of modern analysis by some New Age expert. Now some of that flittered to the surface of her memory. Sentences about changing your life by changing what you think, that if you could change how you saw something, then the object itself would seem to change. Suddenly, those words seemed extraordinarily relevant.

Asher had regarded her with a mixture of fear, pity, and maybe even disgust. What was it that Cal saw when he looked at her?

"When you look at me. What is it that you see?" Her voice was barely a whisper and she peered at him through loose strands of hair.

He was not caught off guard by her question. Before answering, he reached out and tenderly pushed back her hair.

"Well, first I see Vic. First and foremost. Then I see a girl on the brink of greatness who has a curious mind and a caring heart." She opened her mouth to interrupt, but he moved his fingers to her lips, shushing her. "You asked what I saw. I see a daughter who adores her mother and would do anything in her power to save her. I see power that has nowhere to go, so it seems to burn you up from the inside out. And I see a girl who is frightened and confused, but who longs for understanding."

Vic was astounded. "You see all that? In me?"

Cal laughed, low and easy. "I do."

"No one's ever been able to stop me. Not like that. Not like you." Her fingers found Cal's. "It was like a calmness came over me. The dark spots faded and I could see clearly. Granted, I was horrified by what I'd done to Asher. But it was as if you were infusing my body with some sort of calm essence."

Cal squeezed her fingers. "I thought maybe your body was somehow reacting with mine. You know I'm still not completely sure how all this immortal business works."

Vic snorted. "Neither am I." A hyacinth was pressed beneath their clasped palms. "We have to find Persephone. Before it's too late."

"I know. I think we should tell Hades and the other gods about Pythia's prophecy. It could mean something more to them than it does to you or me. Maybe it will help."

"Yeah. Maybe."

The broken pieces shall be scattered.

She hoped those pieces weren't her mother.

Chapter Twenty-Three

Hades called for a carriage to the Above World.

And when Cal thought *carriage*, what greeted him outside wasn't exactly what came to mind.

In the rotunda drive, a shiny black 1966 Cadillac Fleetwood Sixty Special Brougham sat waiting. The back end looked like a jet ready for take-off with its winged rear lights. The front had a massive chrome grill that Cal suspected was shined in case Hades wanted to catch his reflection in it. Its front lights were like bug eyes stacked one on top of the other and the roof was a fine, pebbled leather. The rear wheels were half-covered by shiny, black fender skirts, and its wire rims were a dazzling chrome.

Cal let out a low whistle as they exited the palace front doors.

"What's with your family and cars?"

"It's ironic, isn't it? You're immortal but infatuated with a time long-gone. Did you know this model was the most luxurious non-limo model? Wait until you see the customized interior," Vic grinned.

Four Harleys pulled up in front of the carriage, as though they were horses readying to get bridled. The two front ones were all red and the two back ones all black. Two other hellhounds joined Asher and Brim in formation.

Hades was already seated at the gigantic steering wheel when Cal and Vic slid into the back seat. The entire interior of the car was ebony, crimson, and deepest burgundy and all soft leathers and velvets. Cal couldn't help but wonder why society drove around on itchy nylon and sweaty vinyl, when people could be driving around in this.

"Seatbelts," Hades glanced at them in the rearview mirror.

Cal noticed he was wearing black leather driving gloves.

They both clicked their seatbelts without argument. Cal mainly because he had no idea how going back to the Above World was supposed to work if they had to drive into a tree to get to the Under World. Beside him, Vic bit her lip and stared out the window at the palace looming over them.

She'd handled the meeting well and did most of the talking. By then it was only Hades and Athena. Zeus, Poseidon and Ares having disappeared to wherever it was that gods went. Vic had calmly told her father about the strange reading Pythia had given both her and Cal, and then explained a prophecy—which sounded more like a riddle to Cal—that the oracle had channeled just as they were leaving.

The entire time Hades had stroked his chin in thought—dark stubble beginning to emerge on his angular olive-skinned cheeks. Athena's piercing gray eyes had narrowed with each revelation, but she didn't interrupt. Neither god had ever heard of the House of Snakes, outside of Pythia's shop, but they both agreed it sounded like it could be something more. Something else.

After Vic had explained everything—without omissions this time. Hades and Athena had agreed that a trip to the Above World was necessary. They needed to pay a visit to the House of Snakes. Perhaps Pythia could tell them who had betrayed them and what happened to Persephone—or if she was still alive.

"I'd know," Vic had said. "I'd know if she was dead."

Cal wasn't sure if she was trying to reassure herself or convince herself.

Hades had offered Athena passage to the Above World with them, but she had waved him off mumbling something about not relying on a man for anything. They agreed to meet in Olympia in four days' time. Which Cal realized was the same day as the Apple Festival everyone at school had been talking about before the weekend.

In the meanwhile, Cal was to retrieve his watch and bring it to Hades who would be staying at the manor with Vic. He was also to collect anything else that could be of value in determining Cronus's motivations and Cal's true lineage. Vic had assured him they'd get to the bottom of it before the Apple Festival.

Cal's insides had been a mess since he overheard Athena's suspicions. That he was a Primordial son. He didn't even know what that meant. He vaguely remembered Vic explaining how before the Olympians, there were the Titans, and before the Titans were the Primordial gods.

They were like the original dynasty. The OD. But he couldn't remember much except that they had strange names and represented abstract things like Chaos, Time, Day and Night. The Cave of Nyx—the cave of night. Nyx was a primordial god.

It was bad enough to think his father had been lying all this time, but it was even worse to think that his father wasn't even his father.

–

The motorcycles roared to life.

They were enchanted so that they were linked to the carriage. Hades—as a god—could travel to the Above World without the accompaniment of a hellhound, but if he was anything, it was a showman and he often used the hellhounds to make a statement. It made a statement to the souls in the Under World and a statement to the Above World as they drove past. Four mysterious motorcycles being trailed by an elegant black Cadillac.

Vic watched out the windshield as they pulled away. She could see Asher's curved posture and the way his black t-shirt clung to him in the sweltering heat. When he turned to say something to the hellhound beside him, a purple bruise had blossomed across his jawline.

She would have to apologize. In all actuality, she'd rather stick a pitchfork in her eye than apologize to Asher. But it wasn't his fault he had stepped into the path of her rage.

They drove along, the red and black landscape darting past. The carriage had tinted windows so they could see out, but no one could see in. Mozart's Requiem was her father's music of choice. Perhaps not what one would expect from the King of the Under World and by some interpretations the devil himself. But Vic saw it for what it was. It was a statement on his sadness. They'd even translated the song in her Latin class. It was about justice and the dead resting eternally.

The song would have lulled her to sleep if she wasn't so anxious. Anxious to apologize to Asher, anxious to return to the manor with her father in tow. Anxious to find Persephone and make sure that she was alright—would be alright, somehow. And she was anxious for Cal.

She couldn't help but wonder if Mrs. Williamson had sat him somewhere else—maybe over by Nick and Elaine then he could have been spared this whole mess. Then again, Vic had learned a long time ago that the universe worked in a much different way than that. One way or another, Cal would have found his way into her life and maybe through Vic was the only way that Cal could learn his true identity and what it meant. Vic wasn't even sure what her own identity meant anymore.

The air and the sword.

She hoped it didn't mean that she'd be the death of him.

"Penny for your thoughts," Cal's voice broke through her reverie. She glanced over at him, across the bench seat. He had bluish circles beneath his eyes. When was the last time he'd slept? And he too could use a shave, dark stubble graced his cheeks.

She reached across the seat and intertwined her fingers with his.

"I was just thinking about how anxious I am right now. And confused. Remorseful. Hopeful," she laughed. "I'm a cacophony of emotions."

"You're not alone in that. I am too. I feel scared. And anxious as well. But I also feel determined to learn the truth. And to help you find Persephone and make her well again." He squeezed her fingers.

"Thank you."

It was an altogether different feeling for Vic to have someone by her side in all of this. Besides Asher and lately Richard, Vic had often been alone. She had studied alone, played mainly alone, grew up more or less alone. Then she had moved to the Above World and enrolled in school alone. And then she had Taken alone. But now this—this was different.

For the first time in her life she had an ally. A friend—possibly more than a friend, okay most definitely more than a friend, but a friendship was at the heart of it despite any prophecy—but she had someone who cared how it turned out. Who cared how she would fare at the end of it all. And if that was all Cal's role was in this, then Vic was eternally grateful for that. Even if she knew when it came to the Olympians, nothing was ever that simple.

They were passing the Mendax now. Vic delighted in watching as Cal's eyes widened when they neared the entrance/exit to the Under World. An ancient, gigantic gnarled black tree stood before them, its branches bare except for flakes of raining ash.

Vic watched as Brim and the other red motorcycle accelerated and disappeared into the massive trunk of the tree. Then Asher and the other hellhound followed. Hades punched the accelerator and sped after them, directly hitting the dark tree trunk, which seemed to absorb them up like a sponge. Blackness engulfed them for only a moment, before they were spit out into a grassy farm field.

The sun was setting and the field was cast in shades of crimson, gold, and apricot. They plowed through the field and toward the paved road, no tracks would be left in their wake. It would simply appear to be an old farming field no longer in use, with a deadened tree at its center, struck by lightning more often than anyone cared to keep track of.

Vic rolled down her window slightly, allowing the crisp fall air to flow into her lungs. The smell of dried grass and rotting leaves hung on the wind, and Vic took deep gulps of it as if she could feel the Above World air pushing out the ash and brimstone of the choked Under World air that inhabited her lungs. The wind cooled her forehead and the dry air pricked at her eyes. A small smile played at the corners of her lips. It felt good to be returning home.

–

"Nothing like a pleasant drive to clear the mind!" Hades said snapping off his leather gloves and placing them in the glove compartment. Cal had never seen anyone actually put gloves in that compartment before.

Vic got out of the carriage and stretched. It was late and both she and Cal had school in the morning. How they would get through the next few days was beyond her. In honor of the weekend's festivities there was no school Friday, but three days was a long time. She knew Hades wouldn't sleep as long as Persephone was missing. And that was part of the problem.

Vic didn't trust her Above World life with Hades in it. She could conveniently come down sick, but then if she happened to show her face at the festival it would clearly look like she had faked it. No, it would be better to bide her time and focus on her studies, while doing what she could outside of school hours. At least Cal would be there.

"I should get going, so that my mom doesn't worry. I texted her on the way to let her know we were headed back. Oddly, the reception in the Under World isn't the greatest," Cal grinned.

"We've been trying to work on that," Hades interrupted. "But the veil is very finicky. Is Richard around?"

Vic rolled her eyes. "Dad it's, like, 8 PM here. Richard works early morning to early afternoon. He's usually gone before I get home from school or just after I get home. He has a wife—and a life outside of the manor. Remember?"

"Very well. I'll get myself reacquainted with the house. I assume you haven't taken over all of the rooms?"

Cal gave her a funny look. It was clear Hades had no idea that Vic only inhabited the living room, downstairs bathroom, and kitchen.

She waved a dismissive hand. "There's plenty of space. For you and whoever else."

She glanced over at the four hellhounds who were lingering in the driveway.

"Just me. Two of the hellhounds will be returning to the Under World, while Asher and Brim search for Persephone." Hades inhaled the night air deeply as if he could smell his wife's presence. "She's here somewhere. I can feel it." With that he turned on his heel and disappeared inside the back gardens.

"Well, I better get you home." Vic headed toward the barn. But a voice stopped her.

"I'll take him." Asher. He continued, "It's not a problem. You live on Magnolia Lane, right? We have to go right past it."

Cal looked at Vic for reassurance before turning back to Asher. He picked up his backpack and slung it across his shoulders.

"Yeah. Thanks." He gave Vic one last look that told her he expected to see her in school the next morning, then headed over to Asher's motorcycle.

"Asher. Wait a second."

The hellhound turned, but didn't step any closer. He stood about three feet away from her. The bruise was definitely ugly and Vic felt ashamed at her loss of control.

"Thanks."

"Sure, like I said. It's not a problem." He turned.

Vic had to do it now before she lost all her muster. Admitting she was wrong didn't come easy. Admitting she was wrong to Asher came even less easily.

"I'm sorry."

Her voice was barely a whisper, but hellhounds had impeccable hearing. Asher paused. Vic noticed that he clenched and unclenched his tattooed hands, his right shoulder tilted toward her like he wanted to turn toward her, but he didn't. Instead he gave a single nod of his head, then walked over to his bike and climbed on.

Cal scrambled up behind him. The Harley came to life beside Brim's already idling bike. They took off down the driveway leaving Vic to stand alone beneath the nearly full moon, its bright light illuminating her surroundings on this clear night.

Vic realized that even though she had apologized, she wasn't sure if Asher had completely understood. Was she apologizing for attacking him? For being with Cal? Or was she apologizing because he'd been inextricably dragged into this since they were children?

She sighed. Maybe it was an apology fitting for a little bit of everything, but Vic had the feeling that it still wasn't enough.

–

Inside, everything was just as she had left it.

She could hear Hades moving around upstairs, the old wooden floor creaking even beneath his elegant step. Suddenly, Vic was overcome with exhaustion.

She changed into her pajamas, her favorite bottoms being a pair with bananas and monkeys on them. Then climbed into her bed. The sheets were cold which just so happened to be one of her favorite things. Hot sheets were the worst.

So much had happened in such a short amount of time that Vic was beginning to feel emotionally numb from it all. Which was probably for the best because then maybe she'd fall into a dreamless sleep. She could still hear Hades moving around, so she leaned over the bed where the pile of books still sat stacked on the floor.

At the top of the pile was the book on the Greek dynasties. Vic picked it up, turned on the little reading light clamped to her headboard, and opened to the Primordial section. There was an ancestral tree at the end of the section. She rooted around in her school bag for a pen and her notes. She began to add what she'd recently learned to what she already had written:

-CHRONUS AND CRONUS

-CRONUS=TIME=CAL'S WATCH??? -DEFINITELY THE WATCH

-CRONUS=TITAN GOD OF HARVEST=BATTLE OF THE GODS=SNAKE

-PYTHIA=HOUSE OF SNAKES

-PERSEPHONE=GODDESS OF THE HARVEST=COINCIDENCE?

-APPLE HARVEST COMING SOON—ANOTHER COINCIDENCE?

-CRONUS AND SNAKES/PYTHIA AND SNAKES (WHAT'S WITH ALL THE SNAKES?)

-CRONUS ESCAPED FROM THE CAVE OF NYX—MISSING ARTIFACT (THE WATCH)

-ATHENA THOUGHT CAL COULD BE A PRIMORDIAL SON...BUT WHOSE?

Vic flipped back to the ancestry chart. At the top it showed Chaos. She had heard the mythology that everything originated from Chaos, or what was also known as the Void.

There was Gaia which Vic knew some cultures still used to refer to the Earth. Nyx was there ruling over the night and Erebus over the Darkness. Vic followed the line connecting the two downward to Aether and Hemera. The word *day* was written beneath Hemera, but what shocked Vic was the word written beneath Aether. It was the word *air*.

The sword is the air and the air is the sword.

Maybe she had been wrong all along. Maybe the oracle's prophecy wasn't about Vic and Cal. Maybe it was only about Cal.

Chapter Twenty-Four

The next morning Vic awoke to snow.

She shivered as she climbed out of bed in her flimsy cotton pajama bottoms and thin t-shirt. The wood floor was cold beneath her feet as she scurried over to the window and pushed aside the curtain. What had tipped her off was the unnatural brightness of the living room when she'd opened her eyes.

Outside the world was blanketed in fluffy white snow that glittered in the early morning sunlight. It was at least three inches, so not a ton of snow, but enough to create a stark contrast between the unseasonable weather of the day before. Icicles hung from crimson leaves that had not yet been shed from their trees.

This was peculiar. It was clear that the sudden change in weather had to do with Persephone's kidnapping. She was somewhere in the Above World, they just had no idea where.

Normally, winter and autumn were the seasons that occurred when Persephone was in the Under World, then spring and summer were the celebrated seasons of her time in the Above World. However, the timing of her illness had created some weird homeostasis. Now Vic wondered if spring would suddenly be upon them earlier than usual as well.

She slipped a hoodie over her head, shucked her pajama bottoms, and hopped into a pair of jeans. After tying up her Chucks, she grabbed a granola bar, her keys and her book bag and hurried out the back door before Hades woke up. Typically, he was a late riser. Surely, he would notice the snow and want to talk about it, but all Vic could think about was Cal and all the talk at school of the early snow and how it would affect the Apple Festival.

The roads glistened with snow—not yet plowed—but the truck didn't fight as Vic carefully maneuvered to Magnolia Lane. She slid her phone out of her hoodie pocket and texted Cal. He texted her back immediately and said he'd be down in five minutes.

While she waited, Vic rolled down the window and inhaled the crisp, cold scent of freshly fallen snow. It was one of her favorite things of the Above World. She wasn't sure if it was the stark difference from her own world, where it was always dark and smoldering that made her love snow.

Large fluffy flakes cascaded down from the trees next to Cal's driveway, probably jostled by birds or squirrels, and Vic watched fascinated as the flakes landed on her windshield and melted into tiny puddles. She had the truck's heat on high and regretted not grabbing an actual coat in her haste to get out the door.

Vic looked up at the sound of the colonial's front door opening and closing. Cal trudged over to the truck. He was wearing a black wool coat and blue and black striped knit beanie, and a blue scarf. And gloves. And boots. Someone had obviously better prepared for the weather conditions than she had.

He yanked open the truck door, shoving his book bag across the seat, bringing in a jolt of cold air and wet snow.

"How are you so prepared for snow when you used to live in a beach town?" Vic asked as he slammed the passenger side door closed.

He glanced at her and rolled his eyes in admonishment. "And how are you so not prepared when you've lived here longer than me?"

Vic shrugged. "I was in a hurry."

Cal unfurled his scarf from his neck then flung it around Vic's own neck, wrapping it around once and letting the ends hang across her shoulders.

"Thanks."

"I'd give you my hat too, but I didn't have time to do my hair this morning."

Vic began to slowly back down the driveway. "Sorry about that. I just figured with the snow and whatever that you'd maybe want a ride."

"Thanks. Here I was hoping it was because you wanted to see me."

"That too."

The scarf smelled like Cal and his fresh-baked honey smell made Vic's stomach grumble. She hadn't eaten dinner the night before and a granola bar was not going to be enough to tide her over until lunch. She glanced at the clock as she eased onto the lane. They didn't have to be at school for ninety minutes.

"Want to grab breakfast? I know this great little diner. It's called the Rooster and they only serve breakfast all day long."

"Breakfast all day long sounds like just my kind of place."

Vic eased onto the main road and headed in the opposite direction of the school. The diner was about ten minutes from Cal's house off another state highway heading toward the next town over. She wanted to ask about the watch, but also didn't want to seem annoying about it. She couldn't see if he wore it because of all the layers he was wearing.

Actually, she also wanted to know more about Cal's father, mother, and siblings but didn't know how to ask without seeming like she was prying. Part of it was wanting to know out of self-preservation, but a part of her wanted to know because it was Cal and she found herself wanting to know all that she could about him.

The diner had a huge sign of a red sun with a yellow rooster superimposed on it. The parking lot had a few other cars and the lot hadn't been plowed. The building was a cute red clapboard with cheerful yellow trim. Its door was also painted yellow and had a little bell that chimed when they entered. The diner was warm and inviting.

Immediately, Vic's mouth watered. The air was chock full of the smells of bacon, maple-syrup, burnt toast, and good coffee. She led Cal to the far booth near the front wall, so they could see out the window. There was a lot of older folks, a man who looked like maybe he drove the semi-truck they'd seen in the parking lot, and Vic noticed a table of three teenagers who probably were also Olympia High students.

After they sat down a young woman came over to them. She had red hair piled in a sloppy bun on top of her head and bright green eyes. A smattering of freckles across her nose, a chunky knit sweater with a smiling snowman, and purple velvet skinny jeans with black ankle boots added to her eclectic look. She plopped down two laminated menus in front of them, took their drink orders—coffee for both of them—snapped her gum then disappeared through some swinging doors into what Vic knew was the kitchen.

Cal studied the menu and without looking up said. "She appears to be an interesting woman. *She* also is dressed for the weather." He glanced up at Vic with a dimpled smile.

"*She* also happens to be the daughter of the owner of this fine establishment."

Cal closed his menu and gave Vic a humoring look with one eyebrow raised. "Alright. I'll bite. Who's the owner?"

Vic grinned. "I thought you'd never ask. The owner is a lovely older woman named Leto."

Cal tapped a finger on the menu then shook his head. "Nope. Doesn't ring any bells."

Vic pulled out the book with the ancestry tree and her notes, opened to the Olympians and pointed to a name, turning the book so Cal could see.

"Leto is one of Zeus's lovers. Their children are Artemis and Apollo."

Cal's mouth dropped open a little bit. "You mean the goddess of the hunt is serving eggs and bacon to teenagers, senior citizens, and truck drivers?"

Vic snapped the book shut and shrugged. "Times have changed and it gets old living forever, after the novelty wears off. It's best to pursue different interests for a while, like running a family business."

Cal gave out a low whistle as Artemis came through the doors holding two steaming white mugs of coffee.

"Well, I have to admit. I truly enjoy her style."

–

After eating their fill of eggs, bacon, flapjacks, and black coffee, it was time to discuss the one thing their conversation had skirted around thus far. The watch. Some matters were just better discussed with a full stomach and a caffeinated mind.

Vic took a sip of lukewarm coffee, which was just how she liked it.

Cal pushed up the sleeve of his red Henley shirt, revealing the watch on his right wrist. He unhooked the clasp and slid it across the Formica table top toward her. The little jeweled snake glittered at the bottom of the dark mother-of-pearl face. Cal reached into his pocket and produced a multi-tool device with a tiny screw driver, perfect for removing the back of the watch to replace the battery. Vic flipped the watch over. Engraved on the back was Cal's initials: CAB. She picked up the screwdriver and carefully began unscrewing the back.

"In case you were wondering, my father is on another business trip. He left on Friday and he still isn't back yet. Mom said he isn't sure when he'll be back and that it could be a week or two."

Vic didn't look up from what she was doing but she could hear the tension in his voice.

"What does your mom think about that?"

One tiny screw slid out of place. She placed it on the little paper doily that her chipped coffee mug now sat on top of.

Cal shrugged. "She's used to it. We're all used to it. You know last night, I was thinking about your mom and our trip to the Under World and the things that Athena said, and the more I think about it the more I realize parts of my life don't add up."

Vic placed another screw on the doily and set to work on the third.

"What do you mean? Like what?"

She felt bad that Cal was experiencing this—a change in identity, but then she also felt more camaraderie with him because the feeling was similar to how Vic felt moving to the Above World. The two Vics: one Above and one Below. Now there would be two Cals: the mortal and the immortal. The one Before and the one After.

"Missed birthdays. Missed holidays. Missed vacations. Missed everything." He sighed and ran his hands through his hair, his beanie tossed on the table. "Like, did I even actually *know* my own father? Sure, he came to my little league baseball games when he could or taught me how to golf, but it was always my mom who was there for everything else. For homecoming dances and awkward photos, when Melissa Maineford broke my heart in seventh grade, when I first needed to learn how to shave…all those things that a dad would normally do with his son, were done by my mom."

Vic bit her lip and began working on the last screw. She was thinking about Persephone and how Persephone—for the longest time—hid Hades' fits of rage from her, only showed her the best parts of her father. Until she could no longer protect her anymore. Until Vic had to see the ugly in order to better understand herself. Maybe what Cal was saying wasn't all that different from her own life, in a way.

"Your mom filled in the gaps. She acted as both parents for much of the time, while your dad was gone on business trips. I guess your mom and mine are both guilty of trying to see the good in other people."

Vic pulled the last screw out and set the screwdriver down. For some reason her heart was pounding. This was it. The actual confirmation that Cal's father—or adoptive father or whatever he was—was actually Cronus. She carefully slid the circular stainless steel piece away, revealing the inner working mechanisms of the watch.

Lying across the top was a very tiny, rusted, curved piece of metal. Like a miniature blade.

The blade of a scythe.

Chapter Twenty-Five

Cal's watch sat in her pocket all day.

The tiny scythe blade was taped to a Post-It and stuck to the notes with the ancestral tree, carefully placed inside the dynastic book. Vic felt horrible for Cal. The moment he saw the tiny blade while they sat in the diner and how all the breath had rushed out of him. His expression had been one completely devoid of hope. It was only then that Vic realized that he'd been holding on very tightly to a thin thread that they'd been wrong.

Unfortunately, the thread was only one that unraveled in a web of lies that had been constructed around Cal. She sat through her classes not really listening. Talk of the snow and the Apple Festival swirled around her, but Vic's mind was on the scythe. And on Cal. And what it all meant.

She knew that Cronus was the Titan god of the harvest. She also knew that his symbols were the snake and the scythe. Pythia had said the House of Snakes had risen. Were the Titans planning an uprising? If so, what did Persephone have to do with anything? And what about Cal?

Athena clearly believed that he was a Primordial son and that Cronus had somehow just been his keeper. Or like a guardian. If she was right, and if Vic was right, then it was possible his father was actually Aether. And she feared she was also right and that they were probably planning to use Cal as some sort of weapon against the Olympians.

She tapped her pencil on her notebook. Which also meant that the Titans—at least Cronus since he was the only one who had escaped, and all the other artifacts were in their rightful place still imprisoning their owners, or so they believed—were in cahoots with the Primordial deities. Maybe Vic had it wrong. Maybe this wasn't a plan for a second Titanmachy, but a plan for the Primordial deities to wage war on the Olympians, but why? It also still didn't answer the question of Persephone's involvement or who had betrayed them.

The window in Latin was open, snowflakes floated in on the cold breeze. A fluffy, fat flake landed on Vic's notebook and she watched as it melted into the page leaving a wet spot. In her thinking, she had been absent-mindedly doodling little cartoonish snakes all over the page.

She tried to think like Mrs. Williamson.

In literature what did snakes symbolize? In the Bible, they symbolized sin and temptation. That one was obvious. She thought of the ouroboros and how in ancient Egypt it was a symbol that represented completion and wholeness. Then, of course, there was Voldemort's snake Nagini in Harry Potter.

Which killed people and also contained a piece of the Dark Lord's soul. She drew the Deathly Hallows symbol next to her snake doodles. No, she decided, snakes were definitely more trouble than they were worth. She brainstormed a list of all the snake symbolism she could think of using a combination of what she already knew and what she'd learned in school.

SNAKES

ADAM AND EVE (BIBLE)

NAGINI (HARRY POTTER)

OUROBOROS (EGYPT)

ST. PATRICK (IRELAND)

QUETZALCOATL (MESOAMERICAN GOD)

NAGAS (HINDU MYTHOLOGY)

GREEKS: CRONUS, PYTHIA, HYDRA, APOLLO, HERMES, HADES (TECHNICALLY), AND MEDUSA

She looked at the completed list. It was fair to say that all the non-Greek notes were probably not a viable option. So she put a big X through those. At least the exercise had gotten her juices flowing. She'd forgotten about how many Greeks used serpent iconology. She chewed on her pencil eraser deep in thought.

Well, she knew for certain it wasn't her father. Along with Biblical references, the snake and serpent was often a symbol of the Under World. However, it was an interesting coincidence. She crossed Hades' name off the list.

She circled Pythia's name. Pythia was the most obvious,

but Vic didn't truly believe that the Oracle was referring to herself when she had said that the House of Snakes had risen and would not be slain.

If anything Medusa hated her snakes. She always had to wear a hat or a head scarf and over the millennia she'd turned more than one lover into stone accidentally (and on purpose), so Vic decided to cross her off the list as well.

Vic knew for certain the hydra was fresh-water bound, which they didn't have around Olympia (the lake was salt water), so she crossed it off the list. (Last she'd heard, it kept popping up as the monster in Lake Champlain.)

That left Cronus (another circle), Hermes, and Apollo. She hated to think Hermes had anything to do with this. The one time she'd met him, he'd been so timid and sweet. He was handsome and athletic and Vic was pretty sure he was training for the 2020 Olympics in Tokyo. A piece of eraser came off in her mouth and she spit it out. *Gross.* She stopped chewing on the eraser and went back to tapping, but not before crossing Hermes off the list.

That left Apollo. Unfortunately, she didn't know much about him and what little she did know wasn't very impressive. He helped run The Rooster with Leto and Artemis, but he lacked Artemis's sweet, eclectic nature. Sure, she was the goddess of the hunt—*of a good deal!* she was known to joke—but she could pull out all the stops if need be, or so Persephone had once told her. The image of her dangling, moon earrings came back to Vic and she smiled. No, from what she'd been told, Apollo was handsome where his sister was quirky and he was arrogant where his sister was kind. Other than that, Vic didn't know much about him. She never saw him around the diner—but was under the assumption he helped keep the books or something like that. The sun on the sign was most likely his touch. She shrugged and circled his name.

The bell rang startling her nearly out of her skin. She scooped up her books and headed for the door just as her phone buzzed in her hoodie pocket. Once in the hallway, she slipped it out and saw that there was a text from Hades. Curse whoever allowed the gods to become savvy to teenager technology.

HOUSE OF SNAKES 3PM

—

Vic parked the truck outside of the House of Snakes. A key difference on this visit being the lump of worry that sat lodged in the pit of her stomach.

She had parked next to the Cadillac, but Hades was nowhere to be seen, already inside. Hades trusted Pythia's predictions, but when it came to Persephone his temper was quick to flare. Cal got out of the truck and appeared on the sidewalk beside her. On the way from the school she'd explained her new findings to him and admitted that she knew very little about Apollo, but that he couldn't be ruled out. She just couldn't imagine what above or below would be his motivation. Cronus and Pythia were the obvious choices, but Vic still couldn't pinpoint exactly how all the pieces fit together. And how Cal and Persephone fit into the mix.

The sky was gray and the clouds had bellies full of more snow. The sidewalk along the shops of downtown Olympia had been shoveled. They walked through the heavy wooden entrance to the House of Snakes and were greeted by Apollo the Cat, who wrapped his sinewy body around Vic's legs.

The shop appeared empty.

"Are you minding the shop, Apollo?" she asked and

crouched down to rub the cat between the ears. He purred in response and leaned into her touch. When Cal leaned over to pet him he hissed and darted away, heading toward the back of the shop.

They made their way through the beaded curtain and up the stairwell to the floor above. Hades' angry tenor reverberated through the door. Vic took a deep breath and knocked.

The door swung open of its own accord and they stepped inside. Pythia and Hades were standing in the area between the kitchen and the living space. Pythia had her hands on her hips, which were covered by a magenta and tangerine-colored silk scarf. She had on geometric patterned palazzo pants and raffia wedged sandals despite the freshly fallen snow. Without looking, she snapped her fingers and the door swung shut behind Vic and Cal. Pythia wore a shawl with gold coins draped over her shoulders and it jingled along with the bangles that slid up and down her arms as she gesticulated.

"I understand, Hades. But it's not that simple. You know that."

Hades just glowered at her, like a petulant child, arms crossed protectively over his chest. His suit was more subdued today. A simple gray three piece with a crimson, abstract print tie and a fedora on his head.

"Um, hello. I got your message," Vic said awkwardly holding up her cellphone, imagining that she and Cal couldn't have shown up at a worse time.

"Come in, come in, Children. Don't just stand there like you don't know whether you're coming or going. Go sit and I'll pour us all some tea. Maybe some chamomile to soothe the temper." She gave Hades a curt glare before heading into the kitchen and banging around in the cabinets.

Vic, Cal, and Hades sat down on the floor cushions near the modular table. To Cal, it was strange to see Hades in this place. The manor he could handle because it was technically his and was an old money sort of mansion. But to see the olive-skinned, dark-eyed King of the Under World amidst brightly colored floor cushions and a rainbow of hangings was a bit much. He began to laugh but quickly covered it up with a cough when Vic brushed her knee against his.

Hades didn't engage his daughter and her friend in conversation, he simply scowled and simmered like a scolded teenager.

Pythia placed mismatched mugs of tea in front of each of them. Vic inhaled. Hers was definitely not chamomile. It was cinna-mint, one of her favorites. Both energizing and comforting at the same time. She leaned over Cal's shoulder and inhaled the scent of his tea which to her smelled a bit like Gingko, which her mother had taught her was good for mental clarity. Persephone was the only one in the family who drank tea regularly. Hades liked his coffee black, as did Vic.

Vic sipped her tea, enjoying the slight burn of the peppermint and cinnamon as it washed down her throat and warmed her from the inside out. She was still wearing Cal's scarf and could smell his lingering honey scent on it. She imagined his mother spent a lot of time baking for all those children. Maybe to make up for her very absent husband.

After they all sipped their tea silently—including Hades who glared all the while—Pythia placed her mug down, her long dark fingers still wrapped around its warmth.

"I know why you're all here. But there is not much I can tell you that you don't already know."

Vic's mind drifted to her notes, of Pythia's name with the circle around it and she couldn't help but think if Pythia was indeed involved that she wouldn't be involved willingly. The Oracle did not take sides. Ever. It was in the original decree back at Apollo's original temple, back when the gods and goddesses actually had temples. When mortals actually worshipped them and cared to appease them.

"You said the House of Snakes had risen. That's what you told me the last time we were here. What does that even mean? And what does it have to do with my mother?"

Pythia's violet lips curled into a smile, but her dark eyes were sad.

"I don't even remember most of the messages I deliver. Sure, it's one thing to do typical psychic stuff. Tea leaf reading, palmistry, and Tarot. But to truly channel—to become the Oracle—those messages are not even revealed to me. They simply come through and are gone."

It sounded like a pretty lonely experience to Vic. Hades had been quiet since they arrived, his long fingers running absent-mindedly over his mug. Vic wondered what they had been arguing about before she and Cal had interrupted. Were they arguing about Persephone? About the Takings not working? Or about the message Vic had received?

The messages were always meant for the recipient, that much Vic knew. Even if the message didn't make any sense, it was only a matter of time before it did. Sometimes the meaning was figured out too late. Vic reached into her notebook and pulled out the Post-It with the scythe. She slid the little rusted piece of metal forward across the table.

Hades' breath hitched. He recognized it.

"That's the Scythe of Cronus," Hades finally said, his voice calm and even.

"It was inside the watch." Cal pulled up his sleeve and showed Hades the watch decorating his wrist.

"The watch was protecting it. Well, what remains of it. The scythe is very old. Millennia. The original is long gone. But this is why the watch kept Cronus tethered to the Cave of Nyx."

Hades reached for it and held it between his elegant fingertips with a combination of disdain and reverence.

"And the watch now?" Cal asked.

"Meaningless. This is the true artifact."

"But why a watch?" Vic asked. "He could have built a new scythe or hid it in nearly anything really."

"Because the Titan Cronus and the Primordial Chronus are one and the same being. The stories go back and forth. Some separate their identities and make them two separate men with two separate spellings, and others combine them into one being. Cronus—Cal's guardian—is a god of time and of the harvest, thus the scythe. But really no man is a father to time. Time is an orphan. Perhaps it is the cruelest trick of all."

Hades didn't look up as he twirled the small piece of metal between his fingers.

"So is it possible my father is still my father?" Cal asked.

Hades glanced up as if remembering he weren't alone.

"It's possible. If Athena is correct, and you are indeed a Primordial son, then yes. Your father could still be Cronus. Or it could be one of the other Primordial deities. Although highly unlikely. Cronus is said to have cast them all into Tartarus. Which is where my brethren and I should have cast the Titans when we overthrew their power." Hades' mouth formed a hard line.

Cal looked relieved, but the relief turned to confusion. "Tartarus?"

"It's the Under World below the Under World. It's an ancient system from the Titan Dynasty, only reserved for the entrapment of an immortal soul. It is said to be a fate worse than death." Vic recited the words her mother had used to explain the World Below the World Below to her young daughter. She remembered shuddering in fear. She hoped her soul was never sent to Tartarus.

Something dawned on Vic in that moment as she thought of Persephone.

"Wait. Dad, you said Cronus the Titan god of the harvest. But that's also Maman and Demeter. Surely, that can't be a coincidence?"

Excitement bloomed in her belly. This was the connection that she was looking for. Another piece of the puzzle that fit snuggly against the rest.

Before Hades could answer, Pythia, who had grown very quiet, fell backwards. Her scarfed head nearly slamming into the floor if not for Cal's quick thinking. He slid a floor pillow beneath her head and it landed on the soft cushion.

Her long, dancer-esque body writhed and her eyes rolled back in her head as her magenta make-upped lids slid partially shut. The whites of her eyes shone in the wintry light from the windows and her long, black lashes fluttered rapidly.

"Is she going to be okay?" Cal asked, taking her hand which had gone cold and rigid.

Hades picked up her mug and sniffed. He wrinkled his nose.

"It's an elixir. The Oracle can drink it to force a vision."

Again, Vic thought of the argument they had walked in on. Maybe all Pythia wanted to do was help. Maybe it was all she could do.

A soft humming sound vibrated through Pythia's parted lips and an otherworldly, unfamiliar voice came through her familiar mouth.

"The Harvest is near and all will be revealed. Snow will fall streaked with pomegranate tears. The seeds of War have been planted and will blossom. The broken pieces shall be scattered. The House of Snakes grows stronger in numbers. One has betrayed his own. His own has betrayed one. Heed the words of the Oracle, spoken for millennia, originated in Delphi. The Sword and the Air will rise as one."

Her mouth snapped shut and her eyelids slid all the way down and went still. The rise and fall of her chest slowed and her hand went limp in Cal's warm one. His face had gone pale. So had Vic's, her mouth hanging open in surprise.

The Harvest.

Persephone would be at the Harvest Festival. Seeds being planted and pomegranate tears, those were the things that Vic associated with her mother. Twisted trees heavy with sunset-colored fruit, her mother's hands pushed beneath the soil dropping daffodil, tulip, and hyacinth seeds deep inside the earth.

Hades scooped Pythia up into his arms. She didn't look like the fierce Oracle Vic had come to know and whom Cal had only met a couple of weeks before. She looked small and fragile in the King of the Under World's arms, like a long-forgotten child. He placed her gently inside the hanging hammock, picking up a brightly colored Mexican blanket that Vic had seen often used in yoga studios, and draping it across the sleeping Oracle.

"Will she be okay?" Cal asked, concern still laced in his voice.

Vic didn't hear Hades' answer.

Her heart pounded with anticipation. The Harvest Festival was only three days away. And Persephone would be there. Vic was sure of it. Because the Oracle was never wrong.

Chapter Twenty- Six

The next three days crept by.

Hades resided on the upstairs floor and if she didn't hear the fall of his footsteps, Vic would have thought she was still alone.

The excitement about both the Apple Harvest Festival and the snow had the students at Olympia High in a heightened frenzy. Teachers struggled to get any lessons taught and it was only mid-term time. Cal had come over after school every day and they'd spent time studying for their exams which fell on the Wednesday (even periods) and Thursday (odd periods) of the week. They hadn't discussed anything else. Cal didn't ask about Cronus and Vic didn't ask about the sword and the air.

Vic would often find herself sitting during an exam, staring out the window at the freshly fallen snow, which seemed never-ending, and thinking about Persephone. It felt like she could simply be at home in the Under World or with Demeter, just like before. Vic living in the Above World none the wiser. And then her mind would drift to Pythia's words, *the one has betrayed his own; his own has betrayed one.*

She'd pull out her list and look it over, tracing over the circled names of Apollo and Cronus. She'd crossed out Pythia's name. The Oracle's last reading seemed to have come at a great expense and Vic didn't think she would have risked it, if she was part of the plan.

But what reason could Apollo possibly have for betraying the Olympians, the gods of his own dynasty? Sure, a lot had changed over the millennia. The gods didn't hold the same status that they once had. But cultures changed. Beliefs changed. But just because people stopped believing didn't mean that the focus of the belief ceased to exist.

When one was alive for millennia, learning how to adapt was crucial and Vic felt that the gods, for the most part, did an excellent job at this. Many had built lives for themselves. Even Hades had a lot of investments in tech start-up companies, always trying to stay one step ahead of the game. It was one of the reasons he often consulted with Pythia about business decisions.

Vic thought of Artemis's tired eyes as she waited on them at the Rooster. But she still had seemed happy, hadn't she? You can't live for millennia and be happy *all* the time, Vic rationalized. Her father was a good example of that. Even herself, and she'd only been alive seventeen years so far. She cringed thinking about it.

–

Friday morning Vic woke up early. She knew from the talk at school that there would be a bake-off in the morning, followed by a pie eating competition. Then at noon there would be the parade with the Harvest Queen waving from a float entirely made from apples. The mayor of Olympia would then thank everyone for a wonderful year and thank the tourists for the boost to the economy. Then the atmosphere would become more fair-like as the afternoon wore on—bobbing for apples, tug-o-war, apple picking, guess how many apples in the barrel, face painting, balloon animals and who knows what else these small town folks would come up with. She had been reassured there would be apple cake, apple donuts, apple pie, apple cheesecake, apple cheese, apple bacon, apple butter, apple jam, apple scones, apple juice, apple cider, and even the world-famous apple pie milkshakes from her favorite diner.

Vic stared out the front window at Richard, who was bundled up head to toe in a snow suit and was snow blowing the driveway with an industrial-sized snow blower. More snow had fallen. Nearly twice what had already fallen—just overnight. It was a light, fluffy snow. Not the kind that was heavy and wet, weighing down the tree branches and knocking down power lines.

She reached for an emerald green, cable knit sweater—her father had sent someone out shopping and packages had magically appeared on her bed earlier in the week—and a pair of dark blue jeans, then searched for a pair of chestnut-colored riding boots that were fur-lined and that were also from the magically appearing boxes.

Under normal circumstances, she'd feel the tingle of excitement at the days' events and being able to spend it with Cal. Except now, the event had been tainted and she had an awful mix of hope and trepidation beating in her stomach. Hope that Persephone would be there and be unharmed—well, further unharmed—and trepidation at what exactly was about to transpire. Vic knew in her gut that things were about to come to a head. She thought of Mrs. Williamson, Mr. Chauvice, and Mr. Beckerman. And of all the people she now knew around Olympia, and worried if whatever transpired would harm them in anyway.

After she pulled on her boots, Vic found her knife and slipped her sheath onto her belt before sliding the onyx blade inside. She was thankful that there were no more Takings, but that didn't mean that she wouldn't take a life if it meant saving someone she cared about.

She found fresh-baked apple cookies on a tray sitting on the kitchen counter. A gift from Anastasia. As Vic chewed the moist cinnamon deliciousness she hoped that Anastasia had entered a batch in the bake off. There was a soft knock at the back door, and Vic pulled it open, inviting Cal inside. She peered around him.

"My mom dropped me off on her way to the bake-off," he explained as he slipped out of his navy-colored peacoat and hung it on a chair at the table.

Vic handed him a cookie. And he took a bite, eyes rolling back in pleasure. Anastasia truly was a wizard in the kitchen.

"Did she enter?" Vic asked.

Cal swallowed. "Yeah. Apple bread. But if these are an entry, I fear she doesn't stand a chance."

The sharp click of Hades' wingtips descended the stairs and he entered the kitchen, immaculate as ever. His black hair slicked back and ruby cuff links pinned to his shirt cuffs. He wore a well-fitted, black suit. Probably something from the shopping excursion. But it gave the desired effect, which was Hades' favorite. Well-dressed fear. He shot them a toothy grin as he snatched a cookie from the tray and in that moment he truly looked like he could be the devil himself.

—

The plan was there was no plan. Well, not what Vic considered a good plan at least. Parking for the festival was in an empty field off the main road, about a five minute walk from downtown's main street.

Hades parked and then grumbled all the while about the mud on his wingtips. Vic didn't want to point out that it was a rural town in the middle of nowhere, or mention the half foot of snow that covered everything, and that maybe boots would have been the more practical choice.

She had on a silvery puffy coat that encased her like a giant cloud and a black knit beanie pulled down over her dark hair. Snow continued to fall in fat, fluffy swirls as they walked toward town. White flakes would hit the top of Hades' head and his cheeks, then instantaneously dissolve. His body temperature was much higher than a normal, mortal person's. Hers was too, but not to the same extent. Half her genes were her mother's and Persephone spent six months of the year in the Above World.

When they reached the shoulder of the road, it was blocked off with orange cones, so patrons going to and from the festival could safely walk in the street from the makeshift parking lot. Downtown had transformed into something magical. White holiday lights were strung over every lamp post, tree, and tall, stationary object. Tents with tables lined the sidewalks and the little park. Steam rose from giant cauldrons of kettlecorn and hot apple cider, the sharp, warm scent of cinnamon and whiskey filling the air.

They passed children eating traditional candied and caramel apples, then passed others eating elaborate apples with layers of chocolate and candies covering the pieces. There were giant wooden apples painted red and with holes cut into them and people were sticking their faces through the holes for pictures. Kids ran by with apple-shaped balloons and apples painted on their cheeks, smeared from the falling snow.

Vic had never seen so many people wearing red in her entire life and was thankful her coat was a neutral color that covered her emerald green sweater. Not that green wasn't an apple color, but Olympian apples were red—kind of the color of a Macintosh, but large and round like a pomegranate with the sweetness and crispness of a Honeycrisp.

She saw women with apple sweaters, and wearing apple-shaped barrettes strung through their hair. Men walked by wearing pom-pom knit beanie caps with apple patterns. They passed fresh-baked apple pies and loaves of apple bread, not to mention the other standard fair food of elephant ears, cotton candy, and deep-fried Oreos (one of Vic's personal favorites).

"This place is like an apple orchard upchucked," Hades grumbled.

But Vic was enchanted.

And so was Cal. A bluegrass band complete with fiddler, spoons and banjo player played music that drifted from the sidewalk near the House of Snakes. He slipped his gloved hand into hers as they passed a giant apple being carved out of ice with a chainsaw. And for a moment, Vic's nerves subsided and she thought, if magic was real then surely this was it.

Hades slipped through the crowd, his black suit disappearing among the coats and hats. In her father's true fashion, Vic had been left behind.

Cal noticed the frown on her face. He couldn't understand why Hades refused to acknowledge the intelligence and courage his daughter displayed time and again. Maybe in that regard, Hades was like any other father. He only saw what he wanted to see which was his little girl, and not a young woman ready to stand up and fight.

"Come on." He gave her a gentle tug. "I think the parade starts soon and we want to have a good spot."

Cal knew they were there for something really serious—and that they had no idea what to expect, who would show up, or what would happen—but his optimistic nature figured that they may as well enjoy what they could of the festival until then.

He stopped and dropped some money in an empty coffee canister and received two steaming, Styrofoam cups of apple cider. He handed one to Vic, and they weaved through the pine trees and elated children. Some kids from school stood in a cluster near a local artisan who was using food coloring to dye the snow and create a portrait of what looked like a young woman. To Vic, it seemed to resemble Demeter. Long, braided blonde hair and deep blue eyes, the angular chin. She supposed it was fitting considering she was the goddess of the harvest.

She let Cal pull her along until they found an empty bench beneath one of the lamp posts. Even though it was nearly noon, everything was lit up beneath the overcast sky, cloud bellies still full of snow. A horn sounded and the mayor—an older woman with streaks of gray in her dark hair—stood on a makeshift stage, where they would later announce the winner of the bake-off. Vic couldn't remember her name, but she had both a small town warmness and a schoolmarm's sternness about her. She wore an apple printed scarf over a crimson-colored wool coat.

The bluegrass band ceased play and the mayor held up a

giant bullhorn and spoke:

"Ladies and Gentleman, Olympians, and out-of-town guests, welcome to the 166th annual Olympia Apple Harvest Festival! It's time for what most of you have been waiting for—the parade featuring our own award-winning Olympia High School Marching Band, along with the reveal of this year's Apple Harvest Queen, which has been kept very hush, hush thanks to the Planning Committee. Enjoy some cider because it's my ap-pleasure to get this festival officially started!"

There was polite applause—even with the bad pun—and the mayor took a giant pair of scissors and cut the red ribbon that marked the start of the parade route. It wasn't a long route, since most of the town had come out to the festival, but it essentially made a giant square around the downtown area, sure to pass all the storefronts and cute, Americana style houses lining the side streets.

The marching band flared up with the Olympia High fight song, the silver and navy band uniforms covered with thick winter coats and their hands covered with stretchy white gloves. Cal clapped along, around his Styrofoam cup, enjoying himself way too much. Vic just smiled, letting the anxiety of not knowing what could happen next slip away, as warm cider heated her insides.

Little floats made by the various high school clubs, trailed behind trucks and SUVs. The 4H club members rode out on brilliant, shiny-coated horses and threw apple candies to the children who'd pushed to the front of the sidewalks, and dove for the goodies slipping and sliding across the snow.

Vic wished she could bottle up this moment forever. The marching band and the children's laughter. Cal's face lit up beside her and all the twinkling lights. Along with the falling snow, it made Vic feel as though she were in a snow globe, just like this one movie she'd seen on some sappy television channel once.

And that all began to change as a float rolled into view, a crimson banner draped across the grill of a black truck with tinted windows. It said Apple Queen in gold, sparkling letters. As the truck rolled past, time suddenly seemed to slow down and Vic felt hyperaware. The bat charm hanging at the base of her throat began to throb, as if trying to get her attention. She dropped the Styrofoam cup, golden cider blooming across the white snow like the golden blood of a god.

The wooden trailer following the truck was covered in tiny white and pink flowers—apple blossoms. Millions of them. But the part that startled Vic—and everyone else—was instead of a middle-aged woman waving from a red throne with an apple wand and a tiara on her dignified head, there was a long, seamless glass coffin. Behind the coffin stood a man—a young man with curly strawberry-blonde hair and a shiny, gold circlet around his head. His eyes were a steely gray, his jaw angular and his mouth wickedly amused.

Vic felt her heart clench in her chest as the float rolled to a stop directly in front of them. On a red satin platform, within the glass coffin lay a pale blonde-haired woman with papery skin that appeared to have cracks—as if she too were made from glass, but Vic knew better. She knew it was the effect of the syrupy poison that ran through her mother's veins.

Persephone was dressed in a red satin ball gown, a gold circlet like the man's upon her head. Vic's heart stuttered and she heard a horrible, gut-twisting scream.

Only later would she realize it had been her own.

Chapter Twenty-Seven

A gloved hand covered her mouth, silencing her scream.

A burly man wearing a knit cap pulled low over his forehead and a bulky black parka wrapped his arms around Vic's torso and roughly yanked her down the sidewalk. She bucked and kicked. Tried to grab for her blade or touch her necklace, but the man's arms pinned her own arms to her sides. She watched as Cal stared helplessly, an arm outstretched toward her as if it were all happening in slow-motion.

She was shoved up onto the float where the curly-haired man grabbed her, pinching her arm as he hoisted her up to stand beside him. Now that she could get a good look at him, she noticed the smattering of freckles across his nose and recognized his sister Artemis in the slope of his jaw line.

"Apollo?"

He grabbed her by the neck, not so much to choke her, put as a point of control. Snow fell around their feet, making the plywood floor of the trailer slick. Apollo wore a ridiculous toga with a golden, roped belt that matched his circlet.

"Hades!" His voice boomed over the crowd. "I have your two most precious possessions! Show yourself!"

He pushed Vic forward by the neck, and she stumbled, cursing beneath her breath and cursing at the uproarious beat of her heart. The festival had come to a standstill. From the vantage point of the float Vic could see children—mouths sticky with candied and caramel apples—curling into the coats of their parents and the confused, stunned looks on the faces of the townspeople. She glanced to the spot where she and Cal had stood moments before. It was empty.

Her father appeared in the middle of the street just past the front end of the truck which sat idling. He looked impassive, eerily calm. All the floats and people that came before had turned around or scattered. All eyes on the Apple Blossom Queen's float. Vic wanted to call out, but Apollo's fingers dug into the back of her neck with such strength she wasn't sure he wouldn't snap her neck if she tried.

"Apollo. What nonsense is this?"

If a voice could cut through steel, it was her father's. It did not betray his concern or his rage. It was cool and sharp, like a razor's edge.

Apollo barked out a laugh.

"This *nonsense* is your undoing. The Olympians, you and your brothers have allowed us to grow weak. Cooking in diners…conducting Tarot readings…playing in rock bands. It's embarrassing. You have let our greatness crumble. It is time that you step aside and let a new dynasty emerge."

So, that was it. Apollo—once worshipped as the sun god

and even made a monotheistic deity in Ancient Egypt—had grown restless. He didn't like being shut in at The Rooster. It was beneath him. So he had decided to act. And in the process betray them all.

"It was you," Vic took the chance. Apollo's fingertips dug into the right side of her throat. "You stole the artifact and gave it to Cronus."

Apollo chuckled. "A small deception for an even greater reward."

"And where is Cronus now? Your ally, your leader. Surely, he hasn't left all the glory to you alone, Apollo? To a mere child?"

Hades' voice was taunting. Vic sensed movement in the crowd. Saw the glint of a lightning bolt scar and the wink of seafoam green eyes, a shimmer of black corset and the red tips of a Mohawk.

At the mention of his name Cronus emerged from behind the painted wood slat that stood behind Apollo. He had amber eyes like Cal—so it was true, Cronus *was* his father *and* he was a Primordial son—and dark hair peppered with white. Unlike Cal, his movements were precise and calculated.

And unlike Apollo, who apparently thought his costume was both fitting for the role he played and a bit of irony at the same time, he wore a pristine white suit with a white fur coat over it and carried a white cane with a serpent's head shining in silver at its top.

The House of Snakes.

His skin was pale, not tanned like Cal's, and if not for the dark hair and amber eyes, he'd disappear against the snow.

Vic saw her father's jaw twitch.

"Dad?"

Cal's familiar voice broke through the silence as he

stepped from the crowd onto the snow-covered street.

"Son. Come. Stand beside your father."

"But why? Why would you do this? Why would you lie to us? To mom and to me."

He sounded hurt and Vic couldn't blame him. His dad had lied to him his entire life. Cal's eyes darted to Vic, searching her face. She blinked twice, trying to let him know that she was okay. Apollo's grip tightened. Her blood was boiling, but Apollo's power was stronger than hers, millennia older than hers. His power was controlled execution like her father's, whereas hers was unbridled chaos.

"Because I was preparing you for greatness. For this!" Cronus swept his cane into the air as if encompassing the town. Everyone just stared at him as if they were mesmerized. Maybe they were.

"A new dynasty is emerging. One where the gods no longer have to remain hidden! One where the people will once again worship us as we were meant to be worshipped. We will banish the rest of the Olympians to Tartarus—all perhaps, but this one."

Cronus took a step, running a pale finger along the glass coffin that held Persephone. Vic tried to take a step forward, but Apollo's grip tightened until she had to gasp for breath and black spots formed in front of her vision. She saw Cal's look of panic and he took a step forward, but Hades put out an arm to stop him.

Zeus emerged and Poseidon, each coming up to flank Hades and Cal.

A cross look crept over Cronus' face. He looked old. And tired.

"You stand with them?"

Cal's eyes bore into Vic's. She was tearing up with the

effort to breathe. Cronus tapped the head of his cane onto the glass above Persephone's face.

"You stand with them?" His voice rose in an angry crescendo with each word. "You stand with them. You turn down eternal glory and a new dynasty for what?" He snarled, whipping around. He was incredibly fast and before she knew what was happening, Apollo had let her go and now Cronus stood behind her, his cane barring her throat. Apollo laughed with glee behind them. Vic realized that he may have thought this was his idea, but really it had been Cronus' idea all along. Apollo was as dispensable as the rest of them. He just hadn't realized it yet.

Old is new and new is old. The beginning is the end and the end is the beginning.

"You stand with them for a girl? A stupid girl full of hate and anger." He lowered his voice. "That's right, young Princess of the Under World. I can see inside your soul and it overflows with shame and regret. And longing." He snarled the last word against her ear.

"Don't hurt her!" Cal cried out.

"Christopher? Christopher, what is this?" A tall, beautiful woman with chestnut brown hair and apple earmuffs stepped from the crowd. Five small children trailed behind her. The children all looked like small, carbon copies of Cal.

"This is our new life, my Darling! One of power where we will be worshipped as gods! One I have worked so very hard to bring to fruition. But our son stands against me. He would dare to betray his father. His maker."

One has betrayed his own. His own has betrayed one.

At her husband's words, Mrs. Bishop angled herself protectively in front of Cal. Vic saw Pythia gently lead the children back to the curb, they went obediently, eyes wide and frightened.

“Christopher, you’re scaring me. Stop this.”

Her voice was firm, but even from where she stood Vic could see the hurt and confusion in her eyes.

“Just let her go, Dad. Please.”

Cal’s voice was frightened, but his expression was all fire.

Cronus’ voice was all ice when he replied. “You. You disgust me. In love with an Olympian. They shame us. You are no son of mine.”

Cal’s expression hardened and then everything seemed to happen at once: a child cried out and ruby red snowflakes began to fall from the sky as if the clouds were bleeding. Zeus clapped his hands and a lightning bolt crashed down near Vic’s feet, causing the trailer to shake and Cronus to lose his grip. Apollo made to grab for her, but Poseidon moved his hands elegantly, as if conducting an orchestra, and a swirl of snow blew into his face, blinding him.

Vic scrambled away. Cal climbed onto the trailer and reached for her hand, she grasped his fingers. Blood red snow clung to his hair and his eyelashes. She noticed something, scooping some up in her free hand.

It wasn’t blood snow. She sniffed it. Sweet with a hint of tarte.

It was pomegranate snow.

“We have to save Persephone!”

Cal’s grip around her tightened. The bat charm at the base of her throat began to pulsate with heat. The snow was coming faster now. Coating everything in a glistening, sparkling red. Vic wiped at the glass case as angry and scared voices shouted all around her. She heard the clash of metal against metal.

Poseidon manipulated the snow so that the townspeople

were lost in a blizzard, shielded from whatever was happening. Apollo and Cronus were trying to get away. To hide from the crashing lightning bolts and mass of scarlet snow that was now thickly coating everything. And Persephone lay encased in glass, still dying. Vic began to cry, hot angry tears.

Together, she and Cal tried to push the glass off its base, but it wouldn't budge. Vic tried to hit it with her fists but it had no impact. With each pummel, pomegranate snow fell away. The snow was her father's. She knew it was. All the tears that Hades had never let her see. The frustrations and the manipulations, this was what created the pomegranate snow. *Snow will fall streaked with pomegranate tears.* Vic pounded on the thick glass, her sobs muffled by the chaos that surrounded her.

"Try this."

Mrs. Bishop had climbed onto the snow-covered trailer, her boots slipping and her hair coated in blood-red snow. In her hands she held an axe.

"Mom?"

She shrugged. "It's an outdoorsy town."

Without a second thought, Vic grabbed the axe. Once she was sure her grip was secure and the axe wouldn't go flying into the crowd of people—who she couldn't even see because of the red blizzard now swirling around them—she swung down with all of her strength. The steel blade of the ax landed square in the glass of the case near Persephone's legs.

A satisfying crack emerged.

The base of her throat pulsated with heat and Vic understood. She took a moment and wrapped her fingers around the charm, feeling its familiar angles. Asking for the strength to save Persephone. A warmth trickled through her fingers and down her arms. Vic adjusted her grip on the axe's wooden handle and again she swung with all her strength, hitting the spot with the first crack. The glass reverberated and in the breath of a second, tiny fissures emulated out from the first crack. As Vic exhaled, she pushed her breath—a dark black cloud of smoke—through her teeth and the tiny shards of fractured glass tremored and then collapsed all around Persephone.

Vic watched in horror as some of the pieces began to pierce her mother's skin as they fell. She dropped the axe and ran toward the pedestal, but an unfamiliar hand grabbed her arm.

"No. *Look.*"

And Vic watched in amazement as the tiny punctures bubbled with syrupy black liquid that flowed from her mother's paper-thin skin. The snaking sickness oozed down the pedestal and mixed with the red snow so that it looked like days' old blood.

"The poison is being pushed out of her body," Cal said in amazement.

Persephone's chest hitched with a deep, shuddering breath and a blush of pink bloomed on her cheeks. Her eyelids fluttered. Vic cried out and stumbled forward, out of Mrs. Bishop's grasp and toward her mother's awakening body. But before she could close the distance, a figure appeared out of the pomegranate snow.

A red-stained toga and limp curls stood before her. Apollo's mouth curled into a snarl. His pearlescent teeth were also stained red, whether from blood or snow, Vic couldn't tell.

"Oh, no you don't," he growled, barring her path.

And suddenly dawning fell on Vic. It wasn't enough to steal the artifact from right beneath Hades' nose and then to betray the rest of the Olympians. Hades had erroneously thought that Persephone's illness had been an act of war. But as Vic looked into Apollo's steel gray eyes she recognized something familiar. Something she'd seen in Cal's eyes as he'd regarded her, as his own father had threatened her life.

Apollo loved Persephone.

Which told Vic something else. Persephone wasn't going to die. At least not today.

Vic slipped on the bloodied snow, falling to her knees, and Apollo lunged for her. As he did she focused her attention on the millions of tiny shards of glass and flicked her wrist, they rose up tinkling like wind chimes. Apollo's eyes widened.

She flicked her wrist a second time and the tiny shards hurled themselves at Apollo. They pierced his eyes, his nose, mouth, cheeks, torso and bare legs. Tiny shards, covered in the syrupy black liquid dug into his skin. He howled in pain, trying to cover his face.

The broken pieces shall be scattered.

She scrambled to her feet and held Persephone's body in her arms. Her mother was feather light from the illness, but Cal was there beside her, helping her to pull Persephone's body free from the remaining shards of glass. Persephone groaned, her dress streaked in red and black. Mrs. Bishop reached up and pulled the other woman into her arms, as Cal and Vic jumped off the side of the trailer.

A strong hand grabbed Vic's hair from behind, yanking her across the trailer on her back.

"You cannot have her."

Apollo was still strong. Vic couldn't see behind her, but she still tried to pull away, even if it meant ripping her hair out of her head. She didn't care.

She heard the sickening crunch of what sounded like bone and felt the grip on her release.

"Nor is she yours to have."

Hades.

He grabbed her shoulder. "Are you okay?"

"Fine. Mom—Mrs. Bishop and Cal." Vic nodded at the side of the trailer where the three of them were huddled, flanked protectively by Zeus and Poseidon. Hades jumped off the trailer, the pomegranate snow dying down around them. The sky seemed to open up above them, patches of blue pushing away the clouds.

The trailer smoked, scattered flames licked at the wood, and Cronus was nowhere to be seen. The crowd of townspeople looked dumbstruck at the wreckage around them. Shell-shocked was the word, a vocabulary word from Mrs. Williamson's class.

Apollo writhed on the trailer bed. Vic pulled her blade from its sheath and Apollo's eyes widened.

"Vic." Cal's voice cut through the confused mumbles of the crowd.

But Vic neatly sliced the tangled blond locks that were gnarled around the gold circlet and yanked it from Apollo's head.

"We'll be needing this. Hopefully a banishment to Tartarus is more appealing to you than cooking at The Rooster. By the way, your pancakes suck."

She sheathed her blade and hopped down from the float, the circlet in her gloved fist. As she stood beside her parents, choked laughter came from behind her.

"You may have bested me, Hades. But the House of Snakes cannot—will not—be slain. The Oracle foresaw it herself."

It sounded like the ravings of a mad man, but Vic knew

that Pythia was never wrong. Could never be wrong. After all she had seen and all she could not *unsee*, Pythia's words were the truth.

Apollo had used her predictions to inflate his already gigantic ego. What had the Oracle seen in Apollo's future? Had she seen his rise and subsequent fall? Pythia had said that the House of Snakes were rising in numbers, who else among the Olympians had joined their ranks? Surely, Apollo was not the only disgruntled Olympian.

There was a collective gasp from the crowd of townspeople as a dark shadow fell over the street. The sound of flapping wings filled the air and a giant black crow the size of an automobile descended from the sky. It grabbed Apollo in its scaly clawed feet, glanced at Hades with its beady black eyes, and then rose back up into the sky, flying off with the fallen sun god dangling above the world.

Vic had seen death. She knew what it looked like and had stared into its eyes many times. But this was not death. The fate of Apollo was something far worse than that.

Chapter Twenty-Eight

Zeus had manipulated the minds of the townspeople.

It was decided that it was much easier to replace their memory of the Apple Festival with one of an unseasonable blizzard, after the prolonged summer spell that had cancelled that years' festivities. That evening as the citizens of Olympia slept, more snow covered the town, blanketing it in a peaceful silence.

Each one—from an embryo in the womb to the oldest centenarian—dreamt of apples dusted with snow and frozen orchards where they ice-skated on frozen-hard-cider ponds. They would not recall the pomegranate snow or deranged man in the white suit and the odd fellow wearing the blood-stained toga. Nor would they remember the beautiful woman asleep in the glass coffin.

However, during that following winter, on more than one occasion someone would flinch at the sound of icicles breaking on the pavement beneath a shop awning, and have a vision of shattering glass. But then it would be gone just as quickly as it had come.

The golden circlet was enclosed in glass and under Hades' protection—now with heightened security—as was the scythe, the watch now nothing but an empty vessel. Still, Cal had traded it into a pawn shop and given the money to his mother who was now living with six kids in a small house next to the library. Mrs. Bishop began to sell her baked confections. Vic was pretty sure she would have won the bake-off.

She couldn't afford that gigantic colonial all by herself and Vic understood now that just because a home looked perfect on the outside, chances are you couldn't necessarily tell what secrets laid in between its walls.

Cal—conveniently—got a job at the Rooster to help out his mother with the bills since she was now on a single income. They still hadn't figured out all of what it meant for Cal—to be half-mortal, half-immortal or for his siblings—but for now Cal was just happy to spend time with Vic trying to figure it all out.

Cal's father had somehow eluded the Olympians the night of the Festival. It was as if he'd disappeared into thin air which, Hades said, was quite possible considering that Aether—air—was one of the Primordial deities and Cronus was supposedly one of them.

Apollo had betrayed them. Cronus had betrayed the Titans—freeing himself but not the others who were all still bound to the Cave of Nyx—and Cal had betrayed his father.

Not all betrayals are equal.

Persephone was slowly blooming back to life. She had returned to the Under World for the remainder of the early winter and would return to the Above World in spring, just like she was supposed to, with hyacinths and daffodils trailing her bare feet.

Lauren—still frail and weak from her comatose state—was back home with her family—a miracle in this strange year where there was no Apple Harvest Festival and the snow came in October. It had taken a lot of pleading to Zeus on Vic's part. Explaining how this was all Apollo's fault in the first place and that if he hadn't poisoned her mother, she wouldn't have had to take the Oracle's advice. She couldn't undo all her wrongs, but to Vic this one felt right. In exchange for this act, Zeus had confiscated her onyx blade, but Vic found that she didn't have much of an attachment to it anyways. In fact, she was glad to be rid of it.

Besides, she didn't need a blade. Because after the incident with Apollo—and with Cal's help—she had realized that she could channel her anger into the precision of a blade all its own.

She was the sword and the sword was she.

The Sword and the Air will rise as one.

Vic still wasn't sure how Cal fit into all this—besides having the unfortunate happenstance of having Cronus for a father—but they were going to find out together.

Together. Sometimes the word still felt foreign on her tongue, but she found that her lips often smiled around it.

They would learn what the rest of the Oracle's message meant. Together.

And once they did, the House of Snakes would fall deep into the depths of Tartarus. Never to rise again. Revenge was not something Vic went looking for, but sometimes it found you all the same.

Acknowledgements

Thanks to my ARC readers! It wouldn't be possible to spread the word about my books if you all weren't so generous with your time and kind words! I'd also like to thank my dad who is my primary beta reader and secondary editor on all of my books. A special thank you to Kari, my virtual bff, for coming on as a second beta reader and helping me make my book the absolute best it could be! Also, thank you to my #thebookishflamefam for being amazing and the best group of friends a girl could ask for!

About the Author

Jennifer L. Kelly is a production specialist in the field of technical publishing. In a past life, she was a middle school teacher. She currently resides in Cleveland, Ohio.

When she isn't writing, she can be found fangirling over *Doctor Who*, doing yoga, spending time with her dog, making candles for her shop *The Bookish Flame*, taking photos for #bookstagram, or tackling her massive TBR list.

She is the author of the YA dystopian series *The Lucia Chronicles* and the YA fantasy sci-fi series *The Elementals*. Visit her website ***www.jenniferlkelly.com*** Or come say *hi* on social media!

www.ingramcontent.com/pod-product-compliance
Lightning Source LLC
Chambersburg PA
CBHW020559310726
48979CB00008B/1277/J

* 9 7 8 0 9 9 9 2 0 1 7 2 5 *